Running on Empty

by

DON AKER

Harper*Trophy*Canada™
An imprint of HarperCollins*PublishersLtd*

Published by Harper*Trophy*Canada™, an imprint of HarperCollins Publishers Ltd.

First edition

HarperCollins books may be purchased for educational, business, or sales promotional use through our Special Markets Department.

HarperCollins Publishers Ltd.
2 Bloor Street East, 20th Floor
Toronto, Ontario, Canada
M4W 1A8

www.harpercollins.ca

Library and Archives Canada Cataloguing in Publication
Aker, Don, 1955–
Running on empty / Don Aker.

ISBN 978-1-55468-754-1

I. Title.
PS8551.K46R85 2012   jC813'.54   C2012-900851-6

Printed and bound in the United States
RRD 9 8 7 6 5 4 3 2 1

The author is grateful for financial support from the Province of Nova Scotia through the Grants to Individuals Program of the Department of Communities, Culture & Heritage.

For my parents,
Leslie and Muriel Aker,
no strangers to challenge and sacrifice

"A father's love crucifies."

From *Father and Son*,
a film by Alexander Sokurov

Chapter 1

"Bet you twenty bucks," said Seth.

"That I can't make it in ten minutes?" Ethan asked. "You're on." He floored the Volvo S80 and the tires spun momentarily on the blacktop before grabbing hold, pressing all four teenagers against their leather seats.

"*Give* 'er!" Rico howled from the back beside Seth, his fist pounding the door frame. Pete, in the front passenger seat, grimaced and held on.

They rapidly pulled up on a Chrysler minivan with a "Baby on Board" sign in the rear window—something that never failed to piss Ethan off. It was like a middle-finger salute to the rest of the world while you poked along at ten clicks below the speed limit. He laid on the horn and, despite the no-passing zone, whipped the S80 around the minivan, pulling back into his lane just before an oncoming semi rumbled past.

"Jeez, Ethan," breathed Pete, "I'll give you the twenty bucks myself, okay?"

"Pussy," Rico taunted. "No guts, no glory."

"It's my guts I'm worried about," Pete countered. "*Keeping* them."

"I got this covered," Ethan assured him. He pushed the pedal to the floor again, racing through the next intersection a heartbeat after the yellow light turned red. He glanced over at Pete and grinned at the sight of his friend's whitening knuckles. "Hey, you only live once, buddy," he said.

"I'd settle for the once," muttered Pete, his eyes never wavering from the windshield.

A Jeep Laredo rolled through a stop sign on a side street just ahead of them, clearly intent on merging into their lane. Ethan accelerated and the Laredo seesawed as the driver braked hard, blaring his horn when they blew past.

Pete shook his head. "Look, Ethan, it's no problem if we miss a few minutes of the game. Really."

"Not gonna happen," said Ethan.

The buildings blurred by them, and Rico turned to Seth. "Better get that twenty out," he said.

"Just keep an eye on your watch," Seth replied. "Isn't over 'til it's over."

As if his words had summoned it, a Halifax Metro Police car came into view, parked at the curb. Fortunately, the cruiser was facing in the same direction they were headed. Ethan doubted the cop gave them a second glance as the S80 slowed and drove past at exactly the posted speed limit. Once beyond it, though, he hit the gas again.

Three blocks later, Rico now counting down the time remaining, they approached Cathedral Estates. A sign to the right of the subdivision's ornate stone entrance declared the neighbourhood to be "A Traffic Calmed Community." Ethan cut a hard right, and the S80 fishtailed through the gate onto Monastery Road, the tires making *whup-whup* sounds on interlocking paving stones designed to make the McMansion-lined street look like it had been there for a hundred years.

"Twenty seconds," said Rico.

No sooner had he spoken than the Volvo hit a speed bump and all four friends bounced upward, their bodies slamming against their seat belts.

"Cripes!" Pete shouted. "You'll wreck the suspension!"

In the back, Rico and Seth cackled like lunatics.

"Ten seconds!" yelled Rico. "Nine. Eight. Seven—"

Ethan cursed as he steered onto Seminary Lane, the Volvo's

Michelins squealing through the turn. But he didn't give a damn if the sound drew the neighbours to their windows, and he pushed the S80 forward, speed bumps jolting them like grenades in the undercarriage. He whipped the wheel right and swung the car into his driveway just as Rico called, "One!"

"*Yes!*" he yelled, pumping the air with his fist.

"Ethan!" shouted Pete.

Despite Ethan's foot on the brake, the garage was still approaching, and he yanked the wheel left to avoid a full-on collision with the door. But the front fender clipped the corner of the garage with a *whoomp!* as they tore by, and the Volvo came to a bone-rattling stop.

All four sat for a few speechless seconds before Rico finally drawled, "Looks like you owe the guy twenty bucks, Seth."

Seth grinned. "Worth every penny if I'm around when Ethan's old man gets home. I've paid more to watch fights at the Forum."

Chapter 2

Ethan poured himself a glass of orange juice, preparing for the lecture he knew his father would launch into the second he came down to breakfast. He'd already heard him go out to the driveway to re-examine the Volvo's fender and the corner of the garage that had crumpled it. Had he expected the damage would disappear overnight? Christ.

It turned out that Seth wasn't there when his old man finally got home. In fact, none of his buddies were. The game on pay-per-view had sucked, even with a case of beer and takeout from Mama Rouzolli's, and they'd eventually gone out to play some two-on-two in the driveway instead. But the splintered siding and ruined fender kept drawing their eyes from the hoop, and then Rico had gotten a call from his girlfriend, Ashley, who drove over and picked him up, taking Seth with them. Pete had hung around a while longer until Ethan let him off the hook, telling him he had homework to do. Like he'd actually do it. By the time Ethan's father got home from a function at his firm, Ethan had gone to bed, grateful for the reprieve.

Ethan's younger sister, Raye, shuffled into the kitchen, her slitted eyes filled with sleep, blue hair flaring wildly in all directions. Still in her pyjamas—an oversized Montreal Canadiens jersey and an old pair of Puma soccer shorts—she scuffed bare feet across the porcelain tiles to the high-tech German coffee maker perched on the polished granite countertop. She watched as the dark liquid filled the cup, then sloshed some milk into it, carried it to the table, and eased into a chair. Spooning sugar into the coffee from the bowl on the table, she yawned tremendously, revealing two metal studs in her tongue, and took a sip. Grimacing, she added more sugar.

The sudden rattle overhead told them their father had just turned off the shower. Despite the fact that the house was new, their pipes often clanked and groaned, something Jack Palmer continually grumbled about but repeated visits by the plumber couldn't seem to fix. Ethan, on the other hand, actually liked the laboured sounds their pipes generated. They made the house seem like a living, wheezing thing, another occupant at 37 Seminary Lane that could piss off his old man nearly as often as Ethan did. Not that his father needed anything *else* to annoy him. When he'd come back inside after looking at the damage again, Ethan could tell by his footsteps on the stairs that he was plenty pissed already.

Nodding toward the ceiling, Raye asked, "He said anything to you about it?"

Ethan shook his head. "Haven't seen him yet." Which was intentional. Ethan had waited until he'd heard his father return to the master bedroom before he'd gotten up himself.

They could hear from their father's ensuite the faint *clack* of the heavy glass shower door being closed, then his solid footsteps on the bathroom floor above them, the only sounds he would make as he got ready. Ethan wondered if there really were fathers who whistled or sang in the morning or if those were just Family Channel fabrications. If such parents existed, actually lived and breathed somewhere on the planet, Jack Palmer certainly wasn't one of them.

Ethan took his orange juice to the table and sat down. "All that sugar in your coffee'll rot your molars," he said.

Raye rolled her eyes, slurped loudly, and let the coffee run through bared teeth back into the cup. Some of it dribbled down her chin and onto the table, which she swiped with her hand and then rubbed on her shorts.

"You're disgusting," he told her, but he had to grin. At thirteen, Raye was unlike any of his buddies' kid sisters. Most of them ran around trying to mould themselves into mirror images of whoever happened to be on the covers of those dumb magazines they pored over constantly. Raye couldn't care less about that stuff, or about what anyone thought of her. Ethan would never admit this to his buddies—or to Raye, either, for that matter—but he thought she was okay. For a kid sister.

"You are *so* gonna be grounded," Raye said.

He shrugged. "You better hope I'm not," he said. "Today's Thursday."

He was, after all, the one who usually picked Raye up after her guitar lessons on that day. She had announced one morning a couple of months earlier that her greatest goal in life was to play bass guitar for any rock band that would have her, and she'd been taking lessons ever since from a guy named Winnipeg Joe, the owner of a tiny music store in downtown Halifax. The guy looked fried whenever Ethan saw him, his eyes always half-closed, his head bobbing to music that no one else could hear, but Raye thought he could walk on water. She didn't have her own guitar because their father considered her interest in music a phase and he had "no intention of laying out good money for something else that will just wind up in the back of a closet." But that hadn't stopped her. Winnipeg Joe had loaned her a second-hand bass to practise on, and he gave her a deal on the lessons, which she was paying for out of her babysitting money. Raye always had plenty of sitting gigs, the result of being the only teenaged girl living in a new subdivision where most of the kids were preschoolers. The street sign on their corner might read "Seminary Lane"—which Seth always shortened to "Semen

Lane"—but Ethan figured "Sesame Street" was more like it. Ankle-biters everywhere you looked.

Raye was characteristically unfazed by his comment. "I can take the bus."

Ethan snorted. "Public transit's for losers."

Raye ignored this and spooned more sugar into her coffee.

There was more movement above them and then they heard their father's footsteps on the staircase. A few moments later, he entered the kitchen wearing black slacks with a knife-edge crease, a crisp blue shirt, and a new Ralph Lauren tie that, of course, picked up the shade of the shirt perfectly. An Armani suit coat was draped over the briefcase he carried, the name of the law firm he worked for—Fisher, McBurney, and Hicks— embossed in gold script on the rich ebony leather.

Ethan's fingers tightened around his juice glass and he braced himself for the explosion.

"Hey, Dad," said Raye.

"Morning," their father replied. He set his briefcase on the floor, hung the suit coat over the back of a chair, then opened the side door and returned with the newspaper in his hands, its headline declaring yet another armed robbery downtown. Unfolding the paper, he scanned the front page then took out the business section, laid the rest on the kitchen table, and pressed the single-serving feature on the coffee maker, each movement slow and deliberate. His eyes never left the newspaper as the coffee maker finished its cycle and he brought the cup to his lips.

Ethan waited, but his old man merely sipped his coffee— black, no sugar—his eyes lasering through a financial page.

So that's *how he's going to play it,* thought Ethan: drawing out the moment, something he probably did for effect in the courtroom. Ethan looked at Raye, who did the coffee-through- the-teeth thing again, but this time he didn't grin.

The three of them made a silent triangle in the kitchen: reading, sipping, waiting.

Tiny starbursts suddenly danced across the walls as a five-carat diamond ring caught sunlight from the window and bounced it around the room.

"Hey, Jillian," said Raye.

Ethan frowned. Although his old man had been seeing Jillian Robicheau for more than a year and proposed to her over a month ago, Ethan still refused to mask his resentment of her.

He'd only been eight and Raye nearly four when the car driven by their mother, Olivia Cameron-Palmer, had left the road and rolled twice, killing her. Their parents had separated months before that and their mother was bringing their dad just-signed divorce papers when it happened. "An early Christmas present," she'd told his old man on the phone before she left, Ethan listening in on the extension in the hallway. He hadn't heard his father's reply, wasn't even sure he'd responded since his mother had hung up so quickly. Outside, the first snow of the season had just begun to fall.

Jillian had met their father on a blind date set up by a mutual friend, although she was always telling people, "I really didn't need a man in my life." That comment never failed to activate Ethan's gag reflex because Jillian Robicheau, a former model, clearly enjoyed the considerable attention she always got from men.

Ethan seldom acknowledged the woman with anything more than a pronoun: *she* or *her* or, more rarely, *you*. He'd disliked her the moment they'd met, and his original opinion of her— *pure plastic,* he'd told his buddies—had only been reinforced since the engagement. Even her name grated on him, and he especially hated hearing people combine it with his father's: *Jack and Jillian* made them sound weirdly like fugitives from a nursery rhyme. Or, as Seth once observed, "characters in a porno." And, given Seth Wheaton's extensive experience with online porn, he'd know.

"Give her a break," Raye'd said more than once when Jillian first started coming around. Ethan had mocked his sister, accused her of being a suck-up, but she'd just shrugged. Raye wasn't someone you could coax or even bully into something she'd already made up her mind about.

"Morning, Raye," Jillian said, gently touching his sister's shoulder, and Ethan could almost see the woman force herself not to smooth down errant wisps of Raye's blue hair. "Morning, Ethan," she said as she moved past him. Ethan remembered the time she'd casually placed her hand on his own shoulder. She'd never tried it again.

Ethan watched her turn to the refrigerator, a huge stainless steel built-in with doors only a linebacker could open on the first pull. Bracing herself, she managed to open it on the second try, took out a bottle of unsweetened cranberry juice, then poured herself a tall glass and took a sip. He could almost feel his own lips curl back from his gums as she did it—he'd tasted that stuff and discovered that "unsweetened" was just advertiser-speak for "bitter as hell"—but apparently cranberry juice was an important part of the new diet she was on. Diets were like religion for Jillian Robicheau, her church the Tabernacle of Two More Pounds.

Ethan wanted out of there—Jillian always had that effect on him. "So," he said to his father. "We gonna do this or what?"

His old man laid the business section on the counter and took another sip of his coffee, staring at Ethan as he swallowed.

Ethan, in turn, stared at the single white hair in his father's left eyebrow, something he did during every confrontation because it proved his old man wasn't perfect after all, despite what he liked to have everyone believe. The guy didn't drink, didn't smoke, didn't even swear. It was like living with the goddamn pope. If, that is, the pope wore designer suits and drove a BMW.

Finally, his father set his cup on the granite countertop. "What do you have to say for yourself, Ethan?"

Ethan, of course, was prepared for this question. Whenever he screwed up, his old man always asked him the same thing, always made him feel like he was on a witness stand and he'd better have his story straight because his father would try to poke holes in it. "It was an accident," said Ethan.

"Accidents are unintentional acts."

"You think I ran into the garage on purpose?"

"Ben Cleveland came over to see me when I got home last night," said his father.

Big Ben, thought Ethan, picturing the fat guy who lived in the Georgian Colonial next door, a brick and clapboard monstrosity with columns along the front that made it look like it had been plucked from a Mississippi plantation. *Yeah, I bet that walking heart attack couldn't wait to waddle right over.* "And what did Big Ben have to say?"

"That you were driving far too fast and you barrelled into the driveway practically on two wheels. Norm Elliott confirmed it."

"If Norm Elliott had *his* way," Ethan sneered about their neighbour across the street, "the cops would be ticketing people in wheelchairs."

His father ignored the comment. "As I said, accidents are unintentional acts. When you drive a vehicle with no regard for the law or your own safety, mishaps aren't accidents. And since you can't be trusted to operate a vehicle safely, I'm suspending your driving privileges."

Suspending. Like he was a principal kicking him out of school for a few days. "For how long?"

"Indefinitely."

Ethan felt his face flush, but he tried not to give in to the sudden pulse of anger that ground his jaws together, knowing it wouldn't get him anywhere. Besides, in two more days, none of this would matter anyway.

"And you'll be paying for the damage you caused," his father added.

Ethan winced. "How much is the deductible?"

"I'm not putting it through my insurance."

Ethan's eyes widened. "Why not?"

"My policy allows me one fender-bender every five years. Any more than that and my premium skyrockets."

"So? You haven't had any accidents."

"That's not the point. I have no intention of giving up my freebie to pay for your carelessness."

Ethan felt the heat on his face work its way down his neck, felt it burn red beneath the collar of his Hilfiger shirt. But he kept his voice even. "So how much do you think this'll cost me?"

His father shrugged. "I won't know for sure about the car until I take it to a repair shop, but I imagine you're looking at thirty-five hundred minimum. Probably closer to four thousand."

"For a *fender?*"

"They'll do more than replace the fender, Ethan. They'll have to repaint the whole front end. And it could cost you a lot more than that if there's any damage to the frame. Repairs to the garage will probably run you eight or nine hundred. Less if the carpenter doesn't have a problem matching the siding, but I wouldn't count on it."

"That's almost five thousand bucks!"

"Plus tax," said his father.

Ethan struggled to keep his voice even. "Look, I have fifty-three hundred in the bank, but I'm saving that for—"

"I don't care what you were saving it for. It'll be paying for the repairs."

"But—"

"I wasn't the one showing off for my friends. *You* were. Every action has a consequence, Ethan."

The *Every Action Has A Consequence* speech. One of his father's favourites, second only to his lecture about obligation. Once again, Ethan struggled to keep the anger from creeping into his voice. "I have no problem with the consequence as long as it involves me paying the deductible."

His father shook his head. "Not an option," he said.

Jillian started to say something, but Ethan cut her off. "That's what insurance is *for!*"

His father sighed. "There's no insurance against stupidity, Ethan. Next time, maybe you'll think twice before you pull another stunt like that."

Ethan had been down this road a few times before. *More* than a few. He knew where all this was heading. And glancing at the weary expression on Raye's face, he was pretty sure she knew, too.

"Life seldom allows us the luxury of choosing our consequences," said his father. "A person is invariably defined by his ability to meet his obligations." He leaned back against the countertop and crossed his arms, a gesture Ethan recognized from countless confrontations with his old man as Jack Palmer's Final Word On The Matter.

Ethan glared at him, burning a hole in his father's forehead for a few long seconds before standing up and ramming his chair back so savagely that it toppled onto the porcelain tiles.

"Young man, pick that up," said his father, but Ethan ignored him as he stormed across the kitchen and out the door, slamming it behind him so hard it rattled on its hinges.

He hoped Big Ben Cleveland was taking notes.

Chapter 3

Ethan was seething as he reached the sidewalk. He'd expected to lose driving privileges for a while, but that shouldn't have been a problem two days from now. What Ethan hadn't anticipated was having to empty his entire bank account to pay for those goddamn repairs.

He'd been saving that money for over a year and a half now, putting aside as much as he could from his job lifeguarding at the Harbourside Pool. He'd worked full-time during the last two summers—the payoff for all those lame swimming badges and Red Cross lifesaving courses he'd taken—and he'd stayed on part-time this fall, suffering through those godawful Saturday morning mom-and-tot swims and teaching beginner lessons to losers on Wednesday nights. Not that he'd had a choice. The day he'd turned sixteen, his father had cut off his weekly allowance. "You're old enough now to earn your own spending money," he'd told Ethan, like he'd just given him a second birthday present, something else to go with the gaming unit Ethan had just unwrapped. Ethan had been pawing around in the box for the Gods of Slaughter disc he was sure must be inside. After all, what good was the unit without the game he'd asked for? But it *hadn't* been inside. Instead, he'd found an envelope containing a business card with "Hank Freyer, Harbourside Manager" on it. "Hank's a friend of mine," his old man had told him. "He's hiring now, so give him a call."

The *You're Old Enough Now* speech was just another in a

long line of big life lessons that his father was forever cramming down his throat. Like the one about meeting your obligations. If Ethan wanted Gods of Slaughter, he'd have to earn the money and buy it himself.

He'd gotten the job. And since then he'd been pretty careful with the cash he'd earned. Sure, he'd spent some of it on junk food, weed, the occasional case of beer with his buddies when they could get someone to buy it for them, gas (which his father insisted he pay for whenever he wanted to drive one of their cars), movies and food when he took out his girlfriend, Allie— stuff like that. But he'd still been able to bank a fair chunk of his pay, and that chunk was for one thing only. Until now. All because his old man was too cheap to put the repairs through his insurance.

It wasn't like Jack Palmer had money problems. Only last week, Ethan had overheard his financial adviser in the study telling his father how "well positioned" he was. His old man had more than doubled his investments in the last eight years, and his biggest problem now—according to the adviser—was finding creative ways to shelter his profits from taxes. In fact, his father was so "well positioned" that every few weeks one of those just-call-to-activate credit cards arrived in the mail. Only yesterday, Ethan had seen an envelope on the kitchen counter probably containing another plastic rectangle that would end up like all the others in his old man's shredder. As if an extra few hundred bucks a year in insurance premiums would break Jack Palmer. He'd spent a hell of a lot more than that on the suit he was wearing this morning, not to mention the small fortune his fiancée was wearing on her left hand.

No, this was all about his old man's obsession with teaching him a lesson. *The* lesson, in fact. *A person is invariably defined by his ability to meet his obligations.* Ethan had begun to think of those twelve words as the Dirty Dozen, and hearing them always made him want to kick the crap out of something. *Anything*. How many times had he been forced to listen to that shit? How many times had he heard his old man solemnly deliver those twelve words like he was passing down an eleventh commandment? If Jillian Robicheau worshipped at the Tabernacle of Two More Pounds, Jack Palmer was forever kneeling at the Altar of Ann Almighty.

The toe of one of Ethan's cross-trainers caught a seam in the sidewalk and he nearly face-planted on the concrete. He cursed and kept going. He had no idea where he was heading, but he'd already decided he was skipping school. He'd had his fill of adults for one day.

A person is invariably defined by his ability to meet his obligations. Ethan had his grandmother to thank for the Dirty Dozen, a grandmother who'd died long before he was born. That, he figured, had to be a blessing in disguise. If a dead woman had that much influence in his life, he could only imagine what power she might have held over him if she were actually alive.

Despite never having met her, Ethan sometimes felt as though he knew his father's mother, Ann Palmer, a lot better than some guys probably knew their living grandparents. His old man had talked about her often when Ethan and Raye were younger, and an enlarged black and white photograph of her hung in an elegant rosewood frame above the mantel in their Seminary Lane living room, just as it had in their last house. In the photo, she was standing beside a clothesline, the wind billowing clean sheets around her as she laughed at the person holding the camera. In the last few years, Ethan had grown to hate that picture. Each time he looked at it, he was convinced that dead woman was laughing at *him*. Well, she sure deserved a snicker at his expense this morning. Here he was just two days from getting what he wanted most, but now the money that would have bought it— *his* money—would be spent on something that his old man's insurance could have paid for easily. He cursed under his breath, jammed his hands into his pockets, and walked faster.

"Yo! Palmer!"

Ethan looked ahead to see Pete hanging out the passenger window of a black car that had pulled over at the intersection of Seminary and Cloister. And not just any car. *His* car. Technically, of course, it still belonged to Pete's older brother, Kyle, because no money had changed hands, but until this morning that had just been a formality. For the past couple days, Ethan had pretty much thought of that Mustang Cobra SVT as his.

"Figured you might not have wheels after what happened last night," said Pete, "so I talked Kyle into giving us a ride."

His spirits lifting, Ethan walked over to the Cobra, his eyes following the car's classic lines. Sure, it needed bodywork to patch some holes that rust had eaten away, not to mention a complete paint job, new tires, and a windshield to replace the one with the starburst crack just below the rearview mirror, but Ethan could see beyond those flaws, could visualize exactly what the vehicle would look like after all that work was done. Besides, there was no problem with the guts of the car. The 32-valve 4.6 litre engine still delivered 305 smooth horses, the 5-speed manual transmission shifted effortlessly, and Kyle had replaced the brakes and exhaust system that summer. The only reason he was willing to part with it now was because he and his girlfriend, Selena, were heading out to Alberta to work on an oil rig and, since they needed to get there by Saturday, they were flying instead of driving. Kyle's pogey had run out a few weeks ago and, according to Pete, Selena had zero problem leaving her server's job at The Chow Down, a diner near the waterfront.

Looking at the Cobra now, Ethan could see himself behind the wheel, could feel the thrum of those horses under the hood, could even see screwed to the back of the car the vanity licence plate he'd decided on: ENOUGH. He'd already gotten the application from the Registry of Motor Vehicles and filled the thing out, unaware that he was wasting his time.

He squatted beside the car and crossed his arms on the edge of the passenger window. "Kyle," he said, nodding across Pete at his buddy's brother behind the wheel.

"Hey, man," said Kyle.

"You finally going back to school?" Ethan asked, nodding at the backpack on the seat behind him. Its Velcro flap had opened, spilling a *Physics for the Future* textbook onto the worn black leather.

Kyle didn't crack a smile. Even though it had been three years since he'd dropped out, school was still a sore point with him. When he lost his job at the chocolate factory and couldn't make his rent, he'd had to move back home. The only person in the house who hadn't minded was Pete, who bummed rides from his brother as often as he could. "You're funny as cancer, Palmer," Kyle grunted.

"Where're your books?" Pete asked.

Ethan shrugged. "I'm cutting today."

"You think that's such a great idea after banging up your dad's car?" said Pete.

Kyle rolled his eyes at Ethan. "How do you put up with this guy, Palmer? Sometimes I figure the maternity ward lost my real brother and gave us this pussy instead."

Ethan grinned. "What d'you say the three of us pick up some pints and hang out by the Arm?" He always enjoyed spending time beside the inlet that opened to the Atlantic Ocean, enjoyed watching the water that was always dotted with sailboats during unseasonably warm days like this one in the middle of October. The ultimate revenge of retirees.

"I dunno," smirked Kyle. "That probably means Petey here won't get his perfect attendance medal."

"Screw you," Pete scowled. "Besides, didn't you tell Selena you'd help her finish packing this morning?"

Ethan raised his eyebrows. "She got you whipped already?" he asked Kyle. "Better be careful she doesn't pack up your balls while she's at it."

Pete chuckled as Kyle flushed, his fingers tightening on the steering wheel. "Guess it's nothing she can't handle herself," he muttered.

"Get in," said Pete, opening the door and sliding out. Pulling his seat forward, he added, "Might as well get familiar with the back seat. You and Allie'll be enjoying it soon enough, right?"

The smile on Ethan's face dissolved into a hard line. He'd talked of little else besides the Cobra with Allie during the past two days, only to have his old man ruin everything in two minutes. He thrust himself through the opening behind the front seat, inadvertently bumping his head against the metal door frame in the process. "Son of a bitch!"

"You okay, man?" asked Pete.

"Yeah, yeah," he muttered. "Just whacked my head."

"As long as that's the *only* thing you're whacking back there," muttered Kyle as Pete repositioned his seat, climbed back into the car, and yanked the door closed. Kyle hit the turn signal, punched a hole in the morning traffic, then turned left onto Cloister Drive. Of course, Ethan had stopped thinking of it as "Cloister" ever since Seth had dubbed it "Clitoris Drive." One-track mind, that Seth.

"Your dad give you a hard time this morning?" Pete asked.

Rubbing the side of his head, Ethan replied, "Making me pay for the damages."

Pete turned to look at him over the seat. "How much is the deductible?"

Ethan sighed. "I have to pay the whole shot." He felt the worn leather of the seat beneath his fingertips, felt the throb of the motor pulling them forward. Felt his anger flare again.

Pete whistled. "That'll run you some serious coin, man."

"You *think?*" Ethan muttered.

"Any idea how much?" asked Kyle.

"Everything I've got. Maybe more, depending on what he gets for an estimate."

Frowning, Kyle glanced at him in the mirror again. "So where's that leave *us?*"

Ethan shrugged, turned to look out the window.

"You know I got somebody else who wants her," said Kyle.

"Yeah. I know."

Except for the throaty rumble from the Cobra's muffler, they drove on in silence.

———————

Ethan nursed his second beer—they'd only been able to scrape together enough cash from their pockets for a six-pack of Molson Canadian when the liquor store opened—and watched a sailboat on the Northwest Arm tack against the stiff breeze. As the boat headed toward open water, its back and forth movements reminded Ethan of the dance he and his old man had been performing for as long as he could remember. There must have been a time when the two of them hadn't been at opposite ends of every argument, but he couldn't recall it now.

"So," said Pete, swivelling around to look at him over the back of the bucket seat. Pete had downed both his bottles soon after they'd opened the six-pack, and he released yet another toes-to-tonsils belch before he continued. "Any idea how you're gonna come up with the cash?"

"Yeah," Ethan grumbled, "no sweat. I'm winning the lottery."

Kyle snorted in the front seat. "Too late. I already picked those numbers," he said, patting his chest pocket. A slip of paper crinkled inside it.

They sat in silence for a few moments. Then, "You hear about those two from Antigonish who won last week?" asked Pete.

Ethan nodded. He remembered the photo on the front page of *The Chronicle Herald,* a middle-aged couple holding a Lotto 6/49 cheque the size of a sheet of plywood, shit-eating grins on their faces.

"I read somewhere that all those lottery winners end up miserable," offered Kyle, tipping his second bottle and draining the last of the amber liquid.

"You're kidding me," said Ethan.

Kyle turned to look at him. "No, seriously. Losers come out of the woodwork looking for handouts."

"That part I believe. Just not the part about you reading." Ethan winked at Pete, who hooted and high-fived him.

"Asshole," Kyle growled over their combined laughter, but even he had to grin before going on. "Anyway, they did some kind of survey, contacted the really big winners a few years after they claimed their cash and asked them how their lives changed. Every one of them said they were happier before they got it."

"My heart bleeds," said Pete.

Ethan nodded. "I could live with a problem like that."

Kyle slid his bottle back into the box with the other empties. "One problem at a time, okay? If you don't have the money, I gotta let Filthy take her."

Ethan groaned. The thought of Philip LaFarge owning the car—*his* car—made his heart sink. Filthy, who had dropped out of school at the same time as Kyle, drove one of the city's garbage trucks, and Ethan imagined him tooling around in the Cobra now, pictured him installing one of those christly musical horns and hanging furry red dice from the rearview mirror. Filthy wasn't the classiest guy going. Ethan felt his anger toward his father blaze again, and his knuckles whitened around the neck of the beer bottle. "You couldn't maybe wait a while for the cash?" he asked, though he knew what the answer would be.

Kyle shook his head. "Wish I could, but airfare's a bitch. I already maxed out my MasterCard, and no way will Selena fly standby."

Ethan nodded. Looking out the window at the sailboat carving the blue water of the Arm, he imagined the moment frozen in his mind like a video on pause, the Standby command blinking in the lower corner of an imaginary screen. Except, of course, the moment wasn't really frozen. Sails snapped and billowed, a gleaming bow sliced the waves, gulls circled and swooped overhead. Nothing stayed the same. No one waited for anything anymore. No one except Ethan Palmer.

"Where *were* you today?" called Allie as she sprinted down the walkway in front of John C. Miles High. The dismissal bell had just rung so Ethan had no fear of being seen by administrators amid the throng that poured out of the building and flowed toward the street.

As it always did when he saw Allie, Ethan's heart two-stepped in his chest. Her long red hair caught the sun as it rippled in waves over her shoulders, fluid movement matched by every part of the willowy body coming toward him. It was obvious to anyone seeing her walk—even those seeing her for the first time—that Alexis Fontaine was a dancer. Having taken ballet since she was four, the girl lived to dance, and she'd moved on to jazz and alternative forms that made Ethan's pulse race whenever he saw her perform.

And made him wonder what this amazingly beautiful, talented girl ever saw in him.

Okay, he knew he wasn't a troll. At five eleven, he was in good shape, and the big bucks his old man had spent on orthodontics when he was in junior high had paid off—as Allie told him soon after they met, he had a "thousand-kilowatt smile." But no way was he in her league. For one thing, when it came to dancing, he was one of those shuffle-on-the-spot guys. And where she was passionate about everything she did, he was interested in almost nothing, always doing just enough to get by. Mr. Rahib, the senior-high guidance counsellor who had met with Ethan a couple times already this year, had described him as "unfocused," but Ethan suspected what the guy *really* wanted to say was "lazy." Ethan, on the other hand, preferred to think of himself as "unmotivated." There were only two things that ever got him excited, one of them his dream of restoring his own Cobra. The other was coming toward him now.

Dropping her bookbag on the grass, Allie slid into Ethan's arms and kissed him while a mass of bodies rivered around them.

"Missed you," he said when he finally released her, reaching down and picking up her bag.

"You missed more than that," she said, her face flushed as they continued toward the street. "Beaker gave a quiz."

Ethan shrugged. Mr. Becker, their physics teacher, was pathologically fond of pop quizzes, so it was actually more surprising when he *didn't* give one. Ethan imagined him standing at the front of the physics lab that day, his scrawny hands just itching to pass out the papers. The guy was so thin that, in profile, he looked more like a test tube than a teacher, an observation made by a student that had resulted in his unfortunate nickname.

"I had the flu," Ethan told Allie, holding up a sheet of monogrammed stationery he'd taken from his father's study after Kyle and Pete dropped him off at his house. On it was an excuse neatly penned in what Moore-or-Less would assume was Jack Palmer's handwriting when he gave it to her tomorrow.

A shadow passed over Allie's face. "One of these days, Ethan, you're going to get caught." The concern in her voice was real, and just one more thing he loved about her.

"It's never failed me before," he said. After all, he'd been using his father's stationery for the same purpose since junior high.

"At least Ms. Moore won't be there when you pass it in tomorrow," said Allie. "Her sub won't care if it's real or not."

"Three-day weekend, huh? *Please* tell me she's not going back to that museum to load up." Their English teacher, Ms. Moore—Seth had dubbed her Moore-or-Less the first day of classes—had spent a week in New York City that summer, and she was forever bringing in stuff she'd bought at the gift shop during her visit to the Metropolitan Museum of Art. Last week, she'd perched a miniature model of Rodin's *The Thinker* on top of her filing cabinet, and this week she'd brought in a print of a painting called *Freedom from Want* that showed a picture-perfect family all set to scarf down Thanksgiving dinner. Christ.

Allie grinned. "Conference. She told us today she's been looking forward to it for months."

"At least *someone's* getting what they want," Ethan muttered.

"Why? Something wrong?"

His arm around her, he led her to a bench that the Public Works department had given up trying to keep painted green. Anonymous artists in the area considered it their own personal canvas, so it changed two or three times a week. Today it was a fluorescent purple covered with black and white spackles. Seen up close, the spackles appeared random, but from several metres back they formed a face that was surprisingly three-dimensional, reminding Ethan of the dots in newspaper photographs that blended into images. Future anonymous artists would have a hard time topping that.

They sat down and, as the crowd flowed past them, Allie listened while Ethan told her what had happened that morning with his father. "No chance Pete's brother will wait for the money?" she asked when he finished.

Ethan shook his head. "He already called Filthy. The guy couldn't wait to get his hands on it. He's picking it up tonight."

"And you really think your dad won't change his mind?"

"Every action has a consequence."

She groaned. "He used that one, huh?" Then, brightening, she said, "Doesn't matter. I can borrow one of my parents' cars when we need it."

"I don't *want* us to have to borrow a car," he snapped, his tone harsher than he'd intended. Seeing her wounded expression, he squeezed her hand. "Sorry. It's my old man I'm pissed at, not you." They sat in silence for a few moments as the stream of students thinned to a trickle.

"Maybe," she said hopefully, "your dad will have second thoughts. Maybe if you talk to him about it, explain how important it is."

He turned and looked down the street, watched as vehicles approached the four-way stop, everyone taking turns, obeying the rules. "My dad isn't like your parents, Allie. I can't talk to him."

"You talk to *me*," she reminded him.

Ethan smiled. "You *hear* me. You actually listen to what I have to say." He gently slid his fingertips along the curve of her jaw, leaning in to kiss her.

Glancing at the watch on his wrist, Allie gasped, "Jeez! I'm gonna be late!" She jumped up and grabbed her bag. "Ingrid will freak." Ingrid Wolff—whose thick German accent and severe demeanour had generated among her dancers a variety of nicknames, one of them "Ingrid the She-Wolf"—expected nothing less than perfection from her troupe, and that included arriving at her after-school dance classes on time. "Talk to you tonight," Allie called over her shoulder as she sprinted off.

"If I had a *car*," Ethan called after her, "I could've *driven* you," but Allie just waved and kept running.

Ethan jammed his hands into his pockets, kicking at a stone on the sidewalk as he headed toward his bus stop. "If I had a car," he murmured, then thought of what Allie had said: *Maybe your dad will have second thoughts.*

Although Allie had met his father, she really had no idea what it was like being Jack Palmer's son. Her own parents actually gave a damn about their two kids, and Ethan enjoyed watching the way all four carried on with each other, her dad teasing both his daughters non-stop about one thing or another, her mom constantly trying to force food into them. Sure, they nagged the girls and gave them a hard time if Allie or Bethany ever let things slide, but the Fontaines never tried to make their daughters' lapses appear more than they were, never tried to engrave those moments with guilt, make them towering monuments of failure.

What Ethan found most surprising about Allie's family was how much they *talked*. The first time he'd been to their house, he was immediately struck by the sheer volume of conversation he heard during the couple hours he was there: talk about school, work, friends, politics, the price of food, even goddamn global warming.

Allie talked to her parents about personal things, too, like her decision to have sex when she met the right boy. She'd told Ethan about having that conversation with them last spring before the Fontaines had moved to Halifax, before she and Ethan got together, and he wasn't surprised to hear her parents weren't thrilled by her decision. What *had* surprised him, though, was how they talked to Allie about that choice, frankly discussing birth control and STDs, then arranged to have Allie meet with a doctor to learn more about her options.

Ethan wondered what it would be like to have that kind of relationship with his own father. He'd forgotten the last time the two of them had enjoyed each other's company, had actually talked without tiptoeing around conversational land mines. They spoke, of course, but mostly just to pass on information. Or, in his father's case, to criticize and hand out ultimatums.

On one of the walls in his father's study was a collection of framed photos of Raye and Ethan taken each year for the Palmer family's Christmas card. All of them had been shot by a well-known Halifax photographer, and on the rare occasions when Ethan went into that room, he'd find himself standing in front of the photo taken four years ago in Point Pleasant Park. Nine years old at the time, Raye was grinning widely at the camera, a gap in her smile showing where the last of her baby teeth had been. Ethan, however, always focused on another gap in the photo, the physical distance between him and his sister that showed how pissed off he'd been at that moment. He'd argued all morning with his father before meeting the photographer at the park, because he'd wanted to compete that day in a regional skateboarding competition in Moncton. "I can get a ride there with one of my friends," he'd explained, but Jack Palmer had booked the photographer months earlier and refused to postpone the session. His old man's Final Word On The Matter—"She's a very important person"—only reaffirmed what Ethan already knew: anything that might be important to *him* wasn't worth a damn in his father's eyes.

That had been the last of their Christmas photos.

There were other pictures in the study, though. The opposite wall—Ethan called it his old man's "glory wall"—was covered with photos of Jack Palmer: valedictorian when he graduated with his bachelor of business administration degree, valedictorian again when he graduated with his law degree, the day he became the youngest attorney ever to make associate at Fisher, McBurney, and Hicks. Other frames contained prints of photos and articles that had appeared in *The Chronicle Herald*, showing his father winning case after case for his firm. In fact, his litigation record was flawless—every one of his clients had received a favourable verdict. To everyone else, Jack Palmer was perfect. To Ethan, that perfection was a pain in the ass. Who could live up to it? Not Ethan, that's for sure, which was probably part of the reason he fought so much with his old man. A classic case of oil and water. But as ugly as oil slicks might be, at least they floated on top, right?

Standing now at his bus stop, he regretted having snapped at Allie, but he could tell that even she didn't fully understand his dream of owning his own car. What had she said to him? *Doesn't matter.* How could it *not* matter? But, then, how could he possibly explain it to a person who didn't begin and end every day in a power struggle with her parents? And how could she—or anyone else, for that matter—possibly understand how important it was that he own a Mustang? And not just any Mustang. A 1996 Cobra SVT.

Ethan cursed, then cursed again. He wondered what advice Ann Almighty might have given him at that moment, and he recalled something his father had often told him and Raye when they were little. Something his grandmother was supposed to have told her own children time and time again: *Make every obstacle an opportunity.* Ethan was pretty sure that this was revisionist history—he doubted the simple woman standing by the sheets in the photograph above their mantel had ever used those words. She probably said something more along the lines of *When life gives you lemons, make lemonade,* but maybe there was some truth in it after all. Ethan just had to see the loss of the Cobra as less obstacle and more opportunity. Opportunity for *what* he had no idea, but he damned sure was going to find out.

Chapter 4

No matter how many times he entered the building that housed the Harbourside Pool, Ethan was always overwhelmed by the smell of chlorine. It was like an invisible fog forcing its way up his nose and down his throat, and he could taste it on his tongue like copper for the first ten minutes he was inside. Which proved you could get used to pretty much anything—except having to turn over all your savings to your old man.

The estimate for the repairs to the Volvo was even higher than expected, so as soon as the work was done, not only would he have nothing in his bank account, he'd owe his father almost three hundred bucks. Ethan had asked him about getting a second estimate but, sitting in his study, Jack Palmer had shaken his head and said he was too busy, adding, "Time is money." The *Time Is Money* lecture was one Ethan had heard almost as often as the *Every Action Has A Consequence* speech, so he'd been prepared for it and offered to take the Volvo himself to a couple other repair shops to see what they'd charge. But his father had leaned forward, steepling his fingers over his desk, and told him no. "You gave up the privilege of driving that car," he said, "when your recklessness caused the damage in the first place."

Ethan had been livid. "You're saying I can't even take it to get another *estimate?* That's not fair!"

"Life isn't always fair, Ethan. It's about time you learned that."

Ethan had caught himself a split-second before causing a

whole lot more damage, reining in his rage before punching a hole in Jack Palmer's glory wall. And it wasn't just because he didn't want to have to pay for more repairs. He wasn't about to give his father the satisfaction of seeing him lose it. Instead, he'd mustered up an actual smile, one of his thousand-kilowatts, and said, "Gee, thanks." Later, though, in the home gym above the garage, he'd pounded the shit out of the speed bag until he was soaked with sweat, his knuckles raw from connecting with the leather again and again.

His old man was right about one thing, though—time *was* money. It wouldn't do him any good sitting around moaning about not having any cash, which was why he'd come to the Harbourside Pool after school today to see Hank Freyer about picking up some more hours. He'd heard earlier in the week from one of the full-time lifeguards that the pool might be hiring another part-timer, and Ethan was hoping that Freyer might spread any extra work around in-house instead of taking on someone new. And if so, Ethan wanted to make sure he was at the head of the line when those hours were divvied up.

He found the pool office door open and the manager at his desk, the phone wedged between his chin and his shoulder. A bundle of nervous energy, Freyer was never motionless. As he spoke, he plucked paper clips from a container on his desk and linked them together in a chain. Glancing up, he beckoned Ethan in and pointed to a chair while he continued, "I know, Sam. We've been all through this—" He paused as the person on the other end of the line spoke for a bit. Then, "So there's nothing I can do?" Freyer listened again, shaking his head as he began dismantling the chain, dropping each clip into the container one at a time. Finally he said, "Well, thanks for the heads-up. Talk to you later."

He hung up the receiver and leaned back in his chair, his fingers drumming the armrests in an erratic tempo. "I don't have you on the schedule this afternoon, Ethan. What brings you in?"

"I heard there might be some changes in hours coming up, and I wanted to talk to you about it."

Freyer raised his eyebrows. "News travels fast. I just found out for sure myself."

"I really need the work," said Ethan, "so if there's anything you can do to give me more shifts, I'd really appreciate it."

"More shifts?" Freyer looked confused.

"Yeah, I could use the money."

"I thought you said you knew about the changes," said Freyer.

"Just that you might be hiring another part-timer."

Comprehension surfaced in Freyer's eyes. "What you heard is old news. We're not hiring now."

"What other news *is* there?" asked Ethan.

Freyer looked at him for a moment, seemed to consider something, then leaned forward over his desk. "I guess it won't make any difference if I tell you now. Everyone's going to hear about it soon enough anyway."

"Hear what?"

Freyer sighed. "With the increase in fuel prices, heating costs have blown our operating budget and we have to cut back on some of the programs we're offering. Early registrations for the next beginners group are down anyway, so we're not going to schedule that session until later in the winter."

"But that means—"

"—we'll have to cut your Wednesday-evening shift," finished Freyer. "And after that call," he nodded at the phone, "I'm pretty sure your Saturday mom-and-tot swim will be going, too."

Ethan stared at him, dumbfounded.

"Sorry, Ethan. I don't like it any better than you, but there's nothing I can do about it. Only so many dollars to go around." For an odd moment, Ethan expected the manager to recite *Time is money* and *Every action has a consequence,* but Freyer just shook his head. "I know this is probably small consolation, but you're not the only one losing shifts. All the part-timers are. If we're lucky enough to find other funding somewhere, I hope to give everybody their hours back, but in this economy that isn't likely. If it's okay with you, though, I'd like to break the news to the others myself."

Dazed, Ethan nodded. "Yeah, sure." He got up and moved toward the door.

"Everything solid with you, Ethan?" asked Freyer.

Ethan turned. "Solid?"

Freyer looked embarrassed. "You said you needed the money. There's so much in the news lately about companies cutting back, people losing their jobs. Your dad's okay, right?"

"Haven't you heard?" asked Ethan. "He's perfect."

Ethan lay on his bed scrolling through car ads on his laptop, wasting time until Allie got home from shopping with her mother and sister. He'd head over to her place as soon as she called.

Besides wasting time, he was also listening to Raye, across the hall, play an old Deep Purple classic, "Smoke on the Water," and he was impressed by how good she was getting. Her performance was even more enjoyable if he imagined their father in his study trying to work. Jack had told Raye over and over that it would be better if she practised when she got home from school, but she said she preferred playing in the evening after she finished her homework. Ethan, though, had wondered lately if she did it just to annoy him. "Even the powerless," his Global Geography teacher once told the class, "find ways to rebel against authority using everyday forms of resistance. For example, farmers in poor countries without the economic means to increase their property might plow an additional few centimetres of field each year until, several years later, they're farming a much larger area." Ethan liked to think that his sister was plowing her own field each night with Winnipeg Joe's borrowed bass.

Suddenly, the music across the hall stopped, and a moment later the door opened. Raye entered, crossing the room and flopping into the chair beside his desk.

"Surfing porn?" she asked as he closed his laptop.

"Ever heard of knocking?"

"Knocking's for losers," she replied and, recognizing the comment he'd made about public transit, Ethan had to chuckle. Raye lolled back in the chair so her head was nearly upside down.

"Pen explode under your chin?" he asked, nodding at the ink marks on his sister's neck.

"Jazz."

Ethan figured as much. Raye's friend Jasmine had decided she wanted to be a tattoo artist, and she liked to practise new designs on whoever would let her—which meant that Raye had been coming home a lot lately with strange symbols drawn on her skin. Their father had freaked the first time until Raye had shown him they scrubbed off, but he still didn't like the idea of his daughter being, as he put it, "covered in cartoons," to which Raye had responded, "One day when Jazz is famous, you'll wish she hadn't used washable ink." This dogged support of her friend was just one more thing that Ethan loved about his sister—although he'd never tell *her* that, of course.

"What's this one supposed to be?" he asked.

Raye got up and stood by the bed, raising her chin so Ethan could better view the design. "A dragon. See how it's clutching a woman in its claws?"

"That's a woman? Looks more like a squirrel."

"I'm ticklish. I squirmed when Jazz was doing that part."

"Who's the woman?"

"It's *all* women."

"I don't get it."

She sighed. "The dragon's a symbol of misogynistic societal attitudes."

"Deep."

Raye cuffed him, her open palm connecting with the side of his head, which was still tender from his encounter with the Cobra's door frame.

"Hey! What was *that* for?" he demanded.

"I know sarcasm when I hear it," said Raye, returning to the chair.

He grinned in spite of himself. The fact that Raye took crap from nobody, including himself, was yet another of the things he admired about her—and, of course, another of the things he'd never tell her. "So," he asked, "who came up with the dragon?"

"Jazz says it represents male hatred toward women. See how all those pointy parts look menacing?"

"Not to mention phallic," observed Ethan, grinning again.

"Yeah, that too," smiled Raye. "Hey, speaking of phallic symbols, what's happening with the Mustang?"

His grin faded. "It's *not* happening." He told her about Kyle's decision to sell the car to Filthy LaFarge.

"Bummer," said Raye, and he could tell she really meant it. "What'll you do now?"

Ethan pointed to his laptop. "I found another one in the north end that's in pretty rough shape, but I could do a lot of the work on it myself."

"With Pete's help," she said. It was no secret that Raye once had a crush on Ethan's best friend, and one of his many attributes that Raye used to gush about—despite Ethan's efforts to ignore her—was Pete's extraordinary mechanical ability. She was right, though. The guy barely passed math each year, but he could dismantle anything from a toaster to a transfer truck and put it back together so it worked better than ever. He was a good guy, too, always taking the time to answer Raye's questions even when he had his head under a car hood.

"Yeah, with Pete's help," Ethan agreed. He was glad Raye's crush on Pete had passed. Lately, he'd begun feeling protective of her, although she'd split a gut—and probably his lip—if she heard him say it. "The problem," he continued, "is coming up with the cash. My bank account just took a shit-kicking, remember?"

"Every action has a consequence," she said, completely deadpan, and Ethan threw a pillow at her. She ducked it easily.

They sat in a comfortable silence for a moment. Then, "I've got some money you can borrow," she said.

This surprised him. "How much?"

"Over four hundred bucks."

Ethan whistled. "All that from babysitting?"

She nodded. "Been saving for my guitar. Winnipeg says he's got a second-hand bass coming in soon that's perfect for me, but I don't really need it. He'll let me use his loaner as long as I want."

Ethan was touched by her offer. "Thanks, Raye, but it's not nearly enough." He told her what had happened to his job at the pool. "So I guess my car plans are officially on hold," he finished.

"Ever think about working somewhere else?"

"You expanding your babysitting syndicate?"

She grinned. "Don't knock it. Money's good. The Croziers and the Sturks usually stay out the latest, but the Applegates tip the best."

"They'd *have* to, to make up for those monsters." The Applegate twins, boys who'd just turned eight, were known throughout Cathedral Estates for terrorizing sitters and had gone through half a dozen before their parents began hiring Raye. There were even rumours they'd tried to set one poor girl on fire, but Ethan suspected the boys started that story themselves. They'd met their match in Raye, though. No pun intended.

"Seriously," she said, "have you thought about getting another job?"

"None of the other pools are hiring. I already checked."

"What about waiting tables?"

"What about it?"

"Remember me talking about Jazz's sister, Sapphire?"

"The drama student at Dalhousie?"

"Yeah. She works part-time as a server downtown. Makes a ton in tips."

"A ton, huh?" He didn't try to hide his skepticism.

"No, really. Jazz says on some nights she makes over four hundred bucks."

Ethan's eyes widened. "Where's she work?"

"Carruthers."

"Yeah, but Carruthers is really upscale. And they serve liquor, which I can't."

"There's lots of restaurants in the city. Must be a few that need servers. Something to think about, anyway." She got up. "Big French assignment due on Monday. Have to go conjugate me some verbs."

"Jeez, it's Friday night. You've got all weekend." But he knew it was pointless to remind her. She was the polar opposite of Ethan—she took school seriously and put a hundred per cent into every assignment. And never at the last moment.

Moving to the doorway, she said, "Wouldn't hurt *you* to crack a book now and then, Ethan Palmer."

He laughed at her near-perfect impression of their father, who had made that very comment to him many times. Ethan flipped her the finger and she grinned at him, then went out and closed the door behind her.

He opened his laptop and slid his finger across the touchpad to wake up the processor. Watching the car ads fill the screen again, he thought about Jazz's sister. *She makes a ton in tips.*

Ethan stared at the screen a moment longer, then clicked on his browser's search bar, typed *serving jobs in halifax,* and hit Enter.

Chapter 5

"You gotta be kidding me." The owner slash manager slash head server at Kenny's Café—who, weirdly, was not named Kenny— slid the resumé back across the table.

Ethan knew what the problem was. He'd already had four other conversations like this at four other restaurants. "Yeah, I know I haven't done any actual serving, but—"

"Look, kid, you're probably a great lifeguard and all, but I need someone who knows how to operate our computer system, can handle a dozen different orders at once, and won't drop the ball when things get crazy. I don't have the time to train you." He waved his hand around the room where people sat at all but one of the café's tables enjoying a Saturday snack. "We're not big, but we're busy. And up to now we haven't needed somebody with Red Cross lifesaver training."

Ethan looked down at the single sheet of paper that summed up his work history in four words: *lifeguard and swimming instructor.* Pathetic.

The man who wasn't Kenny stood up. "Sorry, kid. Come back when you've got some experience, okay?"

Ethan stood, too. "Thanks anyway," he said, but the man had already moved off to seat two more people who'd just walked in. Sighing, Ethan reached for his resumé and slid it back into its folder. He wasn't sure why, though. It wasn't like it was doing him any good.

But he still had one last place to try.

"A friend 'a Selena's, huh?" said the thin woman in the pink uniform and white running shoes as she gestured toward a table. She looked to be in her forties and wore a name tag that said "Lil" and an apron around her tiny waist that was splattered with a bunch of faded stains, one of them either ketchup or blood.

Sitting down, Ethan found himself wishing her apron was a little longer because her bony kneecaps looked eerily like doorknobs. For a moment, he couldn't help thinking how this woman and Beaker, his physics teacher, were made for each other. Not only were they both maybe ninety-eight pounds soaking wet, they even had the same sharp nose and close-set eyes. In a sudden weird leap of imagination, Ethan pictured the two of them naked in a heated, horizontal frenzy, and it was like picturing two sticks being rubbed together to start a fire. Struggling to erase that mental image, he said, "I've known her for a couple years. Her boyfriend, Kyle, is the brother of a buddy of mine."

Lil nodded, then set a glass of water on the table before sliding into the seat across from him. "Welcome to The Chow Down," she said.

Looking around the diner, Ethan counted more than a dozen tables arranged on worn red and white tiles. Several booths lined two walls, one of which had a plate-glass window overlooking the harbour two blocks below them. A couple of the booths and four of the tables were occupied by solitary customers, every one of them several times Ethan's age. The tables were made of wood and stained a diarrhea brown, and lying on their scratched surfaces were vinyl placemats with faded pictures of Nova Scotia tourist sites like Peggy's Cove and the Cabot Trail.

"You wanna order?" the waitress asked him.

"No, thanks." Glancing at the menu, he'd been surprised by how long it was, but most of the people eating there now seemed to be going for the All Day Breakfast. The smell of bacon hung heavy and cloying in the air, and behind him he could hear someone spreading something on toast as crisp as cardboard.

"So you're lookin' for a job," said Lil.

Ethan nodded. "Who do I—"

"—see about applyin'? You're lookin' at her. The owner, Mr. Anwar, drops in maybe once a month. He's got places all over the city. The Chow Down ain't at the top 'a his priority list, if you know what I mean."

Ethan wasn't sure how to respond so he just nodded.

"Me 'n' Ike pretty much run the place," she continued, nodding toward the kitchen behind her. "Ike's the cook."

Ethan handed her his resumé. He felt bad now about asking Allie to help him with it last night; they'd spent over an hour trying to find ways to make him sound more hirable, time she could have spent doing something far more worthwhile. Like staring at a wall.

He was surprised when she gave it only a passing glance. "A recommendation means a lot more to me than a piece 'a paper," she said. "If Selena sent you, that carries a lot 'a weight."

Selena *hadn't* sent him. In fact, Selena didn't even know he was there. Last night while he was online copying names of Halifax restaurants that were hiring, he'd suddenly remembered Pete talking about Selena giving up her job at The Chow Down. But if Lil thought Selena had sent Ethan to the diner, he wasn't about to change her mind.

Just then, a bell rang at the diner's entrance. Lil shot a look over her shoulder as a balding, heavy-set guy came in. He gave the waitress a wave.

"Take a load off, Clarence," she told him. "Be with you in a minute."

Clarence nodded and moved toward one of the booths beside the window, the door of the diner shrieking shut on a hinge that clearly hadn't seen oil for a while.

The waitress turned back to Ethan. "You got any servin' experience?"

Ethan's heart sank. He shook his head.

"Ever done any cookin'?"

"For myself. Not in a restaurant, though."

"Dishwashin'?"

He thought about their dishwasher at home, a state-of-the-art stainless-steel tall-tub that did everything but load itself. He shook his head again.

"And I should hire you because . . ."

Ethan took a deep breath. Riding the bus over here, he'd tried thinking of ways to offset his lack of experience, but only one thing had come to mind. It was dumb, he knew, but what did he have to lose? "I'm a blank canvas," he said. "You get to train me exactly the way you want." It sounded even lamer than he'd imagined it would.

Lil threw her head back and laughed, the sound much deeper than Ethan would have expected from such a scrawny woman. With her mouth wide open, he could see lipstick lining the edges of her front teeth and, beyond them, dark fillings in her molars. He took a swallow of his water as an excuse to look away.

"Blank canvas, huh? So now I'm an *artiste?*" She used the French pronunciation, and Ethan couldn't imagine anything more bizarre in that greasy-spoon diner. Except maybe the image of Beaker and the waitress doing the nasty. Yeah, definitely that.

Her laughter subsiding, she scanned his resumé. "Still in high school, huh?" she asked after a moment. When Ethan nodded, she continued, "If you're lookin' for somethin' part-time, why not try Costco or The Brick? Or even that jeezly Bed Bath & Beyond?"

"I need to make a lot of cash fast."

She raised her eyebrows, which were little more than pencilled lines on her narrow forehead. "You musta seen my Mercedes in the parkin' lot, huh?"

"No, I didn't."

"Probably 'cause it looks a lot like a Ford Focus with bald tires and a trunk that's tied closed with a coat hanger." She grinned. "What makes you think The Chow Down's the place to make a lot 'a money?"

Embarrassed, Ethan shared something Kyle had once told him: "I heard Selena cleaned up in tips."

"That's because she had a couple assets you're sorely lackin'."

"Experience and regular customers?" he asked.

"Great tits." Lil shrugged. "Maybe you're right about that blank canvas." She looked across at the heavy-set man by the window. "Clarence," she said, "just be another minute, okay?"

"No hurry, Lil," he told her. "My meetin' with the lieutenant-governor can wait a bit."

She shot him a grin—"Thanks, sweetie"—then turned toward the kitchen. "Hey, Ike!" she called. "Stick your ugly mug out here."

Ethan heard something from the kitchen behind her that sounded like a blend of grunt and snarl, and a second later a guy nearly as wide as he was tall pushed through the batwing doors rubbing a wad of paper towels between his hands.

"Ethan," said the waitress, "Ike Turner. Ike, this here is Ethan Palmer. He's interested in the job."

Ike Turner looked like he'd been a cage fighter in another lifetime. An *undefeated* cage fighter. He had huge shoulders and a massive chest, and his arms were nearly as thick as Ethan's thighs. Even under his apron and baggy workpants, his legs looked sturdy enough to support a truck. He wore a baseball cap and T-shirt that looked the colour of grease, and tattoos covered most of his exposed skin. Ethan wondered what Raye and Jazz would think of the tat on his right forearm, a green dragon with glowing red eyes being ridden by a voluptuous blonde. As the guy got closer, Ethan could see the blonde was having a pretty good time given her lack of clothing and the way she was gripping the dragon's tail. *Nothing phallic there,* he thought as he stood up. "Nice to meet you," he said, extending his hand.

Ike ignored it. "You waited tables before?"

Ethan let his hand drop. "Not really."

"You either have or you haven't. Which is it?"

"Haven't," Ethan admitted.

"Don't let the door hit your ass on the way out," Ike said, turning back toward the kitchen.

"Selena sent him," said Lil.

Ike hesitated and looked back. "You know Selena?"

"Her guy, Kyle, is my best friend's brother."

"And she sent you?"

"That's why I'm here," Ethan lied.

The cook looked at Lil. "Up to you," he said. "You're the one's gotta work with him." He pushed through the batwing doors and disappeared.

Lil turned to Ethan. "Say I give you the job. When can you start?"

"When do you need me?"

"I could really use someone this afternoon. My other part-timer's in Cape Breton visitin' family, 'n' there's an American destroyer and two cruise ships in the harbour. With the city full 'a sightseers, we'll be packed to the rafters when the gawkers get hungry."

"Sure," said Ethan. "Why not?"

Lil grinned at him, unveiling the lipstick on her teeth again. "You got chutzpah, kid. I'll give you that." She pushed back and got up. "Come meet your first customer."

Ethan slid out of his chair and followed her over to the man in the booth by the window. "Sorry to keep you waitin', Clarence," she said. "Meet the new Selena. Name's Ethan. Mind if he busts his cherry on you?"

The guy grinned, his double chin doing a little dance. "Anything for you, Lil."

"Thanks, sweetie. Be right back." She walked over to the cash register and rummaged in a drawer beneath it.

Clarence studied Ethan for a moment. "So you never done this before?"

"Nope," said Ethan, shaking his head. "But how hard can it be?"

Lil returned with a pen and notepad in her hand, and Clarence winked at her. "A real crackerjack, this guy."

"We'll see." She handed the pen and notepad to Ethan. "I figured you'd probably wanna pass on the apron," she said, grinning.

He grinned in return. "You figured right."

"I'll give you this section for now, okay?" She gestured toward a group of six tables, including the booth Clarence sat in. "Everything you need to know is on the menu except for the special." She pointed to the small blackboard to the left of the kitchen doors on which someone had chalked—in surprisingly elegant handwriting—*Liver and Onions*, along with the price. "For now," she continued, "just take the orders, bus the tables, and keep the food comin'. I'll look after the cash register for you. I can show you how that works another time. If there *is* another time," she added.

"Thanks," said Ethan.

"Be gentle, Clarence," she warned the heavy-set guy, then moved off, stopping to fill an elderly man's water glass.

"So," Ethan said to Clarence, "what can I get you today?"

"My usual."

Great, thought Ethan. *A wiseass.* "And what's that?"

"The number four."

Lifting the menu from its metal stand on the table, Ethan scanned it. "Uh, I see we got three number fours. You here for breakfast, lunch, or dinner?"

"I'm workin' the night shift over at the hospital. Whaddya think?"

"Clarence," said Lil from the other side of the diner. "Give the guy a break."

"Just showin' him the ropes," Clarence replied. "He asked me how hard it could be."

"He'll find that out soon enough," she said, nodding toward the kitchen.

Clarence guffawed, his laughter sounding like it came from the bottom of a barrel, both of his chins dancing again. "You sure got *that* right, Lil." He turned to Ethan. "Gimme the Rib-Eye with extra fries, coleslaw, and a side of mayo. And a Diet Coke."

Yeah, thought Ethan as he wrote down the order. *The diet drink makes it the heart-healthy choice. You and Big Ben Cleveland must be on the same program.* He turned toward the kitchen.

"You forgettin' somethin'?" asked Clarence.

Ethan stopped. "What?"

"How I like my steak."

Ethan forced a smile. "How would you like your steak?"

"Close to mooin'."

"Put down 'rare,'" said Lil, who had just come out of the kitchen with a plate in her hand. She frowned at Clarence, who raised his hands in surrender.

Ethan pushed through the batwing doors and found himself in a kitchen that had obviously seen better decades but was unexpectedly tidy. Scarred tiles checkerboarded the floor between a long white countertop and a row of stainless-steel appliances, each nicked and gouged but all scrubbed clean. They included a griddle the size of a small table, two ovens stacked one above the other, a deep fryer, two microwaves, eight gas burners, a fridge and upright freezer, an enormous contraption that Ethan assumed was a dishwasher, and two sinks. Open shelves lining the opposite wall held an assortment of pots and pans as well as plates, saucers, cups, and glasses, and several large bowls on the countertop were filled with ingredients and condiments. And in the middle of it all stood Ike Turner, flipping eggs on the griddle before dropping what looked like hand-cut potatoes into the deep fryer.

"I've got an order," said Ethan, tearing the paper from his notepad.

The cook grunted, nodding toward a length of string looped between two tiny pulleys hanging above the counter. Dangling from it were two similar pieces of paper. "Goes there," he said.

Seeing the other two orders hanging from metal clips, Ethan scanned the countertop. He saw some of the same clips in a plastic container, pulled one out, fastened the paper to it, and hung it from the string.

Ike sighed profoundly. "Ever heard of 'First come, first served'?"

Ethan nodded.

The cook lifted Ethan's order off the string and hung it to the left of the other two, advancing the string toward the right. "Got it?" he demanded.

"Got it," said Ethan.

Ike's eyes suddenly narrowed. "What the hell's that?" he asked, pointing at what Ethan had written.

Ethan shrugged. "The guy's order."

"This here an eight?"

"A four."

"And he wants it raw?"

"Rare."

"With a *man?*"

"A side of mayo."

The cook tore the paper from the clip, crumpled it, and tossed it at Ethan, bouncing it off his forehead before Ethan could react. "Can't cook what I can't read, numbskull."

Ethan flushed. "Looked clear enough to me."

Ike took two broad steps forward, and although he was at least four inches shorter, his physical presence seemed magnified as he glared up into Ethan's face. "Let's get one thing straight right now," he snarled. "I don't give a rat's ass how anything looks to you. This is *my* kitchen and I'm king, got that? If I tell you to cross your legs and shit salmon, you'd better goddamn do it."

Flushing even more deeply, Ethan fought the urge to tell the king where he could shove his crown. "Got it," he replied.

"You'd *better*," continued Ike, "if you wanna keep workin' here. I got zero time for slackers, fancy boy. Now write me the goddamn order so I can read it."

Fancy boy! Ethan fumed as he opened his notepad, rewriting the order with exaggerated care. He tore off the page and hung it carefully to the left of the other two on the string. "Happy?" he asked.

Ike looked as if he was going to backhand him, and Ethan nearly flinched. "Oh, we got a long road ahead of us before I even get in the *neighbourhood* of happy," the cook growled.

Ethan just shrugged and turned to leave.

"You forgettin' somethin'?" Ike nodded at the crumpled paper on the floor.

Ethan gaped at it. "I'm not the one who—"

"You don't walk away from a mess," Ike growled. "Not in *my* kitchen."

Seething, Ethan stooped to pick up the paper, thinking about the mom-and-tot swims at Harbourside that had been such a pain in the ass. Not once during all those Saturday mornings had any of the moms—or any of their snot-nosed brats—pissed him off as much as this prick.

Back in the dining area, he could tell from the looks on everyone's faces that they'd been listening to the exchange in the kitchen. Lil and a couple of the old guys gave him sympathetic smiles, but Clarence uncorked another of his guffaws. "So how hard can it *be?*" he snorted.

Chapter 6

You got chutzpah, kid, Lil had told him. Four hours later, Ethan was pretty sure that whatever chutzpah he might have had was now gone, along with the feeling in most of his toes. In fact, all he was really conscious of below his waist was an ache that began in his arches and spread to his ass. Allie had told him he should dress up a little when he applied for jobs, so along with a sport shirt and a pair of dress pants, he was wearing the patent leather shoes his father had bought him for his cousin's wedding that summer, and those wingtips had been tight to begin with. They were now at least half a size too small, and man, was he paying for it. He could feel a stickiness in his socks that probably meant his blisters were bleeding.

Not that he'd had a moment to check them. Lil had been right about the gawkers. The destroyer and the cruise liners had brought waves of people down to the harbour, all seeming to need to eat at the same time—and non-stop. Ethan suspected that hungry tourists with big money probably went to the more expensive restaurants along the waterfront. The Chow Down, on the other hand, seemed to attract every oddball, cheapskate, and family with kids under five. Kids who screeched at their parents, upset their food, balled up the pages of the colouring books Lil kept on hand, and threw the crayons Ethan brought them in Styrofoam cups. Reaching down for a stub of Burnt Sienna that looked like it had been gnawed on, he could understand why some species ate their young. In fact, by the middle of the

afternoon, he'd begun to wonder why the human race hadn't died out long ago. If the odds were heavy in favour of producing kids like the demon spawn he'd been serving, who would want to take the chance? As much as Ethan loved risk—hell, it kept the blood pumping and let you know you were actually alive— he doubted he had the *cojones* for *that* gamble. The last four hours—*no*, he thought, glancing at his watch, *make that four hours and nine minutes*—had been a hell of a lot more effective than any of those ass-numbing lectures on birth control he'd sat through in school, and he had new respect for Raye's ability to keep those Applegate hellions in line.

Dropping the crayon back into its cup, Ethan began clearing the table. As he stacked the dirty dishes onto his tray, he uncovered the tip the father of that freak show had left him— two lousy bucks. Math had always come easily to Ethan, and a quick mental calculation told him he hadn't even been tipped five per cent on the before-tax total. And that wasn't the lowest he'd gotten. Some people had left him a buck, and a few hadn't tipped him at all.

One reason, he realized, was that he lacked Selena's considerable assets. Some of the oddballs had even asked about her, clearly annoyed those impressive tits had moved on to Alberta. But it wasn't only his flat chest that undercut his efforts. He'd mixed up orders, dropped a tray of dirty dishes, smashing everything but the cutlery (he'd mistakenly pushed through the left batwing door instead of the right just as Lil was coming out), and upset a glass of ice water into a woman's lap. She stormed out shouting that she'd never darken The Chow Down's doorway again if *he* was serving there. Ethan was surprised that Lil hadn't fired him on the spot, but she'd just shrugged her shoulders and told him there were orders up in the kitchen. Ike mostly glowered at him before turning his eyes toward the ceiling as if silently counting to ten. The few times he did speak, it was only

to snarl at Ethan about what he was doing wrong, which was pretty much everything. Ethan had bitten back so many replies that his jaws ached nearly as much as his feet.

"Could we get some *service* over here?"

Ethan turned to see a large, burgundy-haired woman glaring at him from the booth by the window that his buddy Clarence had sat in hours earlier. Despite having given Ethan a hard time, Clarence had left him the biggest tip so far—four bucks— along with some information. "You know what *tip* stands for?" Clarence had asked. When Ethan shook his head, he'd told him, "It's short for 'to improve performance.' You got no place to go but up, kid."

"Be right there," Ethan said to the burgundy-haired woman as he finished wiping off the table, then carried the tray of dirty dishes toward the kitchen, trying not to wince with each step. They'd gone through a ton of dishes that afternoon, and Ike's assistant had certainly earned whatever The Chow Down was paying him.

Lil had introduced the assistant simply as Rake. Ethan didn't know if that was the guy's real name or just some handle he'd picked up, but Ethan guessed the latter because, in his late fifties or so, Rake was as thin as any garden tool and had about as many hairs on his head as the tines on the business end of one. Besides doing prep work for Ike, one of his jobs was to keep the clean dishes coming, which he did. Something he didn't do was talk. He'd barely nodded when Lil had introduced him, and Ethan hadn't heard him say a single word during any of the times he'd been in the kitchen.

"Here's another one," Ethan said to Rake as he set the full tray beside the dishwasher. He grabbed an empty one, loaded it with clean cutlery and paper napkins, and hurried back out to the dining area. An hour earlier, they'd gotten so busy that Lil had given him a few more tables to serve, and all of them were

now occupied as he headed toward the burgundy-haired woman. Across from her sat a man half her size, the expression on his face a lot like the one Ethan probably wore each time he had to return to the kitchen.

The woman was drumming her fingers on the tabletop, the rapid clacking of her long fingernails, like miniature gunfire, audible even above the surrounding chatter. "We've been sitting here for almost fifteen minutes!" she spat.

Liar, thought Ethan, who'd seen the couple come in less than five minutes before. "Welcome to The Chow Down," he said, the greeting now as automatic as breathing. "You had a chance to look at the menu?"

"What do you *think* we've been doing all this time?" she asked. He couldn't place her accent. American Midwest maybe? For all he knew, though, she could have come from Musquodoboit Harbour on the Eastern Shore.

"Sorry," he said, swallowing the sudden urge to upset her ice water. "It's been crazy here all afternoon." He held out his notepad, now noticeably thinner than when Lil had first given it to him. "What can I get you?"

As he wrote down their order—she wanted the Garden Salad while her male companion chose the Mile-High Burger, probably praying for a heart attack to put him out of his misery—Ethan's mind wandered back over the last four hours. Rude customers like this burgundy nightmare hadn't been the worst of Ethan's afternoon. Nor had poor tips, aching feet, or even tongue-lashings from Ike. The lowest point had come when he realized that the largest group he'd waited on—one he'd pulled a couple tables together in order to seat—had stiffed him. Which meant that the cost of three All Day Breakfasts, two Tuna Melts With Fries, a Chicken Alfredo With Garlic Toast, and a Seafood Platter Supreme was coming out of his own pocket. Combined with the cost of the dishes he'd broken,

Ethan might end the day owing more money than he'd earned, measly tips included.

His latest order in hand, he headed to the kitchen and was just clipping the paper to the string when his cellphone vibrated. Easing it out of his pocket, he saw Allie's name on the display. He knew better than to let Ike see him answer it, of course, but at that moment he needed to hear the voice of someone who actually gave a shit about him.

"Where've you been? How'd the interviews go?" she asked him. The phone tucked between his ear and his shoulder as he reached for two plates waiting under the warming lamp, Ethan could barely hear her voice over the clatter of cutlery and the rattle of pans.

"I got a job," he told her. "A place called The Chow Down."

"That's great!" she said. "When do you start?"

But before he could answer, one of the plates in his hands shifted and he watched an All Day Breakfast slide off the chipped porcelain and hurtle floorward. Bracing himself for another roar from Ike, he felt the cell shift along his neck and it, too, fell, landing squarely in the middle of Eggs Over Easy. It didn't even bounce.

"Thanks for picking me up, man," said Ethan as he slid into Seth's ancient yellow VW Beetle. A huge Love Bug decal had once adorned its hood, but the car's previous owner had altered it with Day-Glo paint so it now read *Love Buggery*, which suited Seth Wheaton just fine. "I couldn't've faced that bus." The ache Ethan felt earlier in his feet and legs had migrated to his back, and there was a knot between his shoulder blades the size of a fist. No shift at the Harbourside Pool had ever left him feeling like this.

"No problem, buddy," said Seth as he pulled the car into traffic, the Beetle backfiring twice. "You look like crap."

"Believe it or not," Ethan muttered, "I feel worse than I look."

Seth grinned. "So what was it like?"

"Not as glamorous as you might think," Ethan replied drily, recounting some of the afternoon's humiliations.

"How'd you do moneywise?"

"I owe them nineteen dollars and change."

Seth laughed, then stopped when he saw the look on Ethan's face. "How—?"

"I tend to drop stuff," he mumbled, unlacing his wingtips and gingerly sliding one of them off. He was right—the heel of his once-grey sock was now brown with dried blood. He reached down to rub his foot but then thought better of it. He didn't want to start things flowing again.

Early-evening traffic was heavy as the Beetle coughed to a stop and Seth waited to turn onto Morris Street, scanning for an opening before swinging the car out. The engine hesitated, so Seth floored it, the Beetle belching blue smoke as it laboured forward. "Look on the bright side," he said. "At least you got a day's experience. Maybe that'll help."

"Help what?" asked Ethan.

"When you apply somewhere else."

"Why would I want to do that?"

"You got fired, right?"

"Actually," said Ethan, reaching into his pocket and pulling out a piece of paper, "I got a schedule." He unfolded it to show a calendar page with dates circled in red and times written beside them. "I'm working again tomorrow."

Seth's eyes widened. "It'll take that long to work off what you owe? Just how bad *are* you, man?"

Ethan shook his head. "Lil, she's the person who interviewed me, she gave me the job. She actually wants me back."

"Why? Comic relief?"

"Lil says most people start out like I did," said Ethan, then grinned sheepishly. "Maybe not *exactly* like I did, but not great. Anyway, she says I'll get better with experience." He reached behind him, massaging his lower back. "One thing's for sure. I can't get any worse."

Chapter 7

"We need to talk," Jack Palmer said when Ethan limped through the front door. No "Hello" or "Hi," or even "Hey." Just *We need to talk.*

Looking into the living room through the wide archway flanked by marble columns, Ethan saw his father sitting in a wingback chair. He'd obviously been waiting for him, and Ethan wondered for how long. Hoped it was hours.

Music played through hidden speakers wirelessly connected to their entertainment system. As usual, his old man was listening to '70s rock. Jack and Raye Palmer both loved "oldies," although Ethan thought "mouldies" was more accurate. Despite the low volume, he recognized Jackson Browne, who was often at the top of his father's playlist. This time the rocker was singing "You Love the Thunder" and, judging from the look on his father's face, Ethan figured thunder was in the immediate forecast.

"Where've you been?"

Ethan shrugged. "Out." He hadn't said more than a handful of words to his dad since the No Deductible hammer had shattered his savings. Not that his father would have noticed. He and two other lawyers at Fisher, McBurney, and Hicks were tied up in a high-profile case involving a politician charged with drunk driving and leaving the scene of an accident. The driver of the car he hit had recorded the whole thing on his cellphone and posted it on YouTube, which made building a defence a legal nightmare, and Jack had been working late every night since he'd caught the case.

"Sit down," his father said, pointing to the sofa. Its white upholstery reminded Ethan of the drawings of sheep in Lil's *Mother Goose Activity Book,* which he'd passed out to kids at The Chow Down. He'd given one of them a page to colour from the nursery rhyme section, and the kid had immediately zigzagged purple all over Mary's little lamb. Ethan mused that a few zigzags of purple—or *any* colour—would be an improvement in that living room. On the advice of his fiancée, Jack had had the decorators paint and upholster everything in a colour called "Brilliant Cream." The only thing that wasn't absolutely white was the photograph of his grandmother, its rosewood frame and sepia tones stark against the wall where it hung. When she saw the finished room for the first time, Raye had muttered to Ethan, "Looks like somebody puked January in there." Neither he nor Raye ever used the room. In fact, Jack himself rarely spent time in there unless he was entertaining guests, so Ethan found it odd to see his father sitting in the living room now, waiting for him.

"Got things to do," Ethan said. He intended to go upstairs, run a hot bath in the whirlpool tub, and spend the next half-hour letting the jets pound away that knot in his back.

"They can wait," his father said.

Ethan recognized his *I'm Not Asking You Again* tone and silently promised himself that if he was ever unlucky enough to have kids of his own—even creatures as ungrateful as those little snots he'd served that afternoon—he'd never use that voice on them. Sighing, he trudged into the room and slumped onto the sofa. "What's so important?"

His father pulled his cellphone out of his pocket, pressed three keys, and set the phone on Speaker.

Ethan recognized the beeps of the phone company's automated voice mail, then a recorded voice saying, "You have one archived message. To review your message, press 1."

Ethan's father pressed 1.

"First archived message," said the automated voice, "sent at 11:17 today." Then another voice spoke. "Mr. Palmer? This is Rachel Moore at John C. Miles High School. I'm Ethan's homeroom and English teacher."

"Look—" Ethan began, but his father held up his other hand, cutting him off.

"I'm sorry to bother you on a Saturday," the voice continued, "but I've been away at a conference and am just now getting caught up at school. I found a letter from you on my desk explaining Ethan's absence on Thursday, and I'm wondering if you could give me a call. I have a concern that I'd like to speak with you about."

Ethan's father clicked off the phone and set it on the coffee table beside a white vase filled with dried flowers that his decorators had obviously sprayed with Brilliant Cream latex. He stared at Ethan and waited.

Ethan let the silence hang in the air. He looked above the fireplace at the photograph of his grandmother, at the sheets billowing around her in the wind. At the laughing smile directed at the camera. Directed at *him*. He'd be damned if he was going to speak first. Two could play the drawing-out-the-moment game.

Finally, his father spoke. "What do you have to say for yourself, Ethan?"

"What do you *want* me to say?"

"I think an apology is in order."

"I'm sorry," said Ethan, his response cool and careless.

Jack sighed. "Do you even know what you're apologizing for? It clearly doesn't matter to you, but it'd be nice if you understood *why* you should be sorry."

The ball in his court now, Ethan was tempted to let his father wait for his answer, but he thought again about the whirlpool tub and the knot in his back. "Forging the note," he lobbed back, then added, "Big deal."

His father raised his eyes and appeared to study the ceiling as if reading words on that flawless white expanse. "Ethan," he began, "I once defended a man—another lawyer, in fact— accused of embezzling money from his firm."

"Look, could we maybe save this story for another time? I've had a long—"

"When I asked him about it off the record," his father interrupted, his voice firmer, "he said it all started the day he forged a client's name on a document to meet a litigation deadline. It was innocent enough. He didn't benefit from it other than saving himself and a paralegal some time refiling the case."

Ethan could guess where this was headed. Longing for the whirlpool, he wished his old man would just get on with it.

"But that," said his father, turning to face Ethan again, "just made it a little easier the next time he decided to forge a signature. And before long—" He paused, shaking his head. "Before long, he wasn't doing it just to save time."

"So," said Ethan, "the big life lesson here is that forging your signature is my first step on the road to white-collar crime." *Or Brilliant Cream–collar crime,* he thought, looking at those ridiculous walls.

"Don't trivialize this."

"But you make it so easy." Ethan stood up. He'd had enough. "Sit down."

"Look, I'm tired. I just want—"

"I said, *sit down!*"

Ethan eyed those spray-painted flowers again, considered hurling them and the vase across that pristine January room. Instead he sat.

"I had a long talk with Ms. Moore," his father said.

Since you missed the parent-teacher evening last month, thought Ethan, *I'm not surprised.*

"She says you haven't been applying yourself."

"If by 'applying myself' she means I haven't been hanging on every golden word that falls from her lips, yeah, she'd be right about that."

His father looked at him as though unsure what he was seeing. "What happened to you?"

Ethan didn't respond.

"It's like I don't even know you anymore," his father continued. "Nothing seems to matter to you."

Resentment ignited in Ethan's belly. "Things matter to me," he said.

"Name one."

"The money you took. I would've been able to buy Kyle's Cobra if you hadn't—"

"Listen to yourself," his father interrupted again, his right index finger stabbing the air for emphasis. "If *I* hadn't. Who was the person who lost control of the car in the driveway? Who was the person who ran the Volvo into the corner of the garage?"

This was the part Ethan hated most—that witness-stand feeling as his father machine-gunned him with questions. Although he'd never seen his old man operate in the courtroom, he could guess this was exactly the strategy he used with people who testified against someone he was representing. "And *you've* never made a mistake in your whole *life*," he snarled.

"Sure I've made mistakes," said Jack. "But I owned up to them. I *paid* for them. I certainly didn't try to blame somebody *else* for what I'd done."

Ethan seethed in silence. As usual, Fisher, McBurney, and Hicks's star attorney had all the right words, even if what he said was so much bullshit.

His father seemed to take his silence for agreement. "Look," he said, "I know we haven't seen eye to eye on a lot of things lately—"

Ethan snorted.

"—but," continued Jack, "I only want what's best for you."

"Then give me back the money you took."

Jack sighed and shook his head. "Money isn't what's at stake here, Ethan."

"Then what is?"

"Doing what's right."

Ethan looked down at his hands that had curled into fists. He forced his fingers apart, struggled to keep his voice even. "That would be life lesson number *what?*"

"Ethan—"

"No, really. They're all coming so fast now that it's hard to keep track. I think I need a program."

"For Christ's sake, don't be such a smartass!"

Ethan blinked, astonished to hear his father swear, but that only fuelled his anger. "Just so I'm clear," he said, his hands making fists again, "is 'Don't Be A Smartass' a *separate* life lesson or a subsection of the 'Doing What's Right' material we just covered?"

"Young man—" his father began, then stopped, and Ethan could see his jaw still working as if Jack Palmer were the one groping for words for a change. *Yes!* Ethan did a mental fist-pump, betting that his old man preferred the predictability of courtroom procedure to the uncertainty of what passed for life on Seminary Lane. Somewhere in that attorney's head of his there had to be a white room where everything he ever said got written down first, revised, edited for clarity, rehearsed, and then rehearsed some more.

"Ethan," his father finally continued, "you've had everything you could possibly want."

Ethan thought about that dumb *Freedom from Want* painting

that Moore-or-Less had bought in New York, and his anger rekindled. People like that artist and Jack Palmer didn't know a goddamn thing. "How would *you* know what I want?" he snapped. "You're never *around!*"

"That's not fair," said his father. "Need I remind you, my job pays for the house you live in, the clothes on your back, the food you—"

"I thought you said money isn't what's at stake here."

His father flushed. "You have no idea how lucky you are, Ethan. When I was your age—"

"Don't."

"Don't what?"

"Sing that song again. The ballad of Ann Almighty and the poor little Palmers."

His father's face looked like a sudden scar as he turned toward the picture in the rosewood frame. Drawing a deep breath, he said, "All I ever wanted was to teach you values you could hold on to your whole life."

"Values, huh?" Ethan was surprised by the venom in his own voice, but it gave him strength as he plunged ahead. "Like that case you're working on now? Defending a man the whole world *knows* is guilty? The other driver got it all on video. *Recorded* him staggering at the scene of that accident, for Christ's sake, then recorded him just driving off. And the guy claims he's *innocent?* I'm wondering what value *that's* teaching anyone. How about this? When you drink and drive, don't run into people with cellphones."

Turning again to Ethan, his father spoke evenly, but heat underlined every word. "Everyone is entitled to due process. Everyone is innocent—"

"Until proven guilty? The video's already done that!"

"That video should never have been made public before the trial. It compromises—"

"Everyone *knows* who it compromises. The team of lawyers who have to *defend* that jerk-off."

"It was an accident that could have happened to *anyone!*" Jack shouted, his face crimson.

Now it was Ethan's mouth that hung open. But only for a moment. "You're actually standing *up* for the guy?"

His father's hands gripped the arms of the wingback as though he were holding himself in place. "The man's a respected government official with years of public service to his credit. He made a mistake."

Ethan leaped to his feet. "The guy gets drunk and rear-ends another driver then leaves the scene of the accident before making sure nobody is hurt. And that's a *mistake.* But *I* clip the corner of a garage and receive the full punishment of Palmer law. That's beautiful." He turned and headed toward the doorway.

"Ethan! We haven't finished here yet."

Ethan ignored him.

"Don't you *dare* walk away when I'm talking to you! Do you hear me?"

Ethan grabbed the handle of the front door and wrenched it open. Because he knew his father was expecting him to slam it, he left it swinging wide.

"Getting to be a habit?" asked Pete.

Ethan looked at the joint in his hand. "This?" He took another toke, then handed it back to his friend.

Pete sucked on it, held his breath for a long moment, and then released the sweet smoke, watching it curl over their heads. "No. You arguing with your dad and then running off."

"Seems like it," Ethan said. Then, "Hey, you didn't have plans tonight, did you?"

"Nah."

Ethan frowned. "You turning into a monk or something, buddy? When's the last time you had a date?"

Pete gave an exaggerated sigh. "*Please* tell me we're not going there again."

"Look, I told you that Hailey Pettinger has the hots for you, right?" He'd gotten that from Rico, who played soccer with Hailey's brother.

"Not my type," said Pete.

"And what type would that be? Inflatable with a big round mouth?"

"Funny," Pete replied.

"I mean it, man. You haven't gone out with anybody since you took Corrine to the prom. And that was, like, four *months* ago."

"Can I help it if I'm choosy?"

"There's choosy and then there's celibate." Ethan stuck a finger in his mouth, flicked at something on his tongue.

"Let's get *your* life straightened out and then we'll worry about mine, okay?" said Pete, offering Ethan what remained of the joint.

Ethan shook his head. "I'm good."

The October air made them both tug their jackets around them. Ethan hadn't had time to grab something warmer, but his jacket was the least of his worries. What troubled him more were his shoes. After catching the Metro Transit, he'd walked the block and a half from the stop to Pete's, where he'd ranted about his old man for a good half-hour. Then the two of them had walked to Subway, bought Steak & Cheese footlongs with Cokes, and ridden the bus down to the Arm. After all that activity, Ethan's feet felt like someone had poured acid over them, and despite the cool of the evening, he'd taken his shoes and socks off revealing blisters that had formed, broken, re-formed, and then broken again. He wasn't looking forward to cramming his feet back into those christly wingtips. The joint had taken the edge off, but he knew it would be an interesting walk back to the bus stop.

Pete took a final toke then tossed the burning remnant into the waves. "You think it's safe?" he asked.

"To go out with Hailey?"

Pete pointed at the dark expanse before them. "The harbour."

"How'd we get from dating to that?" asked Ethan, looking at his friend more closely. "You fried?"

Pete's face creased in a foolish grin. "Sorry, man. I goof on good weed."

They sat in silence for a moment. Then, "What'd you mean about 'safe'?" asked Ethan.

Pete nodded toward the Arm. "All those millions they spent cleaning it up. They say the bacteria level's okay now, but would *you* swim in it?"

"Tonight?"

Pete elbowed him. "In the *summer,* fool."

Ethan considered. "There's still plenty of bacteria. They allow so many parts per million, right? There'll always be shit out there." He yawned and looked at his watch. "I should be heading back. Work tomorrow." When he'd finally run out of steam ragging on his old man, Ethan had told Pete about his nightmare afternoon at The Chow Down and the schedule Lil had given him.

"So when do you actually start *making* money at that place?"

Ethan gave his buddy a palms-up *Who knows?* and began pulling his socks back on, his face contorting with each tug. Then came the shoes and a string of profanities.

"Whoa, you *eat* with that mouth?"

Ethan told Pete what he could do with his own mouth— and exactly what parts of his anatomy might benefit from the experience—as the two gathered their things and headed up the street to the bus stop.

"What's Allie doing tonight?" asked Pete.

Ethan shrugged. "I was supposed to call her when I got cleaned up after work, but then this thing with my old man set me off." He pulled out his cell and pressed the power key. "I turned this off at work"—he didn't bother mentioning that Ike had threatened to heave it into the alley behind the kitchen if he didn't—"and forgot to turn it back on." As the screen powered up, both he and Pete could see that Allie had left two messages. Ethan speed-dialed her, but the call went immediately to her voice mail. "Busy," he said, pressing End and returning the phone to his pocket.

"You aren't leaving her a message?"

Ethan looked at him. "Why all the questions?"

It was Pete's turn to shrug. "Just thought she might be wondering where you are."

"Where I am," muttered Ethan, "is *walking* when you and I should be tooling in the Cobra." Despite his buzz from the weed, he was limping again, which only made him more pissed at his old man.

"Yeah, about that," said Pete. "I saw Filthy driving it this morning on Robie."

Ethan halted. "That's *so* not an image I need in my head right now, okay?"

Pete smiled sympathetically. "Sorry, man. Try that one instead." He gestured toward the water behind them, its dark surface twinkling with lights reflected from buildings on the other side of the Arm. "Cool, huh?"

It *was* cool, but Ethan's earlier comment echoed in his head: *There'll always be shit out there.*

And even all those parts per million wouldn't add up to the shit he knew he'd be in when he saw his old man again.

Chapter 8

"Some of us weren't sure we'd see you again," said Lil as Ethan came through the door of The Chow Down the next day. "Hey, Ike!" she called toward the kitchen. "You owe me five bucks!"

The cook stuck his head out through the swinging door, spied Ethan, scowled, and disappeared again.

"I'm not feeling the love," said Ethan.

"Oh, don't mind him. Ike's a sweetheart when you get to know him." Taking chairs down off tables, she nodded at Ethan's feet. "Where're your dancin' shoes, darlin'?"

Ethan grinned. Although still tender, his feet felt better than yesterday thanks to the cream he'd put on them last night and again this morning. Not to mention the cross-trainers he was wearing. They'd cost him close to three hundred bucks at The Running Room, but at the time he'd only been thinking about how great they looked. Moulded specifically to Ethan's feet, the shoes now cushioned them perfectly without chafing the blistered parts. "Like them?" he asked Lil.

She whistled. "Honey, they're a thing 'a beauty."

Then he noticed the shoes on her own feet—no-name athletic wear she'd probably bought at Zellers for fifteen bucks—and felt awkward. "So," he said, quickly changing the subject, "what do you need me to do?"

"For one, keep wearin' those tight jeans you got on. I got lots 'a comments about you from the girls yesterday."

Ethan tried not to shudder. "The girls" were four old women, obviously regulars, who had come in just before the end of his shift. None of them looked under sixty, he doubted any of them still had their own teeth, and he was pretty sure one of them was wearing a wig—a dirt-cheap job with straw-thick "hair" and an obvious seam on one side. But they'd been nice to him, asked him all sorts of questions, and ignored the fact that he dropped their napkins, sloshed a coffee on their table, and mixed up two of their four orders. "What'd they say about me?"

"That's just between us girls," Lil winked, reaching into the pocket of her apron. "But they left you this," she said, and handed him some cash.

"Hey!" Ethan exclaimed as he took the four fives. "That's the best tip I got all day!"

"After you left," said Lil, "the girls were askin' me how your first day went, 'n' I happened to tell 'em how you'd ended up owin' more'n you earned. A few minutes later, they come up 'n' give me the fives and told me to make sure I gave you the money. Said they all knew what it was like to have rough first days." Lil reached out and, much to Ethan's surprise, plucked the bills from his hand. "Now you're all paid up. You're startin' with a clean slate this mornin'."

Ethan sighed. "Easy come, easy go, huh?"

Lil studied him for a moment, glanced down at the money in her hand, then looked at him again. Returning the cash to her apron, she continued, "Just so you know, Ethan, twenty bucks is a whole lot 'a money for those four. One of 'em barely gets by on her widow's allowance and the other three earn minimum wage cleanin' rooms over at the Marriott."

Ethan's eyes widened. "Kind of old to be working, aren't they?"

"People gotta eat and make their rent no matter how old they are."

Ethan felt his face redden.

"Just so you know, okay?" she repeated.

Ethan nodded.

"Now, we got tables to get ready, darlin', so move those sweet jeans 'a yours."

As he helped her hoist off the remaining chairs, Ethan could tell it was going to be another long day, but he was actually looking forward to the work. It would help keep his mind off the bomb his old man had dumped on him that morning.

His second day wasn't worse than his first. He dropped only one meal—and that was because the plate was extra hot when he grabbed it—though he screwed up at least as many orders as before. As Lil had warned him, Sunday was The Chow Down's busiest day of the week when the weather was good, and no sooner did one group leave than another horde took their place. He didn't even have time to wipe off the tables before the next bunch sat down, so he mentioned to Lil that a "Please Wait to Be Seated" sign might be a good thing. Lil had just laughed. "Darlin', customers been seatin' themselves in this place for years. If I put up a sign like that, you'd hear 'em hootin' clear over to Pier 21." So Ethan had wiped around flabby arms and beer bellies, welcoming everyone through clenched teeth as he laid out paper placemats and filled customers in on the day's special, which made him think of Allie.

After she had watched yet another pay-per-view basketball game with him last month, Allie had made Ethan suffer through a program on the Food Network about high-end restaurants. Boring as hell, but he'd learned that one of the first skills servers in fancy places mastered was something called "romancing the food," which involved describing for customers in vivid detail any item on the menu—how a particular cut of meat was prepared, how the ingredients of a sauce complemented an entree, stuff like that. There was, of course, no romancing of food at The Chow Down. "Today's special is Wieners With Sauerkraut," he told each new group and was surprised at the number of people who ordered it. He had trouble just looking at it when he carried it out of the kitchen holding his breath because it smelled a lot like ripe compost.

On the plus side, learning how to ring in the orders wasn't nearly as bad as he thought it would be, mostly because the owner, the elusive Mr. Anwar, had installed a touch-activated computer, similar to an iPad, that fast-tracked the process. During Lil's demonstration of the system that morning, Ethan figured out a couple of shortcuts she hadn't known about herself. "Cute butt and brains, too," she'd said.

As the day wore on, he found himself wondering whether "the girls" would return, but they didn't. Instead he had taxi drivers and truckers on their breaks, clerks and cashiers who worked at the shops down on the waterfront, and family after family who seemed to eat whenever the mood struck them. And then there were the weird ones: a man in a too-big trench coat that he kept buttoned up to his neck like he was hiding explosives strapped to his chest; a woman who hummed to herself, rocked back and forth, and kept slipping food into her purse; and a long-haired guy with fully inked arms that reminded Ethan of snakeskin. For some reason, that last one creeped him out most of all. There was something snakelike about his eyes, too. Cold, like he was studying everyone who came through the door, calculating striking distance. Ethan thought he could feel those eyes following him whenever he came out of the kitchen, but he knew that was just his imagination working overtime. Still, it was a relief when the guy finally left.

Many of the customers who came in greeted Lil by name, calling to her from across the diner as Ethan was seating them.

Few bothered asking him *his* name even though he hadn't yet gotten his tag, but he liked the anonymity. It wasn't like he'd be bragging to people about working there.

During his half-hour lunch, which he finally got at two in the afternoon, Ethan sat on the back step in the alley behind the kitchen revelling in the simple feeling of not standing on his feet. He could go hard on a basketball court for a long time, but he'd never known his legs to be as tired as they were now. At least he didn't have more blisters.

Lil had told him he could ask Ike to make him something for his lunch, but Ethan had served—and cleaned up after—so much food that putting any in his mouth was about the last thing he wanted to do. Besides, he wouldn't have had the nerve to ask Ike anyway. During a brief lull that morning when Ethan hadn't been rushing out of the kitchen, he'd found himself studying a tat on the back of the guy's neck. Ethan couldn't see it all—part of it extended down inside his T-shirt—but the part he *could* see showed a heart with the word *Mike* inside it, which Ethan found more than a little surprising. He'd been standing there grinning to himself when Ike suddenly swung around and barked, "Wha'*choo* lookin' at, dipshit?" Which was when Ethan had grabbed the too-hot plate. The tirade that followed the loss of a Linguine With Mushrooms and the plate it was on still echoed in Ethan's ear.

There wasn't much to see out here in the alley, since it bordered a three-storey brick building. According to Lil, the place had been a lot of things over the years, including a box factory and a brothel, and it was now being converted into condominiums—expensive ones, judging by the big sign out front. He'd overheard a customer asking Lil about it, and she'd told the guy she wasn't the least bit surprised. "Too many young people are headin' out west for jobs," she'd sighed. "Pretty soon Halifax won't be much more'n a summer home for retirees.

When I win the lottery, sweetie, the only things I'll invest my money in around here is pharmacies and funeral homes."

Taking a long swallow of a root beer he'd grabbed from the fridge, Ethan leaned back against the top step and studied the brick building. Since most of the structures in this area had been destroyed in 1917 during the Halifax Explosion, this one must have been built sometime after that. Not *long* after that though, Ethan thought, since the exterior was in pretty rough shape. He briefly wondered why the owner hadn't just torn it down and started fresh, which probably had more to do with city bylaws than preserving historic property. His old man had done some legal work for an architectural firm, and Ethan had heard him tell Jillian over dinner one night how builders often had more leeway when renovating than with brand-new construction. Sooner or later, Ethan thought, everything came down to loopholes, something his old man was an expert on.

Jack had been out somewhere with Jillian when Ethan had gotten home last night, which had postponed the blow-up he'd expected after their earlier confrontation. And, extra bonus, Jillian hadn't stayed over. Ethan figured she went home to catch up on all the beauty-product infomercials she'd PVRed—it was a full-time job being on the cutting edge of cosmetics, right?— and he'd idly wondered if Moore-or-Less had any New York artwork honouring that kind of commitment.

His old man was in the kitchen when Ethan came down for breakfast and was visibly taken aback to see his son up so early. Ordinarily on a Sunday, Ethan didn't drag himself out of bed much before noon. There had been a few awkward moments as Ethan pawed through the refrigerator for orange juice and eggs, and he was surprised his dad hadn't launched into lecture mode already. But that was only the first of his surprises.

"About our talk last night," Jack said.

Standing in front of the open refrigerator, Ethan sighed. "Look, I have to be somewhere in an hour. Can we make this quick?" He waited for his father's usual opening volley.

"I want to apologize for losing my temper," said Jack.

Ethan closed the refrigerator door and turned to him, astonished.

"I should never have shouted at you," Jack continued. "And I shouldn't have called you a smartass. I'm sorry."

Ethan gaped at him. "Yeah, well . . . okay."

"It's not okay," said Jack. "I let my anger get the better of me."

Ethan wasn't sure what was expected of him here. Was this supposed to be one of those moments like on daytime talk shows where family members buried the hatchet, embraced, and lived happily ever after—at least until the next commercial break? Was *he* supposed to apologize now, too? But he'd already said he was sorry for forging the note he'd given Moore-or-Less. What else was he supposed to apologize for? Criticizing his father for defending a prick? Walking out while his father was still screaming at him? Ethan wasn't sorry for either of those things. It was safer not to say anything. He nodded.

A moment passed, during which Jack cleared his throat, got up from the table, and walked over to the window. Beyond the glass, Ethan could see the corner of the garage that a carpenter had repaired the day before, and now the siding was flawless again. Too bad. He'd grown used to seeing the damage. It was evidence to anyone passing by that life at 37 Seminary Lane was less than absolutely perfect, no matter what his father might like people to believe.

"Look, Ethan," his father began, turning to face him, "I had a couple of visitors last night before you came home."

So that explains it, thought Ethan, remembering how he'd found it unusual to see his father sitting in the January room.

His mind ran through a number of possibilities. Moore-or-Less and the guidance counsellor, Mr. Rahib, were the most likely candidates. Although he couldn't imagine teachers making house calls, it would explain his old man's *Nothing Seems To Matter To You* speech. Maybe house calls from teachers were one of the perks of owning a McMansion in Cathedral Estates. If you could call that a perk.

Jack brushed at a non-existent piece of lint on his shirt, an action Ethan had seen him perform a hundred times and had always interpreted as preening but now realized was a way of buying time. "I've been asked to run for public office," his father said, his face crinkling in a broad grin. "A few months ago, a committee was struck to review my work, my political affiliations, and my public persona, and last night two of the committee members officially asked me to represent their party in the provincial election next year."

"That's great," Ethan said. Was it? He didn't know.

And then, suddenly, he realized what was happening here. His father was asking him if it was okay to run for public office. His father was asking for his permission.

Ethan's head reeled. But, as he thought about it in the silence that settled around them, he could understand why his old man would want to ask, would *need* to ask. How many YouTube clips had Ethan seen showing husbands and wives and sons and daughters of politicians caught in the public eye? He remembered a news story not long ago about the teenaged son of a government official who'd wrecked a vehicle that was leased by the province. It had been humiliating for the official, and for the son, too, whose accident wouldn't have been newsworthy if it weren't for his mother's job.

For a moment, Ethan revelled in this new position. After having been told *No!* countless times, he would finally get to know what it felt like to have the power to do the same. Not that

he'd made up his mind—he'd have to think all this through—
but he was going to enjoy watching his father squirm for a
change.

Jack cleared his throat again. "The thing is—"

"I'll have to think about it," said Ethan.

His father raised an eyebrow. "Think about what?"

"Whether it's okay with me and Raye."

"Ethan," said his father, and Ethan could hear something
different in his voice. Embarrassment? "I've already accepted
the nomination."

"You *what?*"

"It's the logical next step in my career, something I've been
grooming myself for."

Ethan felt his fingernails dig into his palms. "And it didn't
cross your mind for a second that it could be a problem?"

"Nothing worth doing is without its problems," said Jack.

"Let me guess," said Ethan. "Another life lesson."

Jack frowned. "Look, I didn't intend for this to be something
else for us to fight about."

"Then why bother telling me about it if you didn't care what
I thought?"

"Because," said his father, "I'm going to need your
cooperation."

"My cooperation," said Ethan softly. Something was building
inside him, and it was easier for him to parrot words than to try
putting his own together. His hands clenched again.

"You're going to have to clean up your act, Ethan. Episodes
like the other night have to stop. I certainly can't have reporters
photographing my son speeding through the streets of Halifax,
or, for that matter, getting involved in *any* activity that would
resonate negatively with voters."

His fingernails now carving half-moons in the flesh of his
palms, Ethan struggled for words but could find none.

"And you'll have to start applying yourself in school. You're graduating this year. You need to start thinking about what you want to do with your life."

Now, at last, his own words came. "Oh, so now you're grooming *me*."

"Ethan, it's time for you to grow up. You're seventeen now and—"

"Seventeen and a *half*," corrected Ethan.

"And a half," repeated his father. "Even more reason to put an end to the kind of ridiculous behaviour I've seen lately."

"You think maybe I should consider the priesthood?" Ethan heard his voice rising, his words caroming off the granite countertop and stainless-steel appliances. "That should get you the *church* vote."

"Ethan—"

"And there's always volunteer work, right? Soup kitchens, food banks."

"For heaven's sake—"

"Better yet," interrupted Ethan, snapping his fingers to signal a brainstorm, "you could send me to some place in Africa. All those AIDS babies, right? Think about the photo ops!"

"I need you to be serious about this, Ethan."

"What about what *I* need? Nothing is *ever* about that, is it?"

"What are you talking about? I'm doing this as much for you and Raye as I am for me."

"You keep telling yourself that," Ethan snarled, turning and heading toward the hallway.

"Can't we have *one* conversation that you don't walk out in the middle of?"

Ethan continued down the hallway. "When did we ever have a *conversation*?" he shot over his shoulder. "And by 'conversation' I mean something that didn't involve you telling me how to live my life."

"Ethan, please—"

"The next time you've got another big announcement to make," Ethan shouted as he strode toward the front door, "save yourself some time and put it in a memo. Your secretary can give it to me." And then he was gone.

Taking a final swallow of his root beer, Ethan shoved thoughts of his father aside and tried to prepare himself for the second half of his shift. He hadn't meant to get all worked up again, but he could feel the heat in his face despite the cool of the alley where he sat. He turned his attention again to the building under construction. The builders certainly had their work cut out for them—lots of the bricks were missing, several more were crumbling away, and the rest needed to be repointed. Funny how everything fell apart eventually. Like his relationship with his old man. There was a time when he'd looked up to his father, admired how sure of everything he always was. He'd even hoped someday to find a job he loved as much as his dad loved the law. After all, people *had* to love something they put that much time into, didn't they?

In the last few years, though, Ethan had come to doubt whether his old man was sure of anything. Most of the time, he just seemed caught up in making sure everyone *thought* he was. And as far as loving the law, Ethan wondered now whether it was the legal profession he loved or the attention it brought him. People were always telling Ethan about seeing news clips of his father, reporters interviewing him about a case he'd just won or a suit he'd just filed. And now he was running for a seat in the provincial government. Christ!

"Break's over, numbnuts."

He turned to see Ike glaring at him through the screen in the kitchen door and stifled a groan. What was that thought he'd had a few minutes ago? *People had to love something they put that much time into, didn't they?* That clearly wasn't the case when you worked at The Chow Down. He pulled himself to his feet and headed back inside.

Chapter 9

"Coming over tonight?"

Hearing Allie's voice on the phone ask that question usually made his legs weak, and any other time he'd be heading over to her place in a second. But not this time.

"I'm beat, Allie," he yawned, the rocking motion of the bus making him even drowsier. "I'm just on my way home now. We got slammed at the diner and it didn't let up all day. I'd be lousy company."

"Really?" she asked, and he could hear the disappointment in her voice. "You owe me, Ethan Palmer. When you didn't call last night, I got stuck taking Bethany and her friends to see that new werewolf movie." Allie's younger sister was infatuated with all things werewolf. She and her friends had read a series of novels about werewolf dudes falling for human chicks, and now that Hollywood was churning out film adaptations, the girls were in tween heaven.

"Was it that bad?"

"You have no idea," moaned Allie. "They're all the same. Werewolf-guy loves her, can't have her but can't live without her, yadda-yadda."

"But did you *like* it?" Ethan teased.

"The drive home was even worse. Bethany and her friends gave play-by-plays of every scene in the book that the director left out."

"I feel your pain, babe."

"You can make it up to me, you know," she said.

"I can?"

"My aunt's leaving on a cruise tomorrow, and my parents are going over to her place tonight to say goodbye. Bethany, too. I'll have the house all to myself." She paused for dramatic effect, then added, "For hours."

His exhaustion vanished. "I'll be right over."

By the time he'd gotten off at the next stop, taken a transfer to Coburg, and walked the two blocks from there to Allie's house, the effect of Ethan's second day at The Chow Down had resurrected itself and multiplied. When Allie let him in, he was in the middle of a yawn that rivalled the surface area of the Fontaines' front door. "Wow. Sorry," he said, embarrassed, and then yawned again.

Allie looked at him with narrowed eyes. "You're sure this isn't because you were out partying with Pete all last night?"

"We weren't out *all* night. I had to get up for work this morning." He yawned a third time. Loudly. "Jeez," he said, embarrassed all over again.

"Maybe you should go wash your face off with cold water or something," said Allie.

"Right." He walked down the hallway to the powder room—Mrs. Fontaine's name for the closet tucked under the staircase where she and Allie's dad had recently installed a small vanity and dual-flush toilet—and ran the water for a moment, cupping it in his hands and splashing some on his face. After a solid minute of this, he turned off the tap, picked up the towel—an expensive microfibre in a decorator colour that he was sure Jillian would have recognized but that, to him, looked like Electric Lime—and dried his hands and face. Peering into the mirror, he was surprised to see how drawn his face looked. Another of his father's favourite Ann Almighty sayings was *Hard work never killed anyone.* Maybe not, but it sure made you look like shit.

"You hungry?" Allie asked when he came out.

He was starving. "What do you have?"

She opened the fridge to reveal a platter of cold chicken and bowls of leftover potato and pasta salads. "And for dessert," she offered breathily through pouty lips, "*moi.*"

He looked at her, his desire for food a sudden second to another longing. "You sure about this?" Although their relationship had grown increasingly physical since they'd begun going steady, Allie had drawn a line in the sand that he'd never pressured her to cross.

Smiling, she reached out and drew him toward her, her lips meeting his, her slim fingers moving through his dark hair. "I'm sure," she whispered when she finally pulled away.

His pulse pounding in his ears, Ethan murmured, "Okay if I have dessert first?"

———

Afterwards, while Ethan was inhaling cold chicken at the kitchen table, Allie asked him about The Chow Down. "So you survived a second day. What's it like there?"

He swallowed a mouthful and washed it down with milk. "It's a job," he said.

"What about the people you work with? Anyone interesting?"

"Lil, the woman who hired me, she's a character. Someone you'd see in a country music video."

"What's she look like?"

Ethan shared his first impression of Lil as a perfect match for their physics teacher.

"So I don't have to worry about losing you to a sexy co-worker, huh?"

Laughing, he shook his head.

"Any other servers?"

"Another part-timer, but I haven't met her. She's on when I'm not."

"Not much of a staff for a restaurant."

"It's not much of a restaurant. Just a hole-in-the-wall diner. Other than us there's just a couple guys in the kitchen. The cook and an assistant named Rake."

"Rake?"

"You'd have to see him."

Allie smiled. "What's the cook's name?"

"Ike Turner," he said, spooning more potato salad onto his plate.

Allie laughed. "Seriously? Ike Turner?"

Ethan stiffened. "You know him?"

"You've never heard the name before?" she asked.

"Should I?" Ethan's earlier cage-fighter impression surfaced again. "He famous or something?"

"Ike Turner used to be half of Ike and *Tina* Turner."

"Ike's *married?*" asked Ethan. He thought about the tattoo he'd seen, the heart with the name Mike in it. Of course, there was also that tat with the blonde. Was the guy bisexual?

Allie sighed. "The Ike I'm talking about is dead. He and Tina were one of the hottest R & B duos in the '60s and '70s."

Ethan's mind conjured an image of Ike at The Chow Down belting out the blues, and he shook his head. There's weird, and then there's *weird*.

"So what's *your* Ike like?" Allie asked.

"A helluva guy. Real prince." He hoped she didn't detect the irony in his voice.

Seeming to sense a sore spot, she changed the subject. "Tips any better today?"

"Actually, they were."

"How much did you make?"

Ethan pushed his chair back from the table. "After I paid for the linguine I threw on the floor—" Holding up his hands, he said, "Don't ask," then continued, "I made almost sixty bucks."

"That's great!"

"And that's not counting my hourly pay, which is going straight into my car account."

"What about your tips?"

"Those will, too, but not today's."

"Why not?"

He grinned. "Pete told me Ragged Ending's performing at the Pier next month." He reached into his pocket and pulled out two tickets. "So I picked these up on the way home."

Allie squealed. "Ragged Ending? Ethan, I *love* Ragged Ending!" She threw her arms around him.

"Hey, I may not know much about '60s R & B, but I know what my girl likes." Actually, Pete was the one who'd reminded him that Allie was a big fan of the group, but she didn't need to know that. After all, *he'd* bought the tickets, right?

She kissed him, her tongue tangling with his, then glanced down at her watch. "I think there's still time for another helping of dessert if you're interested."

He *was* interested.

Chapter 10

"I won't keep you long," said Ms. Moore.

Ethan hoped she meant it. Lil had called him that morning to tell him Jeannie, the other part-timer, couldn't make it that afternoon, and could he fill in. Even after yesterday's gruelling shift, he'd jumped at the chance for more work, but Moore-or-Less had cornered him after last class and asked him to stay behind. Only a handful of students remained in the hallway, the clang of locker doors putting exclamation points on the end of the school day.

"I spoke to your father on the weekend," said the teacher.

His eyes on the wall clock behind her, Ethan shifted his weight from one foot to the other. He could only imagine how Ike would react to him walking in late. "Yeah, he told me you did." Fortunately, he hadn't seen his father since their "conversation" the morning before. Ethan had gotten back from Allie's late, and his old man had left the house today before Ethan was out of bed—"An early meeting with his new media consultant," Raye told him over breakfast. Raye had been characteristically blasé about their father's decision to run for public office, which she'd learned about the night he accepted the nomination. "It is what it is," she'd said. Ethan had begun to wonder if there was anything that could possibly upset his sister.

The teacher opened her record book. "You're a much better student than your current performance indicates, Ethan."

Performance. He hated how adults threw that word around,

like the whole world was a stage. Suddenly, out of nowhere, he recalled a line from a play his class had read the previous year— *As You Like It* or some other damn thing by Shakespeare—and he grinned.

Moore-or-Less raised her eyebrows. "You find this amusing?" she asked, disapproval hardening her voice.

"Sorry," he said. "My mind was somewhere else."

The teacher sighed. "And therein lies the problem, Ethan. Being somewhere else." She held up the note he'd left with her sub the previous Friday. "I'm pretty good at spotting forgeries, especially when they contain misspellings." She pointed to a word—"For future reference, *absence* doesn't have two *s*'s"—then crumpled the paper and dropped it into the recycling bin. "I could have gone directly to the principal about this, you know. He takes a dim view of students who forge letters from parents."

Ethan sobered. "I appreciate that," he told her, glancing at the clock again. "It won't happen again. I promise." *Are we done here?*

"This meeting isn't about your skipping school or forging notes, Ethan."

Ethan suppressed a frustrated sigh.

"Even when you're here, you're not. It's like nothing matters to you. Nothing's all that important."

Ethan groaned inwardly. *Christ, she's channelling my old man.* He wasn't sure whether she wanted him to agree or disagree, and he couldn't take the chance of being wrong and prolonging her lecture. "I'll try harder, Ms. Moore. You'll see."

She took off her glasses, a hideous orange and green pair that looked more like abstract art than eyewear, and laid them on her desk.

"What is it you want, Ethan?" the teacher asked. "*Really* want?"

To get the hell out of here. "Same stuff everyone wants."

"And what would that be?"

Ethan fought a flare of annoyance, tried to keep his voice light. "You know, a good job, nice home, two point four kids, stuff like that."

She stared at him. "That's crap and you know it."

Ethan's eyes widened.

"People who *really* want those things," continued the teacher, "have a plan to make them happen. I don't believe you're thinking beyond the next five minutes."

Ethan looked at the second hand making another sweep of the clock. *You got* that *right*. "So," he said, his mind manufacturing images of Ike berating him at full volume, "I'll make a plan."

"Well, that's just wonderful," Ms. Moore said, her voice thick with sarcasm.

Ethan felt his face grow warm. "What do you *want* me to say?"

"That's the point, Ethan. You're always trying to feed people the easy answer instead of thinking things through." She reached for her glasses and put them back on. "Which is why I'm giving you an assignment."

Ethan shifted on the balls of his feet. "I already wrote it down in class."

"No," she said. "This is a different one."

Great. More work on top of everything else.

"You'll have until the end of the semester to complete it."

Ethan nearly grunted his exasperation. *Must be one hell of an assignment if it takes three months.* "What do I have to do?"

"Find out what's important, Ethan."

He blinked at her. "Excuse me?"

"To *you*. Find out what's really important to *you*."

"This a joke or something?" he asked.

"Far from it." She looked down at her hands folded in her lap. "You can keep doing for me in class what you've done since the beginning of the school year—that bare minimum you're so fond of. I know there's not much I can do at this point to change that." She looked up at him again. "But by the end of the semester, I want you to produce something honest for me. Something you really and truly believe. Tell me what's important to you."

"How long does it have to be?"

She smiled, but Ethan saw no warmth in her face. "For once in your life, Ethan, don't focus on the bottom line."

"How much is it worth?"

She turned to look out the window. "Far more than I can ever tell you."

Puzzled, he waited for her to say more, but she didn't. He glanced at the clock again. "Look, Ms. Moore, I have to—"

"Go," she said. "You're already halfway there anyway."

He left her still staring out the window.

———

"Where the hell you been?" snarled Ike.

Hanging his jacket on the peg by the kitchen door, Ethan replied, "I had to meet one of my teachers after school. She wants me to—"

"You get your ass here on time or leave it the hell home for good."

Clenching his jaws to keep from saying more, Ethan headed toward the dining area.

"I didn't *hear* you," Ike growled.

Ethan stopped in the doorway. "Okay," he said.

"Okay *what?*"

"I'll get my ass here on time."

"Make goddamn sure you do."

Lil clucked sympathetically as Ethan came out of the kitchen and began clearing a table just vacated by a guy in a green jacket with *White Glove Movers* lettered on the back. Although it was in Lil's section, he didn't mind helping her out. Besides, he hadn't forgotten Ike's mantra: *You don't walk away from a mess.*

"Don't take it personally," Lil said.

"How else should I take it?" he muttered. "I got here as soon as I could, okay? Maybe the Incredible Hulk could cut me a break once in a while. " He shrugged. "I guess a guy like *him* has never needed one."

She reached for the mover's dirty dishes that Ethan was stacking on one side of the table. "Ike's had his share 'a troubles," she said.

"Poor him. Looks like he could handle whatever comes at him."

"You'd be surprised," she said. She hesitated for a moment before adding, "I think you remind him of somebody."

"Who?"

Lil opened her mouth to say something else, but just then the bell above the door rang and a short old man in baggy pants and a threadbare sweater entered.

"Hey, Boots," said Lil.

"Afternoon, Lil," he replied, taking a seat in a booth and nodding at Ethan.

"Boots," said Lil, "meet Ethan Palmer. He took over for Selena. Ethan, this is Boots McLaughlin."

Ethan stuck out his hand and the little man took it. His hand in Ethan's felt papery and frail, and Ethan was careful not to grip it too hard.

"Nice to meet you," said Boots.

"Same here," said Ethan.

"You've got big shoes to fill."

Ethan winked at Lil. "I've heard that's not *all* I have to fill."

The little man chuckled. "A sense of humour. I like that. It'll come in handy around this place," he said, nodding elaborately toward the kitchen, and Ethan immediately warmed to the old guy.

"What can I get you?" asked Ethan.

"He'll have the Western Sandwich," said Lil. "No tomato."

"That right?" Ethan asked.

Boots nodded.

"And," added Lil, "take off twenty-five cents because of the tomato."

Ethan turned to her, surprised, and she shot him a look that told him she was serious. "Anything to drink with that?" he asked Boots.

"Just water," the little man said.

"Shouldn't take too long," said Ethan. "I'll be right back with your water."

"No rush," Boots said. "I'm in no hurry."

Later, after Boots had paid his bill and left, Ethan began clearing the table and was surprised to see the old guy hadn't left him a tip. "Jeez," he muttered under his breath as Lil walked by.

She stopped. "Anything wrong?"

"That old guy seemed nice enough."

"He *is* nice," she said.

"To *you* maybe." He nodded at the table. "A tip on a Western Sandwich minus the tomato wouldn't've killed him."

Lil pointed to a small rectangular piece of paper beside the empty water glass. "Boots *always* tips," she said.

Ethan picked it up, turned it over, and then realized what he was looking at.

"Boots don't have a lot 'a money," she said, "which is why he always orders the cheapest thing we got. And why I deduct the quarter for the tomato he never eats."

"You'd think a guy without a lot 'a money wouldn't waste what he has on *these* things." Ethan tossed the paper on the table.

Lil picked it up and handed it to him. "They're not for himself. He buys these dollar lottery tickets to leave as tips when he comes in here."

Ethan scowled. "Someone should tell him about probability."

"Probability?"

"We learned it in math. The odds of winning anything big on these are, like, one in nineteen million. This isn't worth the paper it's printed on. I'd rather have the buck."

It was Lil's turn to scowl. "He may get the cheapest thing on the menu, but Boots has too much pride to leave only a buck for a tip. With the ticket, he's leavin' you a chance for a whole lot more." She looked at Ethan for a moment, and he sensed a story coming like the one she'd shared about "the girls." He was right.

"Boots is a sweet man, Ethan. A real good guy. He worked hard all his life paintin' houses until his back gave out on him, and now he gets by on his old age pension. His wife died a couple years ago, so that cut his income in half." She lowered her voice. "Just between you 'n' me, he came in here once on his way home from grocery shoppin' and all I saw in his bag were cans of soup. *Dented* cans, the ones stores sell real cheap just to get rid of 'em. Can you imagine eatin' soup three times a day?"

Ethan felt his stomach shift uneasily.

"He only comes in here when he's saved up a few bucks," she continued. "It's not much, but it's a big treat for him. He gets lonely."

Ethan looked at her, dumbfounded. "How d'you know all this?"

She shrugged. "People got a whole lot to tell you if you take the time to listen. And you don't just hear it in what they say."

Ethan thought for a moment. "Why do you call him Boots?"

"That's how he introduced himself to me when he first come in here. I don't even know his real first name. I asked him about it once, though. Kind 'a sad." She looked out the window at the harbour. The passenger ferry was halfway across to Dartmouth, a white wake churning behind it. "He grew up dirt poor in Sydney Mines. His parents couldn't afford to buy a growin' kid shoes all the time, so they bought him those black gum-rubber boots. You probably don't know what I mean."

"I know," said Ethan. He'd often seen them lined up on shelves in Canadian Tire.

"His feet had more growin' room in those, so he wore 'em most of the year, except in the summer, when he went barefoot. The kids at school took to callin' him Boots, and the name just stuck." Lil looked at Ethan sharply. "He didn't tell me this in a feel-sorry-for-me way. He was just answerin' my question about his name, tellin' me what I wanted to know."

Ethan nodded.

"So if he comes in here and leaves you a lottery ticket, you gotta know that's a bigger tip than a lot 'a these jokers throw on the table, okay?"

Ethan nodded again. He pulled his wallet out of his jeans and slid the ticket inside, then returned it to his back pocket.

On the way to his bus stop after work, Ethan thought again of Lil's story about Boots's childhood and how, in some ways, it was like his old man's. Jack Palmer had grown up in rural Hants County, the oldest of three children whose father cut pulpwood and whose mother stayed at home caring for their growing family. John Palmer Senior had died without life insurance in a logging accident when John Junior was nine and, as Jack liked to tell people, his still grieving mother had immediately begun cleaning people's houses and taking in laundry to make ends meet. It had been a struggle to keep the family together, but she'd somehow made the mortgage payments on their tiny home—most months, anyway—and kept food in their bellies. Barely, Jack said, but she always managed. And she never once complained. She was, as he frequently described her, "the epitome of grace under pressure who taught her children by example the value of honest hard work and the importance of education." Although Jack was the only one of the three kids to go to university, his sister, Carol, had gone to business school and now worked at an accounting firm, and their brother, Paul, had a good job at the shipyards. Ann Palmer had been proud of all they'd accomplished and so were her children. Jack especially.

When people had asked her how she'd been able to keep going after her husband died, how she'd managed to raise three children all on her own with so little income, she'd apparently responded with the comment about obligation that had become Jack Palmer's mantra, although Ethan figured his grandmother probably said it a lot more simply—*You do what you have to* or some garbage like that. He wondered if all parents prettied up their past to cram down their kids' throats. Probably.

Ethan thought again about Boots, thought about the irony of two guys starting out with nothing and ending up so differently, then froze momentarily on the sidewalk, looking at his reflection in a convenience store window. *Christ,* he thought, shaking his head, *the old man's got* me *doing the life-lesson thing now.*

Grinning at his own foolishness, he glanced at his watch and saw he still had ten minutes before the next bus arrived, so he turned and headed into the store. He had a physics test the next day and knew he'd need a boost later that evening when he finally got around to studying, so he headed toward the cooler at the back and pulled out a couple cans of Red Bull. Opening his wallet to pay for them, he found the lottery ticket stuffed between two fives.

Impossible odds, yeah, but *somebody* wins those jackpots, right? As he handed the clerk his money, he thought again about how different the lives of his old man and Boots now were. *He worked hard all his life paintin' houses until his back gave out on him,* Lil had said. Which pretty much proved that his father's line about "honest hard work" was so much happy horseshit. Maybe what Boots had really needed all along was to catch a break, a chance that would really make a difference. A single run of good luck. Ethan looked again at the ticket in his wallet, then glanced around and saw the lottery scanner to his left. Because he was seventeen (and a half), he knew he couldn't cash a winning ticket, but there were other people lined up behind him so he was pretty sure the clerk wouldn't care who used the scanner. He took the change she offered him, then stepped aside to make room for a pimply-faced kid with a fistful of chocolate bars.

He walked over to the scanner, turned to see if anyone was interested in what he was doing, and was satisfied the roof would have to cave in to get this group's attention. He held the ticket's bar code under the red light but nothing happened. Then he realized the bar code was facing the wrong way, and he turned the ticket around. Holding his breath, he slid it carefully into the beam and saw a message appear in the scanner's display.

Not a winning ticket.

Big surprise. One in nineteen million. He shook his head in disgust, crumpled the paper in his hands, and tossed it into the garbage can beside the scanner, a can he now saw was nearly filled with other crumpled tickets. He was glad no one had seen him make a fool of himself.

On his way out the door, though, he suddenly had the feeling he'd been wrong about that. He sensed eyes staring at him, tracking him, but when he looked back the only person turned in his direction was the pimply-faced kid, and he was busy cramming a Butterfingers into his mouth.

Weird.

Chapter 11

Stretched out on his bed, his physics textbook open on his lap, Ethan took a final swallow of Red Bull then deftly tossed the can across the room into the wastebasket where the other one already lay empty. He turned again to the material in front of him, scanned it, and flipped the page. His pencil drumming against the book, he read aloud: "The maximum possible friction force between two surfaces before sliding begins is the product of the coefficient of static friction and the normal force. Assume that a curve with a radius of 60 metres is properly banked for a vehicle weighing 1338 kilograms travelling 100 kilometres per hour on dry pavement. Using 0.8 as the coefficient of static friction of a rubber tire on wet pavement, calculate the speed at which a car travelling that same curve on a rainy day will—"

Ethan halted the drumming, scanned ahead, frowned, then closed the book with a *thump*. What a frigging waste of time. It all made about as much sense as that crazy *Find-out-what's-important* assignment that Moore-or-Less had given him that afternoon. Well, one thing for damned sure that *wasn't* important was *this* crap. He pictured himself explaining to a cop how the coefficient of static friction of rubber on asphalt helped him determine the appropriate acceleration of his car, taking into account both the horizontal and vertical forces acting on the vehicle. It wasn't the math that bothered him. It was the fact that all of it was such complete and utter bullshit.

If Allie were here, he'd buckle down and slog through it.

He always worked better when she was with him. There was something about her that kept him grounded, focused, made him want to do better.

But Allie wasn't here. He lifted the textbook to eye level, estimated the required force and angle of entry, then sent the book sailing across the room toward the wastebasket. It might actually have made it had it not opened halfway through its arc. The heavy cover bounced off the rim, and the book banged against the wall and landed in a heap under his poster of a fire-red Cobra SVT.

A moment later, his bedroom door opened and Raye stuck her head inside. "Construction or demolition?" she asked.

"People's choice," he replied.

"I'll get back to you with the survey results." She entered the room, noting the physics textbook on the floor. "Test tomorrow?"

He grunted.

She moved toward his desk, saw the ads displayed on his laptop's Web browser, and sighed. "Car porn. You're pathetic."

He grinned at her, but then his smile faded. "The one I told you about? Sold already."

She shrugged sympathetically. Bending down, she scrolled through the site. "Lots more here."

"No other Cobras, though."

She kept scrolling, then stopped when a midnight blue Mustang GT appeared. She bent over the laptop, then whistled when she saw the price. "People really charge that much for old cars?"

Ethan swung his legs over the side of the bed and sat up. "The owner's done a ton of work on her. Check out the specs."

Raye leaned closer to the screen and, as she read, Ethan saw her squinch her eyes.

He sighed. "You gotta tell him, Raye."

She ignored him, continuing to scan the specifications the car's owner had posted.

Ethan recognized a stalling strategy when he saw it. He knew she didn't understand half of what she was reading. "If *you* don't—"

She whirled to face him. "You promised you wouldn't say anything."

"Only because you said you'd do it yourself," said Ethan.

"And I will."

"Any time this decade?"

She turned back to the screen.

"What's the big deal anyway?" he asked.

She scrolled through the site at hyper-speed, not even pretending to read now. "There's this guy in my class," she said finally.

Even from the side, Ethan could see his sister's neck—unadorned by Jazz's artwork this evening—begin to redden. "What guy?" he asked, trying not to grin.

"Brad Clahane."

"What about him?"

"I think he likes me."

Ethan felt a familiar surge of protectiveness move through him. "So do you like *him?*"

Raye turned toward him, and Ethan could see the colour in her neck now blooming in her cheeks. She picked at a thread on her Canadiens jersey, which reminded Ethan of their father—she seemed to be considering her next words. Then, "He was going out with Celia Johnston until last week and—"

"Isn't she the one you said gave—"

"Blow jobs to half the junior boys' soccer team? Yeah, that was the rumour."

"And?"

"Turns out it wasn't a rumour."

Ethan raised his eyebrows. "Brad find out?"

She nodded. "Brad's on the team. The *other* half."

"Ouch," said Ethan.

"Yeah. Ouch."

"So what's this got to do with you not telling the old man about your eyes?"

Raye glanced at the laptop, its screensaver now sending random images of Mustangs hurtling across the display. "Jazz heard Brad tell Colin McAvoy he was thinking of asking me out."

Ethan's eyes narrowed. "I hope he's not expecting—"

She punched him in the shoulder. "Brad's a nice guy," she said.

"Yeah, well, I'm a nice guy, too, but—"

Raye stuck her fingers in her ears. "I can't HEAR you," she said, humming loudly until Ethan waved his surrender. Lowering her hands, she said, "Give me a break, okay? There's only so much my impressionable young brain can handle."

Ethan grinned. "You still haven't told me why—"

"Brad Clahane isn't gonna ask out a girl who wears glasses."

Ethan looked at his blue-haired, tongue-studded, frequently fake-tattooed sister and couldn't believe this was the same kid who, years ago, used to follow him around like a puppy, her short legs pumping madly to keep up. A lot of older brothers would have minded, but Ethan hadn't. He *said* he did, of course, but most of the time it was just an act for his buddies. He actually liked having Raye around. Some of it, he now knew, had to do with their mother dying; they had filled a void for each other at the time. But the rest of it had to do with Raye. Even as a little kid, she'd been her own person, never the annoying cling-on that so many of his friends' younger siblings were, probably because she intuitively knew how far she could push a moment, could always read people better than most adults he knew. Certainly better than their father could read Ethan, anyway.

Ethan wanted to reach out and put his arm around her now, wanted to tell her that if this Brad Clahane was the nice guy she said he was, he wouldn't care about the glasses. But he didn't. They were, after all, Palmers. Hands off. "There's always contacts, you know," he offered.

"Yeah, but they like to start you with glasses first." She nodded toward the Mustangs racing across the laptop's screen. "I still have that money if you need it," she said, changing the subject.

"Thanks," he said, "but your brother got himself a job. One that pays tips." He told her a little about The Chow Down and how Lil had offered him weekend shifts and at least one during the week, depending on the other part-timer's schedule.

"Sounds great," she said. "Dad know?"

"He didn't ask." And why would he? Jack Palmer was the centre of his own universe.

"What about school?" she asked, pointing at the physics textbook on the floor.

"Got it all under control," he said, getting up and retrieving the book. He laid it on his bed and then turned to her. "It might be better, though, if, you know . . ."

"If I don't say anything about it?"

"I don't need the extra grief right now," he said, thinking of what his father had said: *You'll have to start applying yourself in school.* It was a sure bet his old man wouldn't react well to news of his son working even more hours than he did at the pool.

She smiled slyly. "And you won't say anything about me needing glasses?"

Ethan's eyes widened. "Sounds a lot like blackmail to me, Rayelene Palmer."

As he knew it would, his use of her full first name drew an elaborate eye-roll from his sister. Rayelene had been their grandmother's middle name, and more than once Raye had complained to Ethan that it sounded like it belonged to some Arkansas housewife with big hair and ten kids. "We got a deal?" she asked.

He looked at her for a moment, then nodded slowly. "As long as you tell him yourself. You need to get those eyes checked out."

"Got it all under control," she echoed.

"Okay." Just as she was turning to leave, he added, "When do I get to meet this Brad guy?"

"We'll see," she replied, then left.

A moment later, Ethan could hear "Smoke on the Water" floating across the hall, but this time it had an oddly upbeat tempo. He sat on his bed, leaned back against the headboard, and flipped his physics textbook to the page where he'd left off, but it wasn't long before his attention wandered to his screensaver. He reached for the laptop and tapped the space bar. The Mustangs vanished, revealing the specs for the car that Raye had been looking at. Ethan skimmed them, then clicked his browser's Home key. In a moment, he was scrolling through mustangcobra.com. Although he knew the features of the 1996 Cobra SVT by heart, he scanned through them anyway, imagining himself inside the vehicle they described. He was no longer in his bedroom on Seminary Lane. He could smell the leather, could hear the pavement whine beneath his tires, could feel the powerful engine pulling him forward. Just as he was ready to really open her up, the textbook lying on his lap slid sideways and fell to the floor. Sighing, he picked it up and tried once more to care about the physics behind friction coefficients. After a moment he snapped the book shut.

Got it all under control, he thought.

Chapter 12

"So how'd you find it?" asked Allie as they left the physics lab. Already the hallway was filling with people heading toward the exits.

Ethan shrugged. "Okay," he said, but the nonchalance in his voice sounded false even to him. Though he'd tried every question on the test, nearly half of them made him wonder whether he'd looked at the right chapter in the textbook the night before. He'd guessed his way through the whole last section.

"Sweet mother of God," muttered Pete behind them. "Was that stuff even *physics?*"

Ethan turned, grinning. Given Pete's problems with math, everyone had been surprised when he'd signed up for Beaker's course that semester. In Pete's favour, he was great at the hands-on stuff, which made the labs easier for him than for some of the other students in their section, but tests and quizzes threw him—which effectively made Beaker his nemesis.

"You figure the guy lies awake all night dreaming up those questions?" asked Pete. "That vector crap, for instance. What the hell—"

"Hi, Mr. Becker," said Allie loudly.

Pete and Ethan turned to see the physics teacher leaving the lab with a stack of papers under his arm. "Hi, people," he said. "Can't wait to mark these tonight." He pointed at his armload.

"Knock yourself out," said Pete, and Ethan could hear the literal undercurrent in his friend's voice.

Apparently, so could the teacher. "I'm especially looking forward to *yours*, Pete," Mr. Becker said. "Your approaches to the problems are always so—" He paused. "—creative." He flashed Pete a big smile before continuing down the hallway.

Pete looked as though he wanted to flash the teacher something in return, and Ethan snorted.

"Come on, guys," said Allie, "let's go. I'm starving."

Earlier that morning, they'd agreed to a post-test lunch celebration at Perk Up Your Day, a coffee shop a couple blocks from the school. Not only did it serve slab-sized brownies, they were curious to see how much damage had been done there the day before. A video had gone viral overnight, and Ethan had watched it again and again, amazed by what a customer's cellphone had captured: a deer crashing through the coffee shop's plate glass window and stumbling around inside, disoriented, before leaping back out. No one knew how the deer had gotten so far downtown, but fear had clearly sent it scrambling for shelter and, seeing its reflection in the glass, the creature probably thought it was running toward another deer. Fortunately, its wounds turned out to be mostly superficial. Halifax police tranquilized it and released it far from the city.

A few minutes later, Ethan and his friends found themselves standing in a long line of other customers who'd come to check out the mess. There wasn't much to see. A new window had already been installed, and a guy was painting the coffee shop's name and logo on its centre. The only evidence of the deer was some deep gouges on the shop's tiled floor, probably made by its sharp hoofs.

After the trio had gotten their orders and grabbed a table near the window, Ethan nodded toward the buxom redhead working behind the counter. "Anyone notice her tips?" he asked.

"Ethan!" said Allie, feigning a punch to his arm.

"*Tips!* I said *tips!*" laughed Ethan. He pointed toward the glass jar on the counter by the cash register. "She's doing an okay job filling the orders, but you wouldn't know it from the money in her jar."

"You tipped her, right?" asked Allie.

He nodded. "I never thought much about it before, but now it's a whole other story."

"*Your* tips getting any better?" Pete asked.

Allie, who'd heard all this before, left to use the washroom while Ethan told Pete some of his latest experiences. "They're getting a little better," he said. "There are still assholes who don't leave anything, though."

"That's harsh," his buddy commiserated. "How long do you think you'll stay there?"

Ethan shrugged. "Not sure. I'm hoping to use the experience to get a job somewhere more upscale."

Pete looked at him, his expression unreadable.

"What?" asked Ethan.

"I never pegged you for someone who'd be waiting tables. I'm seeing a whole new side of you."

Ethan suddenly felt defensive. "What's that supposed to mean?"

"Hey, man, that wasn't a criticism—" Pete began, but then Allie returned to the table.

"Did you tell him about Boots?" she asked Ethan.

"Boots?" said Pete.

"A guy who comes into the diner every once in a while," said Ethan. He told Pete what Lil had said about the little man, finishing with the part about the lottery tickets. "Crazy, huh?"

Pete shrugged. "I think the old guy sounds kinda cool."

"That's what *I* said," agreed Allie.

"He leave you a ticket?" Pete asked.

Ethan nodded. "One. Didn't win anything."

"Like that's a shock," Pete commented dryly. He drained the last of his coffee and set his cup on the table. "My old man's been playing the same 6/49 numbers since before I was born and never won more than a few bucks and some free plays. Even somebody as bad at math as me knows a losing game when he sees one."

Ethan laughed, but Allie was strangely silent, and their conversation moved on to other things.

"You finished with these?"

The three turned to look up at the redhead standing beside them and pointing toward their empty cups and plates. From this angle, her ample breasts were even more spectacular.

"Yeah, we're done," said Pete. "Thanks."

The redhead leaned over the table collecting their dishes, her upper body inches from his buddy's face, and Ethan looked forward to the comment Allie would no doubt make later about their friend ogling those impressive boobs. But Pete seemed to look right through her as if she wasn't even there before turning to Allie and chatting about the physics test again.

Ethan's eyes widened. *Son of a bitch!* Before this moment, he'd never suspected a thing. He probably should have, he supposed, since Pete hadn't dated a girl for months, and never longer than a couple weeks. *Should I tell him that I know?* he wondered as the three got up to leave. *Or do I just wait for him to tell me himself?* The idea of a Palmer asking someone to open up about his personal feelings almost made him laugh, but Ethan wondered if Pete would ever bring it up on his own. After all, they'd known each other for years. If you couldn't tell your best friend you were gay, who *could* you tell?

Beyond his immediate surprise, Ethan really didn't know what to make of his discovery. He felt detached from it somehow, like his brain hadn't processed it yet. He couldn't picture Pete with another guy. Not that he *wanted* to. Christ!

But why hadn't Pete *told* him? They'd always shared everything, hadn't they? Even the stupid stuff, like all the shit with Ethan's dad. He couldn't imagine not having his buddy to talk to each time his old man pissed him off. Didn't *want* to imagine it. Pete could always cheer him up, could make him laugh no matter how bad he felt.

And suddenly Ethan thought about someone else who could make him laugh—Seth, with his jokes about faggots. And hadn't Ethan told a few of those over the years? More than a few. He couldn't remember Pete ever telling fag jokes, but then Pete never made fun of anyone, queer *or* straight. Were those jokes the reason he'd never told Ethan he was gay? Was he afraid their friendship would be over? That was something else Ethan couldn't imagine. As hard as it might be to accept that his buddy was a homo, it'd be a hell of a lot harder to lose his best friend.

As he followed Allie and Pete toward the exit, his thoughts turned to Ike. The cook had obviously gone through his own coming-out process—a guy didn't tattoo a man's name in a heart on his neck without making it obvious to everyone—so wouldn't he have some advice to offer a teenager who was still in the closet? By the time they reached the street and were heading toward their afternoon classes, Ethan had almost convinced himself that the next time he worked at The Chow Down, he should just come right out and ask Ike how he got the courage to tell people he played for the other team.

But then common sense returned, along with his memory of Ike's face as he'd snarled, "Wha'*choo* lookin' at, dipshit?"

Yeah, he'd wait for Pete to bring it up on his own.

Chapter 13

"You *born* stupid or do you hafta *work* at it?"

His face on fire, Ethan gritted his teeth as he held out the plate, the potatoes with the Roast Turkey Special silently mocking him. "Look, I forgot to ask, okay? He wanted fries instead of mashed. Sorry."

Judging from Ike's reaction, *sorry* didn't cut it. The cook snatched the plate from him, scraped the potatoes into the garburator, and dumped a serving of fries between the turkey and the cranberries while behind him Rake examined the ceiling. "Try not to drop it!" Ike growled, shoving the plate into Ethan's hands.

Ethan fumed as he returned to the dining area. Business was slow, probably because it was Hallowe'en. Even the university students who were always looking for cheap food had stayed away. With just two customers there, at different booths, Lil had taken a half-hour off to run some errands, and the only sound in the diner was the scrape of cheap cutlery on even cheaper plates. There was no way the customers hadn't heard Ethan getting ripped a new one in the kitchen, and the grins on both their faces when he came out confirmed it.

"Sorry again for the mix-up," he said as he set the plate in front of the customer who'd asked for the fries. It was the long-haired guy with the tattooed arms and eyes that seemed to bore holes through you. He looked to be in his thirties, which was unusual. Except for university students, most of the people who came to The Chow Down alone were older types, many of them senior citizens on fixed incomes. Guys in their thirties who ate there usually dragged a pack of bickering kids along with them.

"No problem," the guy said, pulling a well-chewed toothpick from the corner of his mouth and laying it on the table. He nodded toward the kitchen. "Ike's still Mr. Congeniality, huh?" He ran his hands through his black hair, pulling it behind his ears, and the cuffs of his leather jacket slid back to reveal his forearms. The ink encircling his arms was intricately patterned, and Ethan thought again of snakeskin.

"You know Ike?" asked Ethan. He'd only made six bucks in tips so far that afternoon, and he was hoping some conversation might translate into cash later.

The guy grinned—more a smirk than a smile, Ethan thought—and said, "Yeah, me 'n' Ike go way back." He reached for the ketchup bottle and slathered the red sauce on his fries.

Ethan wondered if the guy was just bullshitting him. Ike had to be a lot older than him. "*Way* back?"

"Far enough," the guy said.

"How'd you two meet?"

The guy forked two of the fries into his mouth, then spoke around the gooey mass as he pointed the fork at Ethan. "You ask a lot 'a questions."

Ethan felt himself flush. "Sorry. It's just hard to imagine Ike with a life outside that kitchen."

"Oh, he's got a life all right."

The comment hung in the air making Ethan feel weird. Was that a remark about the cook's *gay* life? "If there's anything else I can get you, just let me know, okay?" he said, moving off to refill salt and pepper shakers.

Later, coming out of the kitchen, Ethan was annoyed to see the guy had left without paying, and he bit back a curse at the thought of having to cover the loss out of his own pocket, especially on such a slow night. When he cleaned off the guy's table, though, he found a ten-dollar bill under his napkin in addition to the money for the meal. It was the biggest tip he'd gotten from a single customer so far, and he suddenly felt like he'd reached a turning point—maybe the time had finally come for him to start applying at better restaurants, like he'd told Pete a few days ago. Of course, he grinned to himself, even Kenny's Café would be more upscale than The Chow Down.

He thought again about the guy's arms, wondering if that was his connection with Ike—buddies who got their ink at the same shop. He began wiping off the table and idly wondered what it was like to be permanently marked in such an obvious way. Seth had a tat on his right shoulder, a Harley-Davidson logo that bled into a burst of flames, and he was considering adding an image of his dream machine, a Harley FXSTSB Bad Boy, to his left shoulder. Seth had tried to convince Ethan many times to get a tattoo of his own, but Ethan had seen enough tats at the pool to realize very few looked good for the long term. He did a flash-forward in his head and imagined the ten-buck tipper fifty years from now in a seniors' home, those inked arms like ruined sticks dangling from a wheelchair. He shuddered.

"Someone walk over your grave?" asked Lil, back from her errands and coming through the batwing doors carrying a large package of paper napkins. She grinned. "A little Hallowe'en humour, honey."

Ethan grinned back at her. "You ever see a guy with sleeve tats come in here?" he asked. "In his thirties maybe?"

"Sleeve tats?" she asked, picking up the napkin dispenser on the table next to his.

"Tattoos that cover the whole arm. This guy had full sleeves on both."

"Long black hair?"

He nodded.

She looked down at the metal dispenser in her hand and pressed a thick wad of fresh napkins into it. "Link Hornsby. Comes in every once in a while."

Ethan thought he detected something in her voice, an undertone he hadn't heard before. He showed her the ten-dollar bill. "Good tipper."

"Mm," she said. She put the dispenser back on the table and moved on to the next one, taking the large package of paper napkins with her. She separated a wrist-thick bundle from it, then hesitated as if unsure what to do next.

"What's up?" he asked, shoving the tip into his pocket.

She turned to him. "This is none 'a my business," she began, then stopped.

"What?" he asked.

She shrugged. "My parents always told me if you can't say somethin' good about a person, don't say nothin' at all."

"Okay," said Ethan, intrigued. "You gotta give me more than that, Lil."

The waitress turned to the single remaining customer sitting on the other side of the diner. "You okay, Benny? Need anything else?"

Benny, a tall man about fifty with stooped shoulders, looked up from his Bacon Burger Deluxe. "Maybe some more water when you get a chance, Lil. No rush."

Lil walked to the sideboard next to the batwing doors and grabbed a pitcher of ice water, then carried it to the man's table and topped up his glass. The *clink-slosh* of water and ice cubes seemed louder than usual.

Ethan moved toward the sideboard and waited for her to return with the pitcher.

"You need anythin' else, sweetie," Lil told Benny, "you just sing out, okay?"

"Thanks, Lil," the man said.

The waitress didn't speak to Ethan right away, busying herself first wiping the sides of the pitcher with paper towels. Then, lowering her voice, she said, "I'm not one for givin' advice. Woman my age waitin' tables in a place like this probably ain't the best person to be tellin' somebody else how to live their lives."

Her comment made Ethan think how different she was from his father, who could definitely learn a thing or two from Lil about offering advice. Jack Palmer subscribed to the Give It Whether They Want It Or Not approach, followed closely by the Repeat Often methodology, although lately he had been too busy with gearing up the campaign machine to harass his son.

"You aren't *telling* me anything, Lil," he said. "I'm asking."

Her next comment came in a muted rush. "I wouldn't be too impressed by anythin' Link Hornsby does."

Ethan raised his eyebrows. "Why's that?"

She shrugged. "Just rumours. Don't know if any of 'em hold water, but I'd steer clear 'a the guy if I was you."

"He left me a tip, Lil. He didn't ask me out."

She shrugged again. "I'm just sayin', okay?"

"Okay." He glanced at his watch and was relieved to see his shift was just about over. "Anything else you need me to do before I go?"

"Nah, it's dead tonight." More Hallowe'en humour, and they grinned at each other. "I got it covered," she said. "You take off."

"Thanks." He went to the register and began cashing out. When he'd finished, he retrieved his jacket from the kitchen—and was floored when Ike actually grunted a goodbye—then went back to the dining room. "See you Friday, okay?"

"You bet," she said, refilling more napkin dispensers.

Outside, the street lights were beginning to wink on, their pink glows easing into white, and the trees around them cast weird early-evening shadows on the pavement. Seeing the lacey patterns of bare branches beneath his feet as he walked to his bus stop, Ethan thought again about the guy with the freaky tattoos. Link Hornsby.

I'd steer clear 'a the guy if I was you.

No problem. Ethan wasn't exactly eager to strike up a friendship with someone whose skin made his own crawl. But he couldn't help wondering about the connection between Hornsby and Ike Turner. Former boyfriends maybe? The sudden thought of the surly cook enjoying a passionate moment with *any*one—man *or* woman—made him laugh aloud, drawing quizzical looks from a couple walking past him.

But he was still thinking about the two as he boarded his bus a few minutes later. And wondering whether that person named Mike knew the guy with the sleeve tattoos.

Chapter 14

"Here!" Ethan thrust the money into his father's hand. "Satisfied?"

Jack Palmer's fingers closed around the wad of bills. "This was *your* doing, Ethan, not mine," he said as he looked up from his desk in the study, another Jackson Browne song playing through hidden speakers. Ethan recognized the track as "Running on Empty," one of his old man's favourites, and felt a fresh flash of annoyance; that title summed up his money situation perfectly now. His father's voice softened. "Now that you're all paid up, I hope we can finally put this behind us. What do you say?"

Ethan glared at him. "If you're looking for another apology—"

His father shook his head. "Over and done with. Time to move on."

Over and done with, thought Ethan. *For* you, *maybe.* After working all those gruelling shifts at The Chow Down, he still had no car and, as of ten seconds ago, had no cash again either. *Hard to move on when I don't have wheels to move on with.* But he kept his mouth shut. What was the point, anyway?

His father nodded toward the money. "I have to hand it to you, Ethan. I'm surprised you were able to pay everything off as fast as you did. I heard the pool was cutting back on its part-time hours."

"I haven't worked there in *weeks*," Ethan spat. He hadn't intended to say anything about his job, but his father's comment pissed him off. Flipping through TV channels in his bedroom last night, Ethan had seen his old man's face appear on the screen, and he'd caught the last minute of a news segment on his father's candidacy. A statement the commentator offered at the end about Jack Palmer having "his finger on the public's pulse" had angered him. This about a guy who didn't have a clue what was happening in his own home. Christ!

"Then where'd you get the money?" asked Jack.

Ethan thought about the robbery downtown that he'd just heard about. The second one in a month. "I hold up convenience stores," he said. "The hours are crazy but the pay's not bad."

"Don't even joke about something like that."

"Might turn off the voters, huh?"

"Ethan—"

"I'm waiting tables at a diner. Happy?"

If not happy, his father looked visibly relieved.

"So that's where you've been," said Jillian, appearing in the doorway in an ivory pantsuit that clearly hadn't come from Value Village. No question about it—the woman had a thing for white. Ethan imagined her wearing that outfit in the January room, pictured her disappearing against those Brilliant Cream walls. Wishful thinking.

"If you'd actually been *interested*," Ethan snapped at her, "you could've *asked* me," and he enjoyed seeing the wounded expression that appeared on her face.

"There's no need to be rude, Ethan," said his father. Then, as if to keep the tension from escalating, he asked, "Which diner?"

Ethan glowered at his father's fiancée a moment longer before replying, "The Chow Down."

"Near the waterfront?"

Ethan nodded.

"I've driven by it," said Jack.

Of course you have, thought Ethan. *Jack Palmer would never actually eat in a place like that.*

"Maybe I'll stop in sometime," his father added, surprising him.

So you can perform the perfect-father routine for the cameras? "I wouldn't bother stump-thumping for *that* crowd," Ethan said, thinking of Ike. "You might get more than you bargained for."

He turned to go. Lil had asked him to cover for her that afternoon so she could leave early. Something about a baby shower. Jillian stepped aside to let him pass.

"Ethan?"

Ethan stopped in the doorway and looked back at his father. "What?"

Jack seemed about to say something, then reached into his pocket. For a second, Ethan thought he might be returning the money, but instead he pulled out a set of car keys, got up, and walked toward his son. "Here," he said. "Now that you're all paid up, you can drive the Volvo again."

Ethan stared at him, surprise rooting him to the spot. Then, just as he was about to reach for the keys, he changed his mind. "Turns out the bus isn't so bad. No strings attached." Then he left.

———

As much as he needed the money, Ethan regretted having agreed to fill in for Lil. Wednesdays were usually the restaurant's slowest times, so they needed only one server, but for some reason there'd been a steady stream of diners through the door for the past two hours. At one point he was almost running between the kitchen and the tables, and Ike told him to slow down. Actually said it without snarling. Of course, not more than ten minutes later, Ethan upset a Spaghetti With Meatballs over an All Day Breakfast as he hurried to load his tray, and Ike's roar seemed to rattle windows, giving new meaning to "Halifax Explosion."

Toward the end of the shift, though, things levelled off and he even had time to chat with some of the customers. "The girls" had returned and immediately launched into questions about girlfriends, because the one with the bad wig had a teenaged granddaughter they all thought would be perfect for him. "Honey," she told him, her synthetic hair glittering under The Chow Down's fluorescent lights, "if this Allie person ever gives you any trouble, you just let me know, okay?"

Boots stopped by, too, ordering the Western Sandwich without the tomato. Ethan forgot to deduct the quarter, but he remembered just as he passed Boots the bill, so he took it back to the cash register and rang it up again. Boots told him not to bother, but Ethan could see he was wearing the same baggy pants and sweater, which, while clean, looked even more threadbare than before. Cleaning off the guy's table, he found another lottery ticket. With zero dollars in his bank account, he might have been even more pissed than the last time, but he thought about the man's sweater and just shrugged, sliding the ticket into his wallet.

All in all, he made over forty bucks in tips by the time he cashed out. Not bad for a Wednesday supper shift. Rather than heading straight for his bus stop, he turned toward Spring Garden Road. At the Ragged Ending concert he'd taken Allie to, the group had announced they had a new album coming out, and he wanted to pick it up for her at HMV instead of downloading it like he usually would. Maybe giving her the CD would help ease some of the tension that had developed between them after he'd cancelled plans with her a bunch of times to take extra shifts. Today was one of those times. Although she'd told him she understood, something in her voice suggested otherwise. She hadn't sounded pissed exactly. Something else. Hurt? Hopefully, the CD would help make it up to her.

On his way to Spring Garden, Ethan passed the convenience store where he'd checked Boots's first "tip," and remembered the ticket in his wallet. He was in a hurry to get to HMV, but he backtracked anyway and headed straight for the ticket scanner, pulling the rectangular slip of paper out of his wallet. He smoothed it between his fingers and slid the bar code under the red light, waiting for the machine's display to tell him *Not a winning ticket.*

His mouth fell open.

Chapter 15

At his locker the next morning, talking to Pete and Seth, Ethan glanced at his watch for the tenth time. It was only minutes until first bell, and Allie always got to school long before that. He was having a hard job not telling anyone else his news before he shared it with her.

Finally she appeared at the end of the hall and headed toward them. He waved to her and was surprised when she didn't respond. He was even more surprised to see her turn into their homeroom instead of coming over to chat with the guys and, more important, to give him a kiss.

Pete seemed surprised, too. "Something wrong?" he asked.

"Beats me," replied Ethan. "Later, guys," he said, then headed into homeroom. Moore-or-Less was putting up yet another godawful print she'd probably bought in New York, this one with watches stretched like putty over tree branches, and he swallowed a snicker as he wove through his classmates toward Allie's seat.

"Where were you last night?" he asked when he reached her.

"Hello to you, too," she replied. She was organizing her books for first class, but there was no mistaking the edge in her voice.

"Sorry, babe," said Ethan, bending down to kiss her, but she pulled away and his lips met air. "Hey," he said softly, "you wanna tell me what's wrong?"

She looked up at him. "You sure you can spare the time?"

He sighed. "I called you three times last night. Why didn't you pick up?"

"Last night? That was, what—the nineteenth?"

Ethan felt himself growing annoyed. "All day," he said.

"I certainly don't know why I'd be hanging around waiting for you to call me on the *nineteenth*," said Allie, and he could see something more than annoyance in her eyes.

And suddenly he knew. November nineteenth. "Jeez, Al, I'm sorry."

Turning away, she asked, "Sorry you couldn't be bothered to call me until after ten? Or sorry you forgot it was our anniversary?"

He couldn't believe he'd been so stupid. Allie had dropped a couple hints a few days ago, but he'd been too caught up in his own shit to realize what she'd been getting at. If he'd been paying attention to the dates rather than just the circles on his schedule, he might have remembered they'd gone out for the first time exactly six months ago last night.

Allie Fontaine hadn't been the warmest person when she'd arrived at John C. Miles last May. Having transferred in from another district during the final weeks of the school year, she'd kept to herself, speaking whenever someone spoke to her but never starting a conversation. Despite this, there was something about her that drew him to her, something more than just her physical beauty, which made his pulse race just sitting beside her in class. It was the way she gave all her attention to whoever might be talking: teacher, student, even one of the school secretaries on the PA. It was like everything was important to her, like she didn't want to miss a thing. During the week that followed, he'd found himself wondering what it would be like to be the focus of all that attention.

When he finally worked up the nerve to ask her out, he took her to see an early show at the Oxford Theatre and, afterwards, to Irene's Ice Cream Emporium, which was spur-of-the-moment on his part because he didn't want the evening to end. Ethan had dated lots of girls since junior high and had gone steady for a while in grade ten, but Allie was nothing at all like those others. She didn't pretend to be something she wasn't, didn't put on an act you knew would falter around the fourth date. And neither had he. That very first evening with her at Irene's, he found himself telling her things he'd never once mentioned to those other girls, and Allie had seemed just as open in the things she'd shared with him. He knew it sounded corny, but it was like he'd been waiting for Allie Fontaine all his life.

Sitting across from him in the booth at Irene's, Allie had remarked how the number of flavours handwritten on the board above the freezer—*Irene's Top 19*—matched that day's date on the photocopied calendar pages that served as placemats. Ethan had teased her gently about being a number nerd, but afterwards he wondered if maybe that had been some kind of sign, if maybe they'd been meant to be there together that night. He'd thought of that coincidence many times later as he passed the ice cream shop, thought of that nineteenth day and how, even after only a few hours together, he'd known she was the one for him.

But he hadn't gone by Irene's since he'd begun working at The Chow Down.

"I'm sorry for both, Al. Really."

Her next words lacked the hard edges of her first. "I thought you were going to surprise me." Turning to face him, she smiled sadly. "Well, you certainly did that."

"Look," he said, his voice husky, "I can't feel worse than I already do. I'll make it up to you, okay?"

"Don't worry about it," she said, but he could still hear the hurt in her voice as she looked away.

The bell rang and everyone began moving toward their seats. Ethan had no choice but to do the same. When he turned to sit down, he found on his desk a small gift-wrapped box, the tag bearing his name in Allie's beautiful cursive. Regret stabbed him again. He glanced over at her, but she was rummaging through her purse, making a point not to look in his direction.

A secretary's voice came over the PA reading the morning announcements, but her words were just meaningless sounds filling the room as he stared at the box. He didn't have to open it to know what was inside. He recognized the store name, Fond Memories, on the gift wrap—it was a small antique shop on Barrington. He and Allie had walked by just after it opened in August, and she'd dragged him—complaining—inside to look around. Allie had seen nothing much that interested her, but Ethan had found an old silver belt buckle bearing the original Mustang logo and "1964" engraved beneath it, commemorating the first year Ford had produced the car. He'd felt like such a geek admiring it—who would wear a silver buckle as big as your fist?—but there was something about it that appealed to him, made him ask the store owner to take it out of the case so he could see it up close. When he turned it over and saw the price tag, though, he handed it back. He'd been saving to buy his own Mustang, and he couldn't afford to spend so much on something he really didn't need.

And now it sat carefully boxed and wrapped on the desk in front of him.

This was so like Allie. Observant, thoughtful, generous, she was exactly the kind of person to have saved her money, gone back to the shop on her own and bought the expensive buckle, then secreted it away until the time was perfect. Until the nineteenth.

And not only had Ethan forgotten to get her anything, including the Ragged Ending CD he'd intended to pick up, he hadn't even gotten around to calling her until after ten o'clock. Happy anniversary, all right. He picked up the box and, looking across the aisle again, he caught Allie's eye. *Thank you,* he mouthed while the school secretary listed the cafeteria specials, and this time she didn't look away.

"So what's your big news?" Allie asked him at recess. She was holding the note he'd passed her in physics class right after Beaker had returned another round of tests, and he was glad she wasn't pissed anymore. He could tell she was still a little hurt, but at least she wasn't mad. "Did you ace it?" she asked.

Ethan flushed. "Not exactly." That, of course, was an understatement. At least he'd passed, which was more than he could say for Pete. "I'm taking you to Carruthers for dinner tonight," he said. "I made a reservation when Moore-or-Less let me leave English class."

Allie's eyes lit up. "Carruthers? Ethan, that's the most expensive place in the *city*." She frowned. "I don't want you spending money on me because you feel guilty."

"You haven't heard my news," he said.

"Wasn't that it?"

Ethan pulled out his wallet. Opening it, he fanned a thick wad of bills inside, some of them fifties.

Allie's eyes were sudden saucers. A couple of students passing by in the hallway eyeballed the money and whistled.

Ethan returned the wallet to his jeans. "Nine hundred bucks," he said.

She gaped at him. "You shouldn't be carrying that much on you, Ethan."

"I was planning on taking a chunk to the bank during my free period."

"But where did you—"

"I won it."

"How?"

He told her about Boots McLaughlin leaving him another lottery ticket and how he checked it on the way home from work. Grinning sheepishly, he said, "Almost threw it away. I'm sure glad I didn't."

"So how'd you get the money? Ticket sellers can get into serious trouble cashing them for people under age."

"Got somebody to do it for me."

"Who?"

"A guy I served at The Chow Down."

Allie's eyes grew wide again. "You asked a customer to break the law for you?"

Ethan shrugged. "He didn't do me any favour, Al. I paid him a hundred bucks."

A bell warned they had three minutes to get to their next class. Lockers on both sides of Ethan and Allie swung open, books either flew in or flew out, metal doors clanged shut once more, and locks threaded through hasps and clicked into place, their combination dials spun for good measure. Everything and everyone around them was in motion, but Allie appeared frozen to the spot, her only movement a slow shake of her head.

"What?" he asked.

"Ethan, I'm happy for you. Really. It's just . . ."

"Just what?"

She shrugged. "It's nothing." She put her hand on his arm. "You're sure about Carruthers? We can go somewhere cheaper. Like Irene's."

He draped an arm over her shoulder. "I was a jerk for forgetting our anniversary. I *want* to do this, okay?"

She looked up at him, her eyes like dark mirrors, and he wondered what was wrong, wondered why she wasn't more excited for him. After all, it was nine hundred bucks, right? Who didn't get excited over something like that? He got the impression that there was something still between them, something more she wanted to say, but then she smiled. "What should I wear?"

Chapter 16

Carruthers was every bit as expensive as they'd heard it was. And it had a waiting list for reservations a month long. Fortunately for Ethan, he'd remembered Raye telling him that Jazz's sister, Sapphire, worked there, and he'd mentioned her name when he'd called that morning to book a table. It was as if the stars had aligned in his favour, because Sapphire didn't have classes that morning and was at the restaurant setting up for lunch. "Raye's brother?" she'd asked when she'd come to the phone. "Your sister's cool. I'll get you a table." And she had.

Looking at the menu now, Ethan didn't see a single appetizer under twenty-five bucks and many of the entrees ran three figures, but the restaurant's decor more than matched the prices. According to the server who seated them, the floor was Italian marble, the gleaming cypress tables were imported from Africa, and three of the dining room's four walls were hand-painted by well-known Maritime artists, so each was its own unique, vibrant canvas. A fourteen-foot-high burnished copper ceiling dazzled with soft light from exquisite crystal chandeliers, but the most spectacular feature was the fourth wall: a single floor-to-ceiling expanse of glass overlooking the harbour. Although the glass at nighttime mirrored the dining area where they sat, beyond their reflections they could see lights from boats and buildings across the harbour winking on the water's surface, and a nearly full moon hung just above the horizon. *If the food's even half as good as the atmosphere,* thought Ethan, *dinner'll be worth whatever it costs me.*

Allie seemed to think otherwise. "It's beautiful," she whispered, and Ethan almost grinned at the awe in her voice, "but I don't feel good about you spending so much money."

He reached across the table and enfolded her right hand in his. "Just enjoy it, okay? Happy anniversary."

"But—"

"Allie," he said, "I was there, remember? I know how much this cost you." He pointed with his other hand toward the buckle he was wearing, the polished silver gleaming in the candlelight.

"It wasn't about the money," she said softly. "I just wanted something to show you how much you mean to me."

He smiled at her, his heart suddenly full, and more than anything he wanted to stand up, take her in his arms, and kiss her, but he could see their server returning with their water, so he just squeezed her hand again. "That's what this is for, okay? So just enjoy it."

They did. After eating amazing salmon appetizers, she had the lamb while he enjoyed a thick steak prepared exactly the way he liked it—just a shade above blue. Their server, a young man with the kind of smile you saw in "after" photos in dental magazines, told him it was Kobe beef, which came from cows massaged daily to improve the quality of the meat. That detail amused both of them, and Ethan briefly wondered what Ike would think of it. He was pretty sure he knew, though—he could almost hear the cook's familiar snarl.

The server seemed to anticipate their every need, appearing from nowhere whenever water glasses needed refilling or plates needed whisking away. Ethan imagined some of his Chow Down regulars eating there, and he caught himself grinning at the image of "the girls" grilling this guy for personal information.

And then, of course, he was thinking about Boots and how they'd ended up at Carruthers in the first place.

It wasn't until dessert arrived—crème brûlée for her and amaretto cheesecake for him—that Allie mentioned the lottery ticket. "So," she said, her spoon making tiny indentations in the crème brûlée, "you said you got one of your customers to cash the ticket for you?"

Ethan allowed a forkful of the incredible cheesecake to melt on his tongue before telling her he'd run into the guy outside the convenience store where, moments before, a scanner had identified the ticket in his hand as a winner to the tune of $1,008.62. "His name's Hornsby. I wasn't paying attention to where I was going, just staring at the ticket as I left the store. I walked right into him."

Allie spooned some of the crème brûlée into her mouth, and he saw her eyes close in that way they did whenever something truly delighted her. Like their first evening at Irene's Ice Cream Emporium when she'd sampled cranberry coffee, which was still her favourite. So he was surprised when she laid the spoon down now, dabbed at her lips with her napkin, then neatly folded it and placed it on the table beside her water glass.

"You don't like it?" he asked.

"It's fantastic."

"But you're not finishing it."

She shook her head. "I shouldn't have let you talk me into ordering dessert," she chided him softly. "I know when I've had enough."

He looked at her and smiled—her self-control was just one more thing he loved about her—but that didn't stop him from putting another forkful of cheesecake into his mouth. Unlike Allie, he would eat until the food was gone, self-control be damned.

Oddly, she didn't return his smile. Studying her face in the soft candlelight, he felt as though something had just happened, had just passed between them, but he wasn't sure what it was. "Allie—" he began, but she'd spoken at the same time. "Sorry, what'd you say?" he asked.

She said nothing for a moment. Then, "How'd that Hornsby guy cash the lottery ticket for you? All the banks were closed when you ran into him, and ATMs don't usually allow withdrawals that big."

"He had the money on him."

"He just happened to be carrying around a thousand dollars?"

"I think," said Ethan, returning to his cheesecake, "he was carrying a lot more than that."

"And that didn't seem a little weird to you?"

Ethan felt the muscles in his jaw grow tense, but he didn't want the evening to take a wrong turn. "The good news," he explained, eating the last of his rich dessert, then leaning across the table for a spoonful of hers, "is that he had the money I needed. I had to get it from somebody. I couldn't cash the ticket myself."

Allie's expression told him she was still hung up on something about Hornsby, but before she could say more, he continued, "When the guy saw how stunned I was, he asked what was up, so I told him about the scanner. He didn't believe me at first, so I took him back into the store and showed him. He offered me eight hundred bucks on the spot for the ticket. I held out for nine."

Allie turned toward that expansive wall of glass, and somehow he knew she wasn't looking at the water or the lights or the moon beyond it. He felt her studying his reflection, watching his mirror image as he watched her. She turned to face him. "I have a problem with lottery tickets," she said softly.

"Why?"

She ran the tips of her fingers across the folded napkin, slowly tracing and retracing a design on it that he didn't recognize. "Do you remember me telling you how my parents moved to Halifax because of my dad's job?"

Ethan nodded.

"That was the truth." She continued tracing the design on the rich fabric. "But it wasn't the whole truth."

He blinked. "I thought your old man wanted to try something different, which is why he took that consulting job."

She turned to the glass wall again, and he sensed her trying to find the words that would explain what had happened, as if she were getting it clear in her own head first. "He did want to try something different. But he didn't really have a choice."

Now Ethan was beginning to understand. "So he got fired from his other job?" he asked.

She frowned. "No. He was really good at it."

Just then their server returned. "Was there a problem with the crème brûlée?" he asked, nodding at what was left in the dish.

Allie shook her head. "It was great. I'm just stuffed."

Looking at Ethan's empty plate, the server asked, "Will there be anything else, sir? More coffee?"

Ethan liked that he'd called him "sir." The guy had just increased his tip by a few bucks. "Only the check, thanks."

The server removed their dishes, skilfully balancing china, silverware, and crystal water goblets. After he'd left, Ethan turned to Allie. "So if your dad wasn't fired, why'd he have to leave his job?"

When she began to speak, there was a sadness in her voice, like a shadow beneath each word. "You know those lottery pools you hear about? How people working at the same place all pay a certain amount of money each month to buy tickets?"

Ethan nodded.

"Dad was in charge of the lottery pool at his office. Ten people belonged to it, and they played the same numbers every week, along with Insta Piks when the prize got really big. Both the 6/49 and Lotto Max. Dad usually bought the tickets several draws in advance, but then I began noticing him stopping at kiosks or ducking into stores when we were going somewhere together. Lots of times. Then every time. He couldn't seem to walk by one." She hesitated, and Ethan could almost feel her forcing herself to go on. "Bethany noticed it, too."

Their server returned and laid something on the table beside Ethan, a leather folder with a stylized C embossed in gold on the front. "I hope you return to Carruthers soon," he said. "Have a good evening."

"You, too," said Ethan absently, ignoring the folder. He turned back to Allie. "Go on," he said.

She shook her head. "Not here." She bent down to get her purse on the floor beside her, then stood up.

Ethan stood, too, reaching for the leather folder and opening it. Seeing the total on the bill inside, he raised his eyebrows, breathing in through clenched teeth as he mentally calculated the tip he'd have to leave. He took out his wallet, grateful that he hadn't made it to the bank that day after all. If he had, he likely wouldn't have kept enough cash. He counted out the bills and placed them in the folder before closing it, thinking of the number of hours he'd worked at The Chow Down to make in tips what he'd just left for their server. Then he turned and took a final look around him. He doubted he'd be returning to Carruthers any time soon.

Outside, he took Allie's hand and they walked in silence. Clouds obscured the moon and there was a bite in the November air. He felt Allie shiver and he released her hand, draping his arm over her shoulder and drawing her close. When they reached her mother's parked Buick, which Allie had borrowed, Ethan knew she had a lot more to say. They continued down toward the harbour a block away, stopping when they reached the boardwalk that followed the water.

As they stood staring across the harbour at Dartmouth on the other side, he felt Allie lean into him. He held her even closer and waited for her to continue. Finally, she did.

"It was such a stupid thing, you know? People buy lottery tickets all the time. Dad did it even before he took over that office pool. Even Mom picked up a ticket now and then if the jackpot got ridiculous, like twenty or thirty million. Doesn't everybody?"

Ethan nodded, his face moving against her hair. It smelled sweet and earthy, like peaches.

"The funny thing—" She shook her head. "No, nothing about it was funny." A moment passed before she continued, "The *ironic* thing was the pool never won any money. Nothing big, I mean. Some free plays and, once in a while, a few dollars they just rolled over into more tickets. Mostly, though, they didn't win anything, you know?"

They stared at the harbour some more, the breeze strengthening, roiling the water so that waves began to slap the piers beneath them.

"I don't know who realized it was a problem first," Allie continued. "Bethany, I think." She paused. "Maybe Mom knew earlier but she didn't say anything. To us, anyway." She reached up and tugged Ethan's arm around her further. He wrapped both arms about her and she turned into him, her face against his chest. When she resumed her story, Ethan had to strain to hear her words.

"One night, Dad was supposed to take Bethany and her friends to a movie, another one of those dumb werewolf flicks that had just opened, but he got delayed, and by the time they reached the theatre, the line up was enormous. Completely sold out, so he ended up having to take them to one of those animated Disney films instead. Bethany was pissed."

"Pretty hard on the guy, wasn't she?"

"That's what *I* thought," Allie explained, "until I heard what had made them late. He'd stopped at a gas station and was paying with his credit card when a glitch put the registers off-line. Took a while to get everything up and running again."

"Bethany and her friends would've been *more* pissed if they'd run out of gas and ended up walking," offered Ethan.

"He wasn't buying gas."

"Lottery tickets?"

She nodded. "*Lots* of them. Bethany said the cashier offered to void all of them so they wouldn't have to wait, but Dad wouldn't let her. He said one of those tickets might be a winner and he couldn't chance it."

"He had a point."

Allie raised her face so she could look him in the eyes. "He'd bought over two hundred dollars worth of tickets, Ethan." She let that sink in before repeating, "Two hundred dollars worth."

Ethan whistled under his breath.

She pressed her face against his chest again. "Turns out he'd been buying tickets like that for weeks. Maybe months. When Mom found out, she asked him to go for counselling."

"Did he?"

"Not at first." He felt her draw a breath, release it. "It was a bad time for us."

Ethan thought about how Russ Fontaine seemed like such a righteous kind of guy, one of those family-first fathers. So *not* like Ethan's old man. Surprising the things you didn't know about a person, how a man could keep something that controlled him—even *defined* him—hidden from everyone he was close to. "What happened?" he asked.

She drew another breath. "Mom finally threatened to leave him if he didn't see someone."

"And he did?"

She nodded, her face moving against him.

"So his counsellor told him he had to quit his job?"

"No. But he had to quit the lottery pool. When he asked if someone else could take it over, they wanted to know why. He could have lied, I guess, but he took his counsellor's advice and told them the truth. It made things pretty awkward around the office."

"Was that why your Dad decided to find another job?"

Allie didn't respond right away. Then, "You know how we talk about everything in our family?"

"Yeah."

"We talked about this, too. A lot. It wasn't easy hearing my dad tell us how let down he felt. How people at work looked at him differently. A lot of people don't understand addiction, don't understand why a person can't just say no to whatever monkey's on their back. The gambling monkey, especially." She shrugged. "Your parents are the ones you count on to take care of problems, right? Your dad isn't supposed to *be* the problem, the reason you have to leave your home, your friends, your school. I was really mad at him for a while."

Ethan felt her sigh, the sound lost beneath the waves and the breeze, and he could sense her struggling against tears.

"When we first moved here," she continued, "I was miserable, stuck inside my own head, feeling sorry for myself. I wasn't very friendly, and I know I put a lot of people off. But then you asked me out." She looked up at him. "You don't know what it meant to me. I know this'll sound silly—"

"Nothing you say to me could ever sound silly," he said, his voice husky.

She hugged him. "It was like turning a corner, like I was finally able to start over again." Despite the tears in her eyes, she smiled. "I love you, Ethan. For that and for so much more."

It was the first time she'd told him that. The words caught him like a stitch. "Allie—" he began.

She looked down. "It's okay. You don't have to say anything."

He put his hand under her chin, drew her face toward his. More than anything he wanted to speak those same words, say the thing he'd never said to anyone before. Instead, he leaned down and kissed her and, in the moments that passed, the cold had no meaning for them.

As they headed back to the Buick a few minutes later, Ethan squeezed Allie's hand. "I'm glad you told me about your dad," he said. "I know it wasn't easy."

"I just wanted you to understand why I wasn't more excited about you winning that money. The lottery thing brought back a lot of bad memories, you know?"

"I know now." He squeezed her hand again.

She brightened. "But at least some good can come of it, right?"

"Me making up for forgetting our anniversary?" he grinned.

She returned his smile. "Big time. But besides that."

"Such as?"

"The guy at the diner," she said. "That Boots person."

"What about him?"

"Sounds like he can really use the money."

Ethan stopped, forcing her to do the same. "What do you mean?" he asked.

"His four hundred fifty dollars."

"What?"

"You're giving him half, right?"

"Why?"

"*He* bought the ticket, Ethan."

"Yeah, but he gave it to *me*. It was *my* tip."

She didn't say anything.

"Allie, I need that money. For my car."

She looked up at him, a measure of disbelief in her eyes. "You'd really do that? Not give half to a guy whose idea of a big treat every couple weeks is a western sandwich with no tomato?"

Hearing her put it that way, he felt like an ass.

"Ethan," she continued, "didn't that woman you work with tell you the guy eats soup all the time? You just spent three hundred dollars on one meal."

He sighed. "You're right. He deserves some of the money."

"You'll give him half?"

"How about half of what's left?"

Her forehead wrinkled. "Ethan—"

He threw up his hands. "Okay, okay, you win. Half."

Grinning, she kissed him again, then reached into her purse and took out her mother's car keys, pressing the button on the remote entry control.

Seeing the Buick's headlights flash on and off, Ethan momentarily felt like he was watching one of those video lottery terminals pay off, the strobe and sound announcing the Next Big Winner. Except that Boots's sudden windfall effectively made Ethan the Next Big Loser. But, of course, Allie was right. The guy could really use the cash.

"I'd give anything to be there when you give him the money," Allie said, moving around to the driver's door. "That'd really be something to see."

Ethan imagined that moment, and he grinned in spite of himself. Yeah, that'd be something to see, all right.

He tugged on the Buick's door handle but nothing happened.

As he waited for Allie to press the lock release again, a gust of strengthening wind off the harbour sent paper and dirt scudding along the street, and Ethan tugged his collar up against the cold. It felt like a storm was coming.

Chapter 17

"So, Palmer!" roared Seth the next morning when he saw Ethan coming down the hall. He was standing beside his locker with Allie and Pete. "Why didn't you tell us about your big win?"

"I planned to," said Ethan as he approached them. "I wanted to surprise Allie with it first. You two goons couldn't keep a secret if your lives depended on it."

Pete faked a powerhouse right. "Nine hundred bucks, man! That's some serious coin."

"Par-tee time, Palmer!" crowed Seth. "And I know just how to help you spend it."

Allie shook her head. "He doesn't have a lot left. We celebrated our anniversary last night."

Seth whistled. "Must've been some celebration." He gave Ethan an exaggerated wink and added, "Hope you got your money's worth."

"Jeez, Seth," Pete muttered. "Way to be crude, man."

"We didn't spend all of it," said Allie, flashing Ethan a bright smile. "Ethan's giving half the money away."

Seth snorted his surprise. "Hey, charity begins at home, right?"

"It isn't charity," said Ethan. "I'm splitting it with the guy who bought the ticket. End of story."

"Who bought it?" asked Seth.

Allie quickly told them about Boots, and Pete grinned. "The ticket tipper? That's *great*, man!" he said, clapping Ethan on the back.

Seth, however, responded with air-kissing noises. "Sounds like a scene from one of those Hallmark movies, Palmer. I can see it all now." He held his hands out, thumbs meeting in a camera-framing gesture, and he fake-panned the hallway, freezing on Ethan's face. "Cue the violins."

Ethan felt heat work its way up his neck. "Funny," he said, his lips tight.

"No, I'm serious," said Seth. "Okay, maybe not Hallmark—a guy probably has to give away a million or more to get a movie made about him. But you're *Live at Five* material at least."

Ethan rankled. He never watched the Halifax news show at home, but last week Moore-or-Less had shown their class some recorded segments in preparation for a video profile assignment. The clip about the woman lobbying for the right to raise chickens on her city property was especially ridiculous. People with an elevated sense of their own importance being interviewed by people who took themselves far too seriously, like they were saving the world one chicken at a time. The only thing missing was a caption crawling across the bottom of the screen proclaiming *A person is invariably defined by his ability to meet his obligations.*

"Right, Pete?" crowed Seth. "I'm thinking we'll need multiple camera angles," he continued, clearly oblivious to Ethan's growing embarrassment. "And lots of voice-overs, right? Testimonials from friends, members of the community, stuff like that. Maybe we could even—"

"Cut it out," Ethan hissed.

Seth blinked at him. "Hey, man. Just joking around, right?"

Allie made a sudden production of opening her backpack and pulling out her physics textbook. "I don't know about you guys, but I've got stuff to do. Didn't have much time for schoolwork last night, and something tells me Beaker's got another quiz on tap."

Pete and Ethan groaned simultaneously, and their unintentional chorus made all four of them laugh, putting the awkward moment behind them.

"See you guys in homeroom," said Allie. She kissed Ethan goodbye and headed off to the physics lab.

"That's cool about the money," said Pete.

Ethan shrugged.

"Seriously, man," continued Pete. "From what you said about that Boots guy, he can sure use the cash. I'd like to see his face when you give him his share."

Christ! Ethan thought, suddenly embarrassed. *Do you have to be so* gay *about it?* What really pissed him off, though, were those last two words—*his share.* The guy spent a goddamn *buck!*

As if reading his mind, Seth said, "That's a lot of coin to be throwing away, man."

Ethan grimaced. "Don't look at *me*. It was Allie's idea."

Pete nodded. "Sounds like Allie."

"That money could really come in handy right now," offered Seth.

"No shit," said Ethan. "Money *always* comes in handy."

"But especially now," Seth said.

"Why?"

"I saw Filthy yesterday."

Ethan held up his hand as if to stop traffic in the hallway. "I don't need to hear about Filthy LaFarge cruising in—"

"He wasn't."

"Wasn't what?"

"Cruising. He was parked outside that medical clinic on Quinpool."

"Yeah? Maybe he's finally seeing someone about his chronic B.O."

Seth chuckled. "Nope. Seems he knocked up Shawna Oliver, and she's planning on keeping it."

Ethan shook his head. "Filthy's never heard of condoms?" He jabbed Pete. "Now *that* guy's *Live at Five* material."

"Seth hasn't told you the best part," said Pete.

"What? You two assholes planning a baby shower?"

Seth looked at Pete, one eyebrow cocked. "I don't think the philanthropist here is ready for the best part, do you?"

"You know, Seth," Pete replied, "you could be right about that." The two stared at Ethan, grins playing at the corners of both their mouths.

"Okay, okay, what's the best part?"

Seth's face split. "Filthy's selling the Cobra. Wants to know if you're still interested in buying it."

––––––––––

Ethan ignored Moore-or-Less droning on about her damn video profile assignment, which she'd been yammering about non-stop for the last hour. Seth had explained that Filthy was desperate for cash and he wanted to unload the Mustang in the next few weeks. Filthy knew he couldn't expect to make any money off it without putting some work into the car first, but he didn't have the cash—or the time, either—so he was willing to sell the Cobra for the same price he'd paid Kyle. And he was willing to take a good-faith down payment from Ethan to hold the car for a few weeks. "Until the end of Shawna's first trimester," he'd told Pete. The fact that Filthy LaFarge even knew the word "trimester" might have come as a shock to Ethan if he hadn't already been reeling with the news of the Cobra.

"What's a good-faith down payment?" Ethan had asked Seth.

"A few hundred bucks and he'll hold it for you 'til Christmas," Seth said. "If you don't come up with the rest by then, he keeps the money and posts the car on Kijiji." Ethan had sworn at that news. The car wouldn't last an hour on that site.

"A few hundred?" he'd asked. "He get any more specific than that?"

"You know Filthy," Seth had replied. "Guy still counts on his fingers. But five should probably do it."

Ethan glanced across the aisle at Allie, who seemed mesmerized by the English teacher's explanation of video transitions. That was the thing about Allie—she was always so accommodating, so aware of how others might be feeling that she couldn't just turn herself off like everyone else did. He remembered going to her house one night and finding her watching a figure-skating championship through fingers spread in front of her eyes. Although she'd never skated herself, Allie loved watching it, loved the way the athletes used their bodies to translate music into movement. But each time a skater began gearing up for one of those difficult combinations, she put her hands in front of her eyes, blocking her view of the screen. When Ethan teased her about it, she'd explained that she couldn't bear seeing the skaters fall. "It's like I'm on those skates with them," she told him. Watching her hands rise repeatedly to her face that evening, Ethan had found one more reason to fall in love with her.

Now, though, Ethan found that same empathy annoying. She'd never even met Boots, yet here she was forcing Ethan to give up a chunk of the cash he needed to get the very thing he'd been dreaming about for as long as he could remember.

Ethan suddenly became aware of silence, and he glanced around the room to see several faces turned in his direction, including Allie's. She mouthed something to him that looked like *praying nation*, but what the hell did that have to do with anything? Standing at the front of the room, Moore-or-Less was staring at him, too, as though waiting for something. Well, let her wait, thought Ethan. He met her gaze and let the silence spool out until the students sitting around him began to grow restless, whispering to each other. The teacher blinked first. "So, Ethan," she said finally, "I gather from your silence that it doesn't much matter to you one way or the other. Am I right?"

Ethan had no idea what she was talking about, so he took the option she'd offered him. "Right."

She smiled. "Okay, then, we'll plan to have you present yours first."

Ethan's eyes widened.

"I'm really glad it doesn't matter to you, Ethan," the teacher continued. "I was *hoping* there'd be people willing to share their work with the class."

Now he knew the word Allie had been mouthing to him: *presentation*. Ethan felt his stomach clench. The only thing he disliked more than the crap Moore-or-Less got them to do was the ordeal of presenting that crap for everyone else to see. "Ms. Moore, I—"

"Thank you for volunteering, Ethan," said the teacher, and he could see behind those ridiculous orange and green glasses a look that suggested she was enjoying herself. Really enjoying herself.

"It's always a shame," she continued, "when I'm the only person who gets to see the results of all that effort. I'd like to make presenting your profiles a requirement of the project but I want everyone to have enough time to do their best work, which is why it's not due until just before the Christmas holidays. Since you'll be working on other units at the same time, there aren't enough class periods available for us to view everyone's. However, I definitely want us to see a few, and I'm glad that Ethan has agreed to show us his first."

"Look, I—"

"So, does anyone else want to present their profiles?" She scanned the class, and thirty pairs of eyes suddenly looked everywhere but at the front of the room. She nodded. "Okay, but if any of you change your mind, please let me know. This assignment is an opportunity to reveal as much about yourselves as about the people whose profiles you'll be compiling. I think it would be a terrific learning experience for all of us to see at least two or three more."

As if on cue, the bell rang and everyone began packing up and heading to their next class. Everyone except Ethan, who remained in his seat. He needed a few moments alone with Moore-or-Less.

"I tried to warn you," murmured Allie as she stood up.

He shrugged. "No worries. I'll see you in a bit."

"Wait for you outside?" she asked.

"Nah, you go. Beaker's probably handing out that quiz already. I won't be long."

She put her hand on his shoulder, squeezed it gently, then left.

Ethan pulled himself to his feet and walked to the front of the room, where the teacher was sorting the assignments she'd collected that period. Everyone else was gone now, and there was no sign of another class coming in. Good. "Ms. Moore?"

She didn't look up. "Yes, Ethan?"

He wondered if she knew he'd be staying behind to talk to her. Probably. And this annoyed him as much as the way she'd tricked him into volunteering. "I'm not presenting my profile."

She continued to sort papers, placing them into neat piles that, Ethan assumed, were arranged by last name. The teacher had a thing about alphabetical order. He could only imagine what her closets at home looked like.

"I said—"

"I heard you, Ethan."

He watched as she finished sorting, then slid the assignments into her briefcase, a sleek blue rectangle with gleaming brass hardware. Ethan half expected it to have a Metropolitan Museum tag on it somewhere, but he didn't see one. "So," he said, "we clear on me not presenting?"

She lowered the lid of the briefcase and clicked it shut, then looked up at him. "How's that assignment coming?"

For a moment he had no idea what she was talking about, but then he remembered: the *Find-out-what's-important* assignment. "Oh," he said, thinking of Filthy's Cobra. *His* Cobra. "I got a handle on that one already."

"I'm pleased to hear that," she said, and her words sounded genuine. "Care to talk about it?"

"I'm kind of in a hurry," he said. "I think Mr. Becker's giving a quiz."

She nodded. "Another time then."

"Look, about that presentation. I didn't volunteer."

"A roomful of people heard otherwise. Or, more specifically, heard you say it didn't matter to you one way or the other."

He hated that she was playing him. She knew he hadn't been paying attention. Did she just want him to admit it? "I didn't hear what you said."

"Really." The word was more statement than question.

"Yeah, so I'm not sharing any profile. Just wanted you to know, okay?" He turned and headed toward the door.

"Ethan?"

He'd reached the hallway by the time he looked back. "Yeah?"

"The presentation is on a volunteer basis only. I'd never force anyone to share it." She took off her glasses and laid them on her briefcase. "But why not try stepping outside your comfort zone for once in your life? Show us what you can really do. Stretch yourself."

Ethan swallowed the urge to tell her what *she* could do, something he was pretty sure would involve some stretching on her part, too. "I don't want to be late for physics," he said.

"No," she said, "you certainly wouldn't want that." But there was something in her voice that suggested otherwise.

Screw you, he thought, then left.

Chapter 18

"Got a minute?" asked Ethan.

Link Hornsby looked at him over the remains of his Spaghetti With Meatballs, his garlic toast untouched. Few customers ever ate the crusty bread, but it was included with the Number 7, and Ethan had gotten used to carting it back into the kitchen along with the dirty plates. Hornsby nodded. "Maybe even two minutes."

Ethan wished there were more people in The Chow Down so their conversation would be covered by clatter, but Lil had taken her break and there was only Boots, sitting at his usual place. Ethan hadn't expected to see the old guy for at least another week, but he'd told Ethan when he'd come in ten minutes earlier that he'd found a bag of bottles that had fallen off a garbage truck. Having cashed them in for a few bucks at an Enviro Depot, he was celebrating. With a Western Sandwich, no tomato.

Which made Ethan feel even guiltier about what he was doing now.

That afternoon before coming to work, he'd deposited the money he'd won in the bank, including the four hundred fifty bucks he promised Allie he'd share with the old man. He'd had every intention of following through on that promise. In fact, he was carrying in his wallet a cheque for that amount, which he'd made out to "McLaughlin," leaving a space for the first name he didn't know. But Link Hornsby had walked in at the beginning of Ethan's shift, and thoughts of sharing his windfall had taken a back seat to an idea that he'd been mulling over.

Ethan glanced toward the little man. "Anything else you need, Boots?" he asked.

Boots shook his head. "I'm fine, Ethan. Don't worry about me," he said, biting into the second half of his sandwich.

Ethan thought of Allie, knew how she'd respond to what he was about to do if she found out, but shrugged it off. How could Boots miss something he'd never had? And besides, if things worked out, the old guy might get the money yet. Ethan turned to Hornsby and lowered his voice. "I still have some of that money left." He paused. A few minutes ago, he'd planned out in his head what he was going to say, but suddenly it all seemed like lines from a bad sitcom.

Something like a grin played at Hornsby's mouth. "You lookin' for a gold star?"

Ethan flushed. "I was wondering if maybe you could, you know, tell me what I should do with it."

Hornsby settled back in his chair and stared at Ethan for a few hard seconds before replying. "Buy low and sell high."

Ethan blinked. "Seriously? That's your advice?"

"I look like an investment broker to you?"

Ethan shook his head. "That's not what I meant. I'm not talking about investing."

Hornsby took a long swallow of his Coke, wiped his mouth with the back of his free hand, then set the glass on the table. "Why're you askin' me?"

Ethan hesitated. "You had a lot of"—he lowered his voice even further—"cash on you the other night."

Hornsby pulled a toothpick out of his leather jacket, wiped a piece of pocket fuzz off it, then stuck it in the corner of his mouth. "Tryin' to quit smokin'," he said, then nodded at Ethan, signalling for him to continue.

"Look," said Ethan, "I don't mean to offend you, but—"

"Never a good opening," said Hornsby, bringing his hands up and locking his fingers behind his head. The movement pulled the sleeves of his leather jacket back, and the inked undersides of his arms seemed to writhe under the diner's fluorescent lights.

Leaning back like that, his face lit by those glowing overhead tubes, Hornsby suddenly looked older than Ethan had previously thought. Maybe it was the long hair that had thrown him off before, but seeing him up close now, Ethan could tell the guy was closer to forty than thirty. His father's age, which nearly made Ethan laugh aloud. Link Hornsby clearly didn't spend his life obsessed with rules, like Ethan's old man. Link Hornsby looked like the kind of guy who'd never met a rule he hadn't broken, a thought that sent a sudden undercurrent of excitement through Ethan. "Like I said," he began again, "I'm not disrespecting you, but you look like someone who knows how to make a quick buck."

"I do, do I?" asked Hornsby, deadpan.

This was turning out to be even harder than Ethan anticipated. He glanced again at Boots, who seemed oblivious to both of them, then turned back to Hornsby. "Look," he said, "if you can help me, great. If you can't, sorry I wasted your time." He took Hornsby's plate and cutlery but left the half-empty glass of Coke. "You want anything else?"

The man reached for the glass again, drained it without removing the toothpick from his mouth, and passed the empty to Ethan. "Nah, I'm good," he said.

Ethan waited a moment, but when Hornsby offered nothing more, he turned and carried the dishes back to the kitchen. When he returned with the check, Hornsby didn't even glance at it. A twenty-dollar bill lay on the table in front of him. "I'll get your change," Ethan said.

Hornsby waved it away. "Keep it," he said. Then, "How serious are you about makin' some money?"

Ethan grinned. "Very."

Hornsby studied Ethan for what seemed like a long moment, his cold eyes almost glittering, then pulled himself to his feet and nodded toward the door. Ethan followed him, glancing again at Boots, who was finishing the last bite of his sandwich. "Back in a second, okay?" he said. Boots nodded and smiled.

In the parking lot, Hornsby asked, "You willin' to take some risks?"

―――――――

"Just take the picture," said Ethan.

Raye let the camera dangle from its strap. "Not 'til you tell me what you need it for."

Ethan sighed. "I told you already. It's for a project I'm doing in English."

"Oh, yeah," drawled Raye. "The project that's not due for, what, at least a month, right?"

"How do *you* know when it's due?"

"I saw Allie at the library this afternoon."

"Liar," said Ethan. "Allie left right after school. She went away for the weekend with her family."

Raye shook her head. "She found out her dad was running late and they wouldn't be leaving the city until after six, so she thought she'd get a jump on her English assignment. She told me all about the profile, Ethan. She also said Ms. Moore gave you 'til Christmas to do it."

"Maybe I'm getting a jump on *my* work, too."

Raye rolled her eyes. "Like I'm supposed to believe that."

"Doesn't matter to me what you believe. Besides, what were *you* doing there?" Raye, he knew, never went to the public library. Disciples of Winnipeg Joe hung out at All Things Vinyl, his hole-in-the-wall music store on Argyle.

Raye stuck her chin out. "I was working on a science project." After a brief moment, she added softly, "With Brad."

Ethan's eyes widened. "The Bradster, huh? How'd you arrange that?"

A grin slid across her face, and then she frowned at him. "Don't change the subject. You've never started working on a school assignment this early in your life."

He grimaced. Raye knew him, all right. "First time for everything," he said through clenched teeth.

"And what's with the tie? The last time you put one of those on was—" She paused. "I can't *remember* the last time." Her eyes narrowed. "Is that even your tie?"

He ran his hand over the expensive Armani silk, a pale grey that seemed to shimmer in the white landscape of their living room. Ethan had needed something plain for a backdrop, and nothing was plainer than those Brilliant Cream walls. "It's the old man's," he told her.

"And since when do you part your hair? More to the point, since when do you *comb* it? You always just run your hand through it."

Ethan was losing his patience. He wanted to finish here before Jack and Jillian got home with even more questions. They were at a hospital fundraiser, an event their father's media consultant recommended Jack be seen—and photographed— at. And Jillian, of course, would do anything for a chance to get her picture taken, even if it meant drinking watered-down wine and moving stale canapés around on a paper plate. Ethan could usually depend on them not returning from a public function until late, but their father had been even more irritable than normal when he'd gotten home from work, so who knew when they'd be back? "Just take the damn picture, okay?" he snapped.

Raye sniffed. "Jeez. Touchy." She held up the camera. Ethan

saw her squint and bring the LCD screen closer to her face before snapping the picture.

"Take a few more," he said.

She took seven altogether before handing Ethan the camera.

"Time's running out," he said as he took it from her. "If you don't tell him about your eyes soon, I will."

Raye frowned again. "Just wait a couple more weeks. If Brad doesn't ask me out by then, screw him."

"You know," said Ethan, "you could always ask *him* out."

She shook her head. "Might be too soon after the Celia thing. I don't want him thinking I've been stalking him, waiting for my chance."

"Which you *have*," said Ethan.

She grinned. "Yeah, well, whatever. I just think it's better if he asks me." She turned and headed toward the stairs, then stopped and looked back at her brother. "Ethan, you're not doing something you shouldn't, are you?"

Ethan raised his eyebrows. "What makes you say that?"

She sighed. "I'm not an idiot. I know this picture isn't for any English project."

He looked at her for a moment, once more marvelling at his sister's perceptiveness. "No," he lied, "I'm not doing something I shouldn't."

———

Later, paging through the headshots on his laptop, Ethan thought about Raye's question: *You're not doing something you shouldn't, are you?* Why shouldn't he? Didn't everybody? Who didn't tell a lie or misrepresent themselves in some way? Hell, that's what resumés were for. He thought again about the politician his father was defending: if a public servant could drink and drive, get filmed doing it, and then deny it before everyone in a court of law, what was so bad about what Ethan was doing? Besides, hadn't Moore-or-Less told him it was time he stepped outside his comfort zone? He figured what he was doing now certainly qualified.

Paging through the images a second time, he chose the first picture Raye had taken, his expression serious but not pained like in the others, when he'd been increasingly self-conscious. He wondered how his old man handled being in front of the cameras so often. Not everyone was a photo-slut like Jillian.

Looking at the picture again, he was surprised by how much he looked like his father, probably because of the tie and how he'd combed his hair. Funny how photographs could hide the truth—he was, after all, *nothing* like his old man. They were oil and water, fire and rain, any metaphor where Jack Palmer was the drizzle to Ethan's dry day.

He rooted around in his desk for a flash drive, deleted everything on it, and saved the image, then slipped it into his jacket pocket so he'd have it on him when he saw Hornsby on Monday.

Chapter 19

"What'd he say?" asked Allie after she'd kissed Ethan hello. She'd been away with her family all weekend at her uncle's wedding in Prince Edward Island and hadn't gotten home until late the night before, but she'd texted him several times, and was dying to know if he'd seen Boots at The Chow Down. Following his reply—*saw him*—she'd sent one final message: *cant wait to hear.* Which was an understatement. Standing in the school corridor, she was nearly vibrating with excitement.

Ethan shrugged. "He liked it."

"That's all?"

"A lot," he said. "He really liked it a lot." He groped for something more. "And he thanked me. He kept saying 'thanks' over and over. It was embarrassing."

"But in a good way, right?"

He nodded. "Yeah, in a good way."

Allie put her arms around his neck and stood on tiptoe to kiss him again. When she finally pulled away, she said, "I know how much you wanted that money for your car, Ethan, but it was the right thing to do. I'm so proud of you."

Ethan hated lying to her, especially after she'd used the L-word with him. But what else could he do?

"Hey, buddy!" Ethan said over her shoulder, relieved to see Pete loping toward them. "You got time to shoot some hoops later this afternoon?"

Pete glanced at Allie and then back at his friend. "Uh, sorry, Ethan. I'm tied up." He looked at Allie again.

"Pete's working with me this afternoon," she said.

She might just as well have said Pete was manning a mission to Mars. "What's up?"

"You know Ms. Moore said we could do the profile assignment in pairs if we wanted, right? As long as we cleared it with her first?"

Ethan *didn't* know that—something else he no doubt missed during Moore-or-Less's scintillating lecture last week—but he nodded anyway.

"Pete and I are doing ours together," she said.

"How'd that happen?" he asked, then wished he hadn't. It wasn't just the question but the way he said it that made him sound like he was jealous, which was dumb. Hell, who could you trust to work with your girl more than your best friend? Answer: Your *gay* best friend.

"We just decided on Friday," Pete said quickly. "I was in the library and ran into Allie and we got talking about it. Seemed like a good idea at the time."

Ethan wondered why the earth wasn't shifting beneath their feet, wondered why tremors weren't already radiating from the unnatural collision of forces too bizarre for mere mortals to comprehend. Pete in the public library. On a Friday afternoon. Christ!

"We were both there checking out information in the media room," said Allie, "and it turned out we had the same idea for our subject. Didn't make sense for two people to do two different profiles on the same person, so we emailed Ms. Moore to ask if we could work on it together. She was okay with it."

It made perfect sense, sure, but a part of him—maybe the same part that had lied to Allie about Boots—was still having trouble with it. "You could've asked *me* to work with you," he said, hating the tone of his voice. He sounded like a ten-year-old in gym class watching teams being chosen. *Pick me! Pick me!*

"No, I couldn't," she replied.

"Why not?"

"Because of the person we're profiling," Allie explained.

"Who is it?" he asked.

"Your dad."

"Why in hell would you want to do your profile on my old man?" asked Ethan, taking his physics book from his backpack and shoving it into his locker, replacing it with his English binder. Several loose pages snagged on the zipper, but Ethan jammed the binder inside anyway, ignoring the sound of crumpling, tearing paper. Allie would have remarked on it if she'd still been there—she was on an environmental kick and hated to see anything wasted, especially paper—but she had an appointment with the guidance counsellor before homeroom, and she'd just left.

"Why not?" Pete replied. "Your dad's always in the news. And this latest trial he's involved in? The one with that politician who was driving drunk? Man, that's a powder keg. Lots of people want to see how that one turns out, including me. And besides," he added, "your old man's running for office in the spring. Who knows? If the political thing works out, he might even become the premier of Nova Scotia one day. Hell, maybe even the prime minister! Who *wouldn't* want to do a profile on the guy?"

Ethan knew Pete had a point. At breakfast that morning, Raye had told him that a reporter was coming to their house to hold a sit-down interview with their father for an upcoming television spot. What Ethan *didn't* understand was why Pete and

Allie hadn't said anything about the project before. "When were you going to tell me?"

"We just decided Friday afternoon. You went to work right after school, and we didn't see you again 'til this morning." Pete stopped, his face reflecting sudden awareness. "Look, man, me working with Allie isn't going to be a problem for you, is it? The only reason we're doing it together is—"

"I know," said Ethan. "'Course it's not a problem. You're my buddy, right?" He raised his arm and they fist-bumped in the hallway. "Look," he said, "I know I've been tied up with this job, but ..." He struggled to finish the thought, suddenly wishing he'd kept his mouth shut. He sucked at the whole share-your-feelings crap.

"What?" asked Pete.

Ethan looked at the floor—*Just do it!*—then forced a smile. "You know you can tell me anything, right?"

"Yeah, I know."

"I hope so," said Ethan. "I mean *anything*. Anything at all. I'm there for you, man, no matter what. Okay?"

Pete glanced down the hallway, and Ethan could see his buddy's ears and neck turn bright red.

Ethan clapped his friend on the back, then turned to get the rest of his books ready for morning classes, the clang of metal lockers opening and closing along the hallway making everything normal again.

"So," Pete asked a moment later, "you decide what you're going to do about the Cobra?"

Ethan nodded. "Giving Filthy the down payment."

"That's great, man! You think you'll have that much in time?"

"I've got it now."

Pete looked puzzled. "I thought you were giving most of it to that old guy who bought the ticket."

Ethan looked around, lowering his voice. "I'm going to, but ..."

"But not yet," finished Pete.

"Right."

"Does Allie know?"

Ethan shook his head. "I told her I already gave it to him."

"You *lied* to her?"

Ethan scowled. "I'm *going* to give it to him," he said. "Eventually. I just need some time to grow the dough."

"And how are you planning to do that?"

"I'm meeting a guy later today about it. Somebody I know from the diner."

"What makes you think he can help you?"

"Look," snapped Ethan, suddenly pissed, feeling like he was being grilled by his old man, "save the questions for Jack Palmer, okay? Or are you doing a second profile for extra credit? If you are, you'd better let Allie know."

"You might want to take your own advice," said Pete. "The letting-Allie-know part, I mean."

Ethan watched as his friend turned and headed toward homeroom and wondered what the hell had just happened.

Moving down the walkway amid the throng of bodies leaving school that afternoon, Ethan saw Link Hornsby sitting on the bench just beyond the school property. To the city's credit, the bench had actually been green for two days during the past month, but right after both "repairs," anonymous artists had covered the fresh paint with their own creations. This latest was clearly by the same artist whose trademark spackles, when viewed from a distance, merged into faces. Walking by it this morning, Ethan had recognized the features of the politician who was on trial for drunk driving, and now Hornsby was leaning against an image of an enormous cellphone pointed in the direction of that bleary face.

"Yo," said Ethan as he stopped in front of the bench.

"Keep *walkin'*, asshole!" Hornsby hissed.

Confused, Ethan did as Hornsby told him. In a few moments, he was beyond sight of the school, wondering what to do next. He didn't have to wonder long. Hornsby materialized wraithlike on the sidewalk beside him.

"What was *that* all about?" Ethan asked, the two of them continuing along the street.

"There's always at least one plainclothes prowlin' that place at the end 'a the day."

As at most high schools in recent years, uniformed police were often seen in and around John C. Miles looking for drug dealers, investigating gang violence, or just making their presence known, but the thought of plainclothes officers there surprised Ethan. "Weren't you worried about them seeing you?" he asked.

Hornsby snorted. "Free country. Guy's got a right to sit on public property," he said, referring to the bench. "Which, I gotta say, takes graffiti to a whole new level. Quite the political commentary there."

Ethan shrugged. "Yeah, whatever."

"You got it?" asked Hornsby.

Ethan was reaching into his pocket when Hornsby snarled, "Not here!" He glanced furtively at the traffic moving past them, then jerked his head toward an alleyway between a real estate office and a dry cleaners.

Ethan turned into the alley and walked toward the rear of the buildings. Seconds later, Hornsby appeared. Ethan reached into his pocket again—this time hearing no complaint—pulled out the flash drive, and handed it to Hornsby, who just stared at him.

"You forgettin' somethin'?" he asked.

Ethan frowned. "You want the money now?"

"This ain't Sears, kid. I don't do COD. Money upfront or no deal."

It was a good thing Ethan had returned to the bank and withdrawn the money. Opening his wallet, he pulled out three hundred bucks and handed it to Hornsby, who counted it and slipped it along with the flash drive into his jacket. Then he turned, heading toward the alley's back entrance.

"That it?" Ethan called after him.

Hornsby didn't look back. Didn't even break his stride.

All Ethan could do was watch him and his money walk off. And think of the warning Lil had given him: *I'd steer clear 'a the guy if I was you.*

Chapter 20

Ethan studied the plastic card in his hand, marvelling again at how authentic it looked. Hornsby had given it to him earlier that afternoon at The Chow Down, and they'd arranged to meet again this evening, at seven o'clock, inside the main entrance of Casino Nova Scotia on the waterfront. More than a little jazzed by what they were going to do, Ethan had shown up half an hour early, and he'd spent the last few minutes memorizing the name, address, and date of birth on the driver's licence in case someone asked him the information. The birth date made him nineteen two months ago, and the photo Raye had taken seemed to corroborate that fact. Funny how something as simple as wearing a tie and combing your hair could make such a difference in a person's appearance. And wasn't his old man forever reminding him that appearances were everything? Who knew he'd ever be right about something?

Ethan hadn't liked spending half of the six hundred bucks left of his lottery win on the licence, but he'd liked the alternative even less. When he'd first talked to Hornsby a few days before in the diner's parking lot about making some quick money, the guy had offered to take all of it to the casino by himself and keep a share of the winnings. "Payment for services rendered," he'd said. Confident guy, that Hornsby, but Ethan wasn't about to turn his money over to someone he hardly knew, especially someone he'd been warned to steer clear of. If Hornsby was going to gamble with his money, he sure as hell wanted to be on hand to see it happen.

"How old are you?" Hornsby had asked him.

When Ethan told him, Hornsby had pointed out that getting him into the casino would require some cash upfront. "I got a buddy who charges two hundred for a driver's licence."

"Already got one," Ethan had said.

Hornsby pulled the ever-present toothpick out of his mouth exposing the chewed end, then flicked it onto the oil-stained pavement. "One that says you're nineteen?" While he let that information sink in, he slid a pack of Craven A's and a lighter from his leather jacket, tapped out a cigarette, and lit it inside cupped hands, no small feat in the stiff breeze off the harbour that afternoon. He took a long drag, then released it and said, "If you're serious about makin' some quick cash, the casino is the place to do it. You wanna be on hand to watch it happen, bring me three hundred bucks and a JPEG headshot."

"I thought you said the licence cost two hundred."

"It does," said Hornsby. "The other hundred's mine. Services rendered, right?"

Standing now in Casino Nova Scotia's huge foyer, Ethan could easily see and hear the activity unfolding across from him in the main gambling hall. Of course, it wasn't like he'd never been there before. He and his buddies had walked through the complex last year on their way to the Schooner Room, for a concert by Toxic Rosebud, but as he looked out across the enormous space now, it felt like his first time. The place was probably a fraction of the size of those big casinos in Nevada and New Jersey, but it was impressive nonetheless. Row after row of VLTs whooped and jangled incessantly as people fed them coins; stainless-steel balls clattered against spinning roulette wheels; dealers in tuxedos called for cards at dozens of tables; gorgeous women wearing high heels and very little else carried trays of drinks to players; and the players themselves added to the noise by calling to the dealers and the servers and each other, shouting bets, chattering on their cells, clinking ice cubes as they drank. Many of them hacked and coughed, clearly craving cigarettes, but they'd have to go to a special room for that since smoking wasn't permitted in the main area. Not many of these people would want to walk away from a hot deck of cards or a smoking VLT. And if they happened to be losing, their luck had to change soon, right?

Looking at them now, Ethan was reminded of a science project he'd seen when he was in fifth grade: a kid had brought in an ant farm, and for the next few days every student's attention was glued to the activity under that glass. Watching the activity in the casino was a lot like watching that ant farm, like he was seeing a strange new species perform its daily routines in its own glass-enclosed habitat. The only difference was that the ants' movements always seemed purposeful and controlled. Here there seemed to be only chaos. And noise.

"You ready?"

Ethan jumped slightly at the voice beside him and turned to see Hornsby, wearing a pair of dark slacks, a blue dress shirt, and a navy blazer. His long hair looked wet, the obvious result of product that held it back from his face, and he'd even shaved. Ethan was grateful to see the transformation since he felt awkward in the clothes that Hornsby had ordered him to wear. In addition to the outfit he'd worn to his interview at The Chow Down, he'd put on one of his father's suit jackets, surprised that it fit him perfectly. He'd consciously avoided looking at all the glass on his way into the casino, reluctant to see his reflection.

"Yeah, I'm ready," replied Ethan. He reached into his pocket and pulled out the three hundred bucks that remained of his lottery winnings and another four hundred he'd earned working at the diner, earnings that had accumulated faster since his shifts had increased. Some of those earnings he'd planned to spend on Christmas presents in the next month, but he figured he might as well put it to good use now.

The money folded inside his fist, Ethan dangled his hand casually at his side, then slipped the money into Hornsby's waiting palm. "Seventy-thirty, right?" he asked.

Hornsby shook his head. "Sixty-forty."

Ethan shot him a cold glare. "That's not what we agreed on."

"We live in uncertain times," said Hornsby. "Up to you," he shrugged, extending his hand with the palmed bills. "You wanna do this yourself, go for it."

Ethan stared at the outstreched hand for a moment as if he really had a choice. "Just win," he muttered, "okay?"

Hornsby's face creased in a one-sided grin that seemed more sneer than smile. "That's what I do."

It turned out that winning was exactly what Link Hornsby did.

He went straight to the blackjack table while Ethan watched from a discreet distance, occasionally putting coins into a VLT. When Ethan had asked earlier how this evening would unfold, Hornsby had made it very clear what Ethan's role would be: "You stay outta my way."

Ethan's three-hundred-dollar piece of plastic paid for itself in the first five minutes when a security guard approached and asked him for some ID. He held up the driver's licence, comparing Ethan with the photo, and, satisfied, gave it back to him with a smiling "Have a good evening, sir." Returning the card to his wallet, Ethan tried to act nonchalant, but he had to work hard to keep his face from splitting into a grin. Fooling that guard had been a hell of a rush.

Ethan had thought Hornsby would choose roulette or craps because those were the games he'd seen most often in movies set in Las Vegas and Atlantic City. After all, what could beat the sheer drama of that ball circling the roulette wheel or those dice rolling in the pit? Talking outside The Chow Down during Ethan's break that afternoon, however, Hornsby had been blunt. "Roulette and craps you play for entertainment. Same as the slots." When Ethan had asked why, he'd replied, "Odds are too much in favour of the house. May as well buy a lottery ticket."

Ethan was going to remind him it was a lottery ticket that had given him his stake in the first place, but he didn't. Instead, he listened as Hornsby explained that, while they had their risk, poker and blackjack involved skill as well as luck. "And I'm not just talkin' about bluffin' or readin' tells," he'd said, referring to the signals that players sometimes unconsciously gave opponents about their cards. "It all comes down to strategy. That's why professional gamblers play poker and blackjack. No such thing as a professional roulette player."

Watching now from the VLTs, Ethan wondered if gambling was, in fact, the enigmatic Link Hornsby's chosen profession. Sipping his drinks—"Whisky, neat," he'd told the server—the guy sat impassively on his stool, almost as if the whole thing was a frigging bore, and Ethan wondered if the attitude he projected had anything to do with the business of bluffing.

Although there were many things about Hornsby that made him uneasy, he couldn't help but admire the way the guy seemed to own the table. For part of the time, only the dealer was with him, but as he continued to win, interested onlookers drifted over, and a few of them joined the game. From his position by the VLTs, Ethan couldn't see how much Hornsby was winning, but judging from the pile of chips in front of him, it was substantial. He didn't win every hand, of course, and sometimes it seemed like he lost as many hands as he won, but the chips continued to accumulate beside his whisky glass. At one point, a man in an obviously expensive suit came and spoke in low tones to the dealer, and shortly after that, Hornsby pushed away from the table, collected his chips, and headed to the teller's cage to cash them in. Ethan followed but took care not to talk to him, as Hornsby had warned.

Once outside the casino, Ethan could hardly contain himself. "So how much did we make?"

Hornsby gave him a casual glance, but the look in his eyes made Ethan uncomfortable. The man walked briskly, forcing Ethan to lengthen his stride to keep up.

Ethan, though, was undeterred. "Not counting the seven hundred I staked you, how much did you cash in?"

Hornsby ignored him, and Ethan fell silent as they continued along the boardwalk beyond the casino, the late November air off the water making him wish he'd brought his winter jacket. Finally, Hornsby turned right into the Park 'n' Pay and approached a sleek, black Saab, exactly the kind of vehicle Ethan pictured a high roller driving. But Hornsby continued past it, stopping beside a rusted Toyota Echo with a deep gouge along the driver's side that looked as though someone had keyed it. In the harsh glare of the overhead light, it made Lil's Ford Focus look almost classy.

Hornsby unlocked the car and motioned for Ethan to get in, then did the same himself.

Closing the door behind him, Ethan found the inside of the car slightly better than the exterior—only the console was scratched, but everything showed signs of wear. Clearly, Link Hornsby didn't believe in wasting his money on wheels. The Echo was point-A-to-point-B transportation and nothing more. Ethan thought it best to keep his surprise to himself. "So," he tried again, "how much did—"

"Look," Hornsby growled, "let's get somethin' straight."

Ethan nodded.

"This ain't high school. We don't compare notes about the big game over a latte or whatever it is you assholes drink nowadays."

Ethan was stunned by his vehemence. All he'd done was—

"And somethin' else. I don't *work* for you. We had a business arrangement. Understand?"

Ethan nodded.

"I can't hear you."

"Yeah," he replied, beginning to feel pissed. "I understand. Loud and clear."

Hornsby nodded. "Good," he said, shoving the key into the ignition. The Echo churned to life and the heater began blowing cold air that gradually warmed, but he made no move to shift into reverse and back the car out of its space. "I cashed in a few dollars shy of twenty-four hundred bucks. That's close to seventeen hundred profit. Your share of the winnings is eight fifty."

"But that's not a sixty-forty split," said Ethan. "That's—"

"Half," said Hornsby.

"But—"

"Consider it an aggravation allowance." He reached into his jacket and pulled out the cash, counting out the original seven hundred in the light from the instrument panel and then adding Ethan's share of the winnings to it.

Son of a bitch! fumed Ethan silently, but he took the money without comment. Smoothing out the bills, he squeezed the wad between his palms. Over fifteen hundred bucks! Even after Hornsby's "aggravation allowance" combined with the cost of the driver's licence and dinner at Carruthers, he had more in his hands now than he'd won with the lottery ticket in the first place. He turned to Hornsby. "How soon can we do this again?"

Hornsby stared ahead as the engine rattled. "You can't afford me."

Yeah, like your overhead is killing you, Ethan thought, his gaze sliding over the car's interior. "Fifty-fifty *is* pretty steep—"

"Kid, that was a one-time low introductory offer."

"What?"

Hornsby turned in his seat to look at him. "You think I don't have better things to do with my time than top up your college fund or whatever it is you Cathedral Estates kids need money for?"

Ethan's eyes widened at Hornsby's mention of his subdivision. But that thought was immediately replaced by another. "Look, I need to make four thousand bucks in the next three weeks, and it seems to me you could do that easy." *Even if you choose to drive a shitbox like this.*

Hornsby's eyes glittered coldly. "I don't do *easy*. I do *smart*. You should try it sometime."

Ethan had no idea why their conversation had gone south so abruptly, but he wasn't about to let this opportunity slip through his fingers. "Okay, you're right, I don't always do smart. But, hey, I work at The Chow Down, so you already know that." Encouraged by the trace of a grin on Hornsby's face, he pressed on. "I really need that money."

"Look, kid, I don't have the time—"

"You said that already. What can I do to change your mind? I need you to work with me just a little while longer."

Hornsby stared at him for a moment, and what had been a trace of a grin grew into a broad smile. He turned off the Echo's motor and the sudden silence in the car was nearly palpable. "Could be you don't need me at all," he said.

Chapter 21

"Where were you last night?" asked Allie as she met Ethan on the school steps. "When you didn't answer your cell, I called your house and Raye said you were probably out with friends. But Pete didn't know where you were, either."

"Pete's not my only friend, Allie."

"Yeah, like you two aren't practically joined at the hip," she teased, threading her arm through his. "So where were you?"

Holding the door open for her, Ethan said, "Doing some research."

She looked up at him, and the expression on her face revealed her surprise. "I'm impressed! Is it for your profile assignment?"

Ethan had made up his mind he wasn't going to lie to her again, but he also couldn't tell her about the casino, not after what she'd shared about her dad's gambling problem. "It *could* be," he said. "I don't know for sure yet."

"What were you researching?"

"A business on the waterfront. A guy I met at the diner took me through it. I got to see how it operated."

"I didn't think that restaurant of yours was the sort of place where business people ate."

"Low blow." He grinned, then added, "This guy's not your average businessman."

"What's he do?"

Ethan was surprised at how easily this next part came. Avoiding her eyes, he said, "He generates venture capital." He'd heard that line when the news came on the flat screen in his room as he was getting ready for bed last night. Something about the government trying to kick-start the lousy economy.

"Sounds interesting," she said.

"You have no idea," he replied, thinking of the long conversation he'd had with Hornsby in his Echo. Hoping to change the subject, Ethan asked, "How's your project going? You and Pete haven't come around to interview my old man yet."

"Oh, we've got lots to do before we're ready for that," she explained. "There's tons of stuff about your dad on the Web and in the library's media room. We're watching as much of it as we can before we finalize our questions. It's pretty interesting stuff, especially the CBC news clips. Did you know—"

"Spare me," he said, holding up his hand. "I get enough of his life story at home."

She smiled, understanding in her eyes.

"Hey, Palmer!"

"Just the guy I was looking for," Ethan called to Seth, who was heading toward them. "Look, Allie, I need to talk to Seth about something. Catch up with you in homeroom?"

"Talk to him about what?"

"Guy stuff. You know."

"Let me guess. Most of it has to do with cars, and the rest involves the two of you standing around making gross noises."

"That's what you get for having such a deep guy for a boyfriend," he quipped.

She laughed. "Go ahead, have your little car talk. I want to ask Ms. Moore something about the profile anyway. I'll see you in a few minutes."

She kissed him and moved off down the hallway, clearly unaware of the attention she got from other guys as she passed their lockers.

"What's up?" asked Seth.

"I got that down payment Filthy wanted. You know where he'll be this afternoon?"

Seth whistled. "You rob a bank, man?"

Ethan shook his head. "Even better."

"Hey, Filthy."

All six feet four inches of Philip LaFarge filled the open doorway of his basement apartment. "Palmer," he replied. He was dressed in sweatpants and an old wife-beater, both mottled with stains. "Seth said you'd be by. Got the cash?"

Standing in the roofless stairwell, Ethan nodded toward the Mustang in the driveway, its rusted wheels at eye level. "Five hundred will hold her for me 'til Christmas?" he asked.

"Non-refundable."

Ethan shrugged. "Not a problem. I don't plan on defaulting." He reached into his pocket and pulled out a wad of bills and handed it to him.

"You don't mind me countin' it, do you?" asked LaFarge, but he'd already begun flipping through the bills anyway, his mouth moving as he added.

"Go for it," said Ethan, turning his attention toward the driveway. He much preferred to have his eyes focus on the Cobra than linger on Filthy's sweats. One of the stains, just above Filthy's crotch, looked fresh and suspiciously non-foodlike.

"All here," said LaFarge finally. "You wanna receipt or somethin'?"

Ethan didn't think he needed one—everyone called Filthy a stand-up guy—but he nodded anyway. "Sure."

LaFarge stepped back into the apartment and Ethan could

hear him moving around inside. "Got a pen here somewheres," he muttered. "Might as well come in 'n' shut the door. Rent don't include the heat."

Ethan stepped through the door and closed it behind him, surprised by what he saw. Although small and sparsely furnished—the single space he now stood in served as kitchen, dining area, and living room—the apartment was clean and tidy, the walls spotless and the cheap laminate floor looking freshly mopped. "Nice place you got here, Filthy," he said. The moment had seemed to call for conversation, but Ethan suddenly wondered if Filthy might think he was making fun.

Apparently, he didn't. Rummaging through one of the two drawers in the kitchenette's only cupboard, LaFarge shrugged. "It ain't Cathedral Estates," he said, "but it's home."

Just then, a toilet flushed, a door off the dining area opened, and a young woman appeared. "Hi, Ethan."

"Hi, Shawna," he replied. He'd known Shawna Oliver for most of his life. They'd started school the same year and were in some of the same classes, but the truth was he really didn't know her much at all. When she was in the third grade, she'd been diagnosed with a learning disability—dyslexia, maybe, or ADHD, something like that—and had dropped out a year or two ago. She hadn't changed much, though. Her hair was still brilliantly dyed—purple with orange highlights this time—and there were still at least half a dozen piercings on her face alone. But what made these details stand out even more vividly was her skin, currently the colour of chalk.

LaFarge went to stand beside her and rested one of his large hands gently on her shoulder. "How're you feelin'?"

She slid one arm around him, stained wife-beater and all, and leaned against his huge body. "Puked again," she said.

LaFarge looked at Ethan. "We're expectin'," he said.

Ethan nodded. "Yeah, I heard." He wasn't sure if he should

say "Congratulations" or "Tough luck," so he offered neither.

LaFarge put his other hand on Shawna's belly, covered by a long housecoat that had seen better days, and patted it gently. "I'm gonna be a daddy," he said.

That single action, that simple caress of Shawna's slightly swollen abdomen, tugged at Ethan's memory, and suddenly the sounds around them—the water refilling the tank of the flushed toilet, a muffled voice from the apartment above, traffic on the busy street outside—receded, leaving him in a pool of muffled silence. Something about that big hand on Shawna's stomach. The gentle caress. The shared smiles—

And then the moment ended as Shawna's hand darted to her mouth and she disappeared into the bathroom again.

"First trimester's the worst," said LaFarge, turning to Ethan, who was surprised all over again that Filthy knew the word. Here he was standing in a basement apartment talking with Filthy LaFarge about fetus development. It couldn't feel any weirder if he were to suddenly find himself standing in that painting Moore-or-Less had hung in her classroom, the one with the watches melting over tree branches. What had she called it—*The Persistence of Memory*? Dumb name. Nothing in it reminded Ethan of memory. In fact, there was something in the centre of the painting that he'd prefer to forget, something Ethan now felt looked a lot like a rotting fetus. Whatever it was, he didn't think it was something expectant parents should spend a lot of time looking at.

LaFarge turned back to the cupboard drawer and resumed digging for a pen. "Got one," he said, pulling out a Bic medium point. "Now for somethin' to write on."

"Look, don't bother," said Ethan. "I know you won't screw me over."

LaFarge nodded. "Just so you know, though, I need the rest by Christmas or I'm puttin' her on Kijiji. We clear about that?"

"We're clear," said Ethan. "Thanks, Filthy. See you around." He went out and closed the door and was surprised to hear it open again, the big guy coming up the steps behind him.

"Wanna check her out?" LaFarge asked, pulling on a jacket. A piece of its lining dangled below the hem.

"Sure," replied Ethan. He'd already stood looking inside the locked Cobra for several minutes before knocking on the apartment door, but he jumped at the chance to sit in her again.

LaFarge took keys out of his pocket and unlocked the driver's door, then stepped aside to allow Ethan to slide in.

Settling back in the bucket seat, Ethan put one hand on the steering wheel and the other on the stick, and for a moment he was seeing open road instead of the back of another apartment building, feeling the air rush past the windows instead of blowing in the open door from the northeast. The weather forecast called for high winds and flurries that evening—the first of the season—and LaFarge shivered in his jacket with the ripped lining. Seeing the grimace on his face, Ethan reluctantly pulled himself out. "Sorry. You're probably freezing."

LaFarge nodded, but it turned out that his expression had less to do with the cold than the car. "Hate to part with her. I pestered Kyle about her for a long time. She's somethin', huh?"

Ethan grinned. "Yeah, she's something, all right."

"Don't make 'em like this anymore," said LaFarge, hugging his arms around himself.

Ethan nodded in return, admiring the car's lines. Even the rust along the rocker panels didn't mar the vehicle's classic beauty.

"Ahh," muttered LaFarge, "it'd be a hassle gettin' a kid in 'n' out 'a that back seat anyway. Definitely not a family car."

"You're right about that," said Ethan absently. "My mother bought one after she and my old man broke up. Her gift to herself in the separation."

LaFarge turned to him. "Puttin' herself back out there, huh?" he asked. "Set 'a wheels like that would sure do the trick."

Still looking at the car, Ethan shook his head. "I think it had more to do with pissing off my old man."

LaFarge grinned. "That why *you* want one so bad?"

Ethan shrugged. "It's a bonus."

Later, walking to the bus stop, Ethan thought again about Filthy's question. Not that pissing off his old man didn't have its own reward, but that wasn't the real reason he'd longed for his own Mustang. And not just any 'Stang. A 1996 Cobra SVT. His mother's car.

She'd bought it used but in mint condition, a private sale from some guy who, like Filthy, was having his first kid and needed a more practical ride. Ethan's mother had taken him with her when she'd gone to look at it, and he'd been awed by the way the colour on the car changed. "It's called a Mystic finish," said the owner. "Cost me a whole lot extra, but it was worth it." He'd seen Ethan walking around the Mustang, watched him moving back and forth, back and forth, following the colours of the car as he altered the angle he viewed it, mesmerized as they melded from green into purple and then brown into gold. "Paint's got the same colour-changing pigments they use in American money," he explained to Ethan's mother. "If a person wants to repaint one 'a these, an inspector's gotta come and figure out how much paint you need, and then you gotta send back any you don't use. And the guy who paints it has gotta be Michelangelo if you want it to look good." He paused. "But you don't need to worry about that. See?" he said, pointing out their reflections in the gleaming door. "I keep her covered whenever I'm not drivin' her. And I'll throw in the cover with the car. I'd hate to think of the sun dullin' that finish."

Later, during their drive back to the Herring Cove house his father had moved out of, Ethan had begged his mother to get the car, but his pleading had been unnecessary. She'd told him she'd already made up her mind to buy it, adding something his eight-year-old brain didn't understand at the time, something about the Mystic finish being a lot like what her life had come down to. "Nothing stays the same, Ethan," she'd told him. "The one thing you can count on is that everything changes."

Even then, even as an eight-year-old, he'd realized she was sharing something important with him, something grown-up, and he'd wanted to pay attention, wanted her to know that he understood what she was saying to him. But he didn't. All he could think about were those colours, how his reflection looked like it was trapped inside a rainbow.

Not long after, his mother had ended up trapped inside that rainbow herself, the crumpled car like a metal W around her lifeless body.

Chapter 22

As usual, Ethan was the only person getting off the bus at the entrance to Cathedral Estates. Despite the whole environmental awareness movement and the push to use public transit, he figured no one else living on Seminary Lane, Cloister Drive, Monastery Road, or any of the other streets in his subdivision ever took the bus. As if to underscore that point, a Lexus GS450, an Acura ZDX, and a Mercedes SLK350 drove past him, each carrying only the driver. Watching them cruise by—all of them probably going to the same frigging place, one of those big box stores out at Bayers Lake—Ethan couldn't help wondering when vehicles started getting names with numbers instead of nouns. Cobra, Corvette, Beretta, Stealth—now *those* were names that grabbed you. Hell, even place names like Sonoma and Santa Fe were better than combinations of letters and numbers that looked like something you'd see on a pharmacy prescription. He shrugged and kept walking.

Not knowing the people on his bus was actually an advantage—it meant he didn't have to talk to anyone. Like always on a Sunday, he had run flat out at The Chow Down, so he liked being able to close his eyes and let the motion of the bus ease some of the stiffness from his body. Even though this was his sixth Sunday working there, he still found himself wiped afterwards. But the good news was he rarely messed up orders now, he hadn't dropped a meal in quite a while, and Ike hadn't bellowed at him in nearly a week, which in itself was cause for celebration. He had yet to see evidence of the "sweetheart" that Lil claimed the cook could be, but Ethan was just grateful not to have a strip torn off him every time he entered the kitchen.

And there was another improvement: the tips were even better since he'd gotten to know some of the regulars. A lot of them he called by name, and he knew without asking what their orders would be. Boots McLaughlin wasn't the only one who got the same item again and again, and Ethan found it funny how people could get locked into patterns, like always ordering the All Day Breakfast. Would it kill them to try the Philly Steak With Fries once in a while?

Some of the regulars could be a pain in the ass, and he felt like he was earning an Academy Award whenever they showed up, pretending he actually gave a shit to see them. But there were some he looked forward to, like "the girls," who'd been in that afternoon. Evelyn, the one with the wig, had asked him again whether he and Allie were still a couple because her granddaughter was still between boyfriends. She'd even shown him a picture that she carried in her purse, and Ethan was surprised by how pretty the girl was—so pretty, in fact, that if he and Allie weren't together, he might have been tempted to let Evelyn set him up. Of course, the moment that thought flashed through his head he felt lousy, and not just because it was disloyal to Allie. It suddenly made him feel like his old man, whose belief in *Appearances are everything* bordered on the fanatical. Like father like son? Christ. Too bizarre even to think about.

Something else that was bizarre was that conversation he'd had with Link Hornsby in his Echo. He'd been thinking about it a lot and, as he walked down Seminary Lane now, he replayed it in his head. The whole idea seemed crazy, but the way Hornsby had explained it made it seem like the answer to his money problems.

When Ethan had asked him that night how he'd been able to win so much money at the casino, Hornsby had told him about a negative progression system called the Martingale. "One of the oldest bettin' systems around," he'd said. "And it's foolproof, as long as you follow it to the letter." He'd explained how it was based on the law of averages, that a person can't lose all the time, just as he can't win all the time. "A gambler usin' the Martingale decides how much money he'll bet and, if he wins, he bets the same amount again. He continues bettin' the same amount each time 'til he loses."

"What's the negative progression bit?" Ethan had asked.

"If the guy loses a hand," Hornsby explained, "he doubles his last bet. If he loses that one, he doubles the previous bet, and so on. When he eventually wins, that bet earns him back all he lost so he can go back to bettin' the original amount."

Ethan had been skeptical. "But all you ever hear about gambling is how often people lose. Their homes, their jobs, everything. If this Martingale system is such a sure thing, why don't we hear about gamblers getting rich?"

"First," Hornsby had explained, "not everybody knows about it. Matter of fact, most people do just the opposite of the Martingale. When they lose, they get nervous and start reducin' their bets. So when that law of averages finally kicks in and they start winnin' again, those smaller bets don't cover their losses. They got way too much ground to make up before they start turnin' a profit again. But it can't happen 'cause that law of averages don't let it."

The explanation had made a lot of sense to Ethan as he'd sat listening in Hornsby's Echo.

"And there's other reasons why you don't hear about gamblers makin' a killin'," Hornsby had continued.

"Like what?"

"A lot of 'em gamble online."

"So?"

"Not many people want their picture in the paper for gettin' rich doin' somethin' illegal."

"Online gambling is illegal in Nova Scotia?"

Hornsby's eyes had gleamed in the light from the Echo's dash. "Online gamblin's against the law for everybody in Canada. The States, too."

Ethan was confused. "I've seen hundreds of pop-ups online for gambling sites. If they're illegal, how do they get away with it?"

"They're set up offshore."

Ethan had let that thought sit for a moment. Then, "Why're you telling me all this?"

Hornsby had shrugged. "You got a stake now," he said, nodding toward the wad of bills in Ethan's hands. "Try it yourself."

"I'm underage."

"So?" Hornsby had let the question hang there.

Ethan was stunned. "How can teenagers gamble online?"

"You never surfed porn?" asked Hornsby.

Ethan reddened. "I'm a guy, right?"

Hornsby nodded. "You clicked a button that said you were an adult before you could get on the site. Same thing with online casinos." To prove his point, he got out of the Echo, went around to the trunk, and then slid back in with a laptop that looked out-of-the-box new and even more powerful than Ethan's at home. Hornsby booted it up—during the log-in process, Ethan saw the username, *Samantha,* appear in a window and wondered who the hell she could be—and then started the car and backed it out.

"Where're we going?" Ethan had asked.

"Look for a signal," said Hornsby, pointing at the Network Center icon on the laptop's toolbar.

"You don't have a mobile Internet stick?"

Hornsby glanced at him like he'd just asked if he bought air. "Why pay for something when you can get it free?"

Ethan shrugged. Made sense. He was so used to his old man paying for everything that he took things like Internet access for granted.

They cruised the streets for a few minutes until they found an unencrypted wireless signal. Hornsby pulled over to the curb, turned off the motor, and took the laptop from Ethan, showing him how easy it was to log into various online casinos, set up an account, and deposit money with a bank card or credit card. Some sites, Ethan was surprised to see, even offered sign-up bonuses, crediting money into your casino account to be used for gambling. He'd thought about the rush he and his buddies got when they played dice at lunchtime, masking the game whenever a teacher or monitor strolled by—kids' stuff compared to what Hornsby was showing him now.

But Ethan still wasn't convinced. "How do winners get their money?"

"Adults have them transfer it into accounts set up for their winnings. That can be a problem, though, if it ends up bein' a lot, so some of 'em do what kids do."

"What's that?"

"They get the casino to mail them a cheque."

Ethan had shaken his head, amazed. "Sounds simple enough."

"It *is* simple."

Parked beside the curb, Ethan found it hard to believe that a person could make a lot of money doing what Hornsby was explaining, especially given the ruined Echo he was sitting in. If Internet gambling was such a cash cow, why wasn't Link Hornsby driving something like that Saab he'd seen back at the Park 'n' Pay? But, then again, wasn't his old man always saying *Waste not, want not?* Hornsby's

Why-pay-for-something-when-you-can-get-it-for-free philosophy was the same kind of thinking, wasn't it? But something was still bothering him. "You said the Martingale was foolproof as long as you follow it to the letter. Why *wouldn't* people follow it? Where does it break down?"

"Two things: balls and bankrolls."

Ethan already knew about the balls, how losing gamblers had to fight the natural instinct to reduce their bets, but he didn't understand the other. "Why should bankrolls be a problem?"

"Law of averages again. You can't win all the time, so you gotta be able to lose, and you gotta be able to keep doublin' your last losin' bet so you'll win back everything you lost. It's all long-term, kid. Go big or go home."

And now here Ethan was going home. He turned into the driveway, surprised to see his father's Beemer—a new M3 he'd bought the week before—sitting in front of the garage. His old man always kept his cars parked inside, so Ethan guessed he and Jillian must be heading out somewhere shortly. And then he remembered hearing something about a fundraiser for his father's campaign. Ethan scowled. Jack Palmer had the cash to throw at a brand new BMW, yet this evening he'd be attending a fancy dinner with his hand out for political donations. Ethan's scowl suddenly morphed into a grin as he imagined an event like that being held at The Chow Down. Hell, he probably could have gotten his father a deal: All You Can Eat Philly Steak With Fries. Of course, it would have meant cramming Ike into a tux for the event, but that sight alone would have been worth the price of admission.

Opening the kitchen door, he saw his father getting water from the refrigerator's dispenser. And wearing a tux. Ethan snorted, shaking his head.

"What's so funny?" asked his father.

"You had to be there," said Ethan, removing his jacket and draping it over a chair.

"Speaking of being there," his father said, "are you home for the night?"

"Yeah, why?"

"Raye's babysitting for the Loebs, and I don't want her coming back to an empty house. There was another robbery last night not far from here."

"A house this time?"

His father shook his head. "Gas station, but who knows what's next?"

"Isn't that what you paid the big bucks for?" asked Ethan, nodding at the electronic keypad by the door.

"Those places all had security systems, too, but it didn't stop the thieves. Do you remember Hank Cavanagh?"

Ethan vaguely recalled a lawyer at his father's firm. "Yeah."

"Hank's got a friend on the force, and he says the police are checking into whether someone's leaking security details that help the thieves circumvent the systems."

Ethan wondered at the weirdness of their exchange, surprised at how long his old man had been talking without launching into a lecture. "I'm home for the night anyway," Ethan said.

"Good." His father drained his glass and put the empty into the dishwasher.

Ethan thought about Raye and wondered if she'd told their old man about her eyes yet. It had been a few days since the last time he'd mentioned it to her, and he'd warned her he wasn't going to wait much longer. "Has Raye said anything to you about—"

"How do I look?"

They both turned to see Jillian standing in the doorway, gorgeous in a low-cut red dress that would stop traffic—and, more to the point, would open wallets. His father gave an appreciative whistle. Ethan just shrugged.

Jack looked at his watch. "We need to get a move on, sweetheart."

"We have plenty of time," said Jillian.

But Ethan knew his old man, knew he had to arrive at least a half-hour early for any function. Watching his father reach for his keys, Ethan said, "Look, I wanted to ask you if—"

"Can this wait?" asked Jack.

Ethan blinked. "Huh?"

"We can talk about whatever it is you want when I get back."

"I don't *want* anythi—"

"Ethan, a lot of important people will be at this event tonight. It wouldn't look good for the guest of honour to be late, now would it?"

Ethan felt his face grow warm. "Look, I just wondered if—"

But his father was already holding the door open for Jillian. "I said we'll discuss it when I get home, okay?" and there was no mistaking his Final Word On The Matter tone. Then, just before he shut the door, "This is Sunday night. You must have schoolwork to do."

Ethan stood staring at the closed door, surprised at himself for thinking his old man might actually have spent five seconds listening to what he had to say. But in a contest between himself and "important people," there *was* no contest.

He reached for the fridge door. As usual, it didn't open easily, its ultra-strong magnetic seal requiring him to brace his feet against the porcelain tiles before he gave it a yank. It reminded him of the physics test he'd studied for and barely passed a month ago: *The maximum possible friction force between two surfaces before sliding begins is the product of the coefficient of static friction and the normal force.* He sure as hell didn't know what "normal" was, but there always seemed to be maximum friction between him and his old man, some unseen force that kept them grinding against each other at every turn. He wondered idly if Beaker had a coefficient for *that*.

The fridge door opened on his second pull and, surveying the various fruit and health drinks inside—Jillian's contribution to the family's dietary needs—he shut it in disgust. Then he grinned. A moment later, he was in his father's study opening the beer and wine cooler built into the floor-to-ceiling cabinet that lined the far wall and contained, along with his father's law library, several bottles of spirits. Although his father never touched alcohol, he always kept it on hand for guests, which Ethan knew had everything to do with appearances. The perfect lawyer couldn't be anything less than the perfect host.

As he'd expected, Heineken bottles filled several shelves of the cooler. His old man would never miss one—or two or three, for that matter. Ethan reached in and grabbed one, twisted off the cap, and brought the bottle to his lips, taking long swallows as he thought again about how his father had just brushed him off. For the hell of it, he stood there estimating the amount of time he and his old man had spent talking during the weeks since he'd clipped the side of the garage with the Volvo. Christ, he could add the month before that and still come up with less time than he'd spent talking with Link Hornsby in his Echo. Not that Link Hornsby would ever snag a Father of the Year award, but at least he took the time to listen to what Ethan had to say, showed him how he could get the money he needed, explained the Martingale system that guaranteed he'd come out a winner. Lil had warned him to steer clear of the guy but, hey, at least he was accessible, hadn't shut him down with *You must have schoolwork to do.*

Ethan drained the Heineken, took two more, then headed down the hallway and climbed the stairs to his bedroom. What had his father asked him? *Can this wait?* No, he'd waited long enough. Now was the time to *do.*

Ethan's cell rang and he saw it was Pete again. This time he answered it. "Hey," he said.

There was dead air for a moment. "You surprised me," said Pete. "I was expecting your voice mail again."

"I can hang up if you want." Ethan could have made his voice lighter, made it sound like he was joking, but he didn't.

"Right." There was a sound—a kind of huff—on the other end of the line, and Ethan recognized Pete's fake laugh, the one he used for parents and teachers whose lame attempts at humour fell flat.

Ethan waited.

"You get my messages?"

"No," Ethan lied.

"Figured you didn't," but there was a hesitation in Pete's voice that suggested otherwise. "There's a fight on pay-per-view tonight. You want to come over and watch it, maybe raid some of my dad's brew?" A few months ago, Pete's old man had begun making his own beer, and he'd filled several shelves in their basement with malt that wasn't half bad. According to Pete's dad, anyway. Ethan doubted it was half as good as the three Heinekens he'd downed.

Raye had just gotten home from babysitting so there was no reason why he couldn't go, except for the beer-buzz he was already enjoying. And his laptop open on the bed beside him, all but one of the fields completed on the application that was now running.

"Sounds great, but I can't. Got stuff to do tonight."

There was another pause. Then, "Look, man," said Pete. "Can we talk?"

"Aren't we talking now?"

"No. We aren't."

Ethan sighed. Things had been awkward between them since that day at school when Pete learned he'd lied to Allie about

Boots McLaughlin. Not that the awkwardness had been much of a problem—they'd spent little time together since then anyway. When Pete and Allie weren't working together on Moore-or-Less's profile project, Ethan was working at The Chow Down—or hanging with Link Hornsby.

"Ethan?"

"Yeah?"

"What's going on, man?"

Ethan looked at his laptop, wondered what Pete would say about *this* project. It used to be he could tell Pete anything, but things had changed. He wasn't exactly sure how, but they had. Was it the gay thing? Maybe. After Ethan's big *I'm there for you, man* speech by their lockers, he'd been waiting for Pete to open up about it, but he hadn't. Now there seemed to be a distance between them. "What do you mean?" asked Ethan, tapping his touchpad to keep the window active.

There was another sound on the line. Not the huff Ethan had heard earlier, though. A wordless murmur. Or maybe a sigh. Then, "You avoiding me, buddy? We haven't hung out in a while."

"I've been busy. So have you and Allie." Ethan had meant to keep the edge out of his voice, but it was there anyway.

"Look, I asked you if me working with Allie would be a problem. Is that what all this is about?"

"All what?"

This time there was no hesitation in Pete's voice. "Christ, Ethan! You've been acting weird for days. No, it's been *weeks* now. Ever since you started that job of yours. Allie's noticed it, too."

There was no denying the edge in his voice now. "So you and Allie spend a lot of time talking about me, do you?"

"I knew it. This *is* about the project, isn't it. You're jealous of me working with her."

Like I need to be jealous of a fag, Ethan thought. "You're crazy," he said, his fingers tightening around his phone.

"Good, 'cause you shouldn't be," said Pete. "Allie loves you, man. Although, to tell you the truth, Ethan? Lately I've been wondering why."

"Go to hell." He hadn't meant to say the words. He'd thought them, but he hadn't realized his mouth was in sync with his brain until he heard them out loud. A result of the Heinekens, probably. He half expected to hear a click and a dial tone, but Pete surprised him.

"Guess I had that coming," he said, and Ethan heard him take a long breath. "Sorry, man, but you got such a good thing with Allie I don't know why you'd want to risk it."

"What makes you think I am?"

"Lying to her, for one thing. She's still so proud of you for giving that old guy the cash. How do you think she'll feel when she finds out the truth?"

"How would she find out?"

"*I'm* not going to tell her, if that's what you think. But lies have a way of catching up with a guy, you know?"

Ethan rolled his eyes. "You've been spending way too much time researching my old man. You sound just like him, life lessons and all."

"It's not just the lie, man. Seth told me you saw Filthy."

"It's no secret."

"Yeah, well, Allie doesn't know."

Ethan sensed the unspoken *Something else* before *Allie doesn't know,* and he fought the urge to tell Pete to go to hell again. "Maybe I want to surprise her when I get the Cobra."

"It'd be cool, man, if that was the reason."

"What makes you think it isn't?" Ethan snarled.

Pete continued, unaware of—or perhaps because of—the anger in Ethan's voice. "You forget I know what the Cobra means to you, man."

Ethan had been preparing to ream Pete out, but he paused. It was true—Pete did know why that particular car was so important. He was the only person Ethan had ever told about his mother's Cobra SVT. How his mother had helped him write down the year and the model, how she had gone online with him to find out as much as they could, the two of them scrolling through sites together, talking, planning, laughing. It was the last thing he and his mother had shared.

"It's like you want that car no matter what," continued Pete. "Including taking the money you promised that Boots guy."

"I *didn't* promise him."

"You promised Allie. And now Seth says you gave Filthy five hundred bucks. Where's the rest coming from? Money doesn't grow on trees."

Ethan snorted. "Do you *hear* yourself?" he asked. His next words were laced with scorn. "*Money doesn't grow on trees.* That's one of my old man's top twenty favourites. You know, I think maybe Kyle was right. The hospital switched us at birth. You're the son Jack Palmer was hoping for."

There was a moment of silence on the other end before Pete spoke again. When he did, his voice was strangely even despite the obvious intensity in his words. "You think *I* sound like your old man? You need to take a hard look at yourself, buddy. You sing the same song over and over. At least your dad says what he does to *teach* you something. All you think about is yourself. You're so wrapped up in what you want, what you think you *need,* that you don't give a damn about anyone else. An old guy lives on soup and you can't even give him back the cost of the ticket he bought you. That's cold."

Ethan felt as though a hand had reached through the phone and slapped him. His head reeling from Pete's comments, he opened his mouth to defend himself, but Pete launched in again.

"And the thing is, it's all pointless anyway. No way can you pull together all the cash you need in time. Seth says Filthy needs all of it by Christmas. You can't make what you need before then. Not waiting tables at a diner."

"Maybe you don't know everything. Maybe I've got other options."

"Yeah? Options like that sound a little too good to be true."

"What would *you* know about options?" growled Ethan. "What've *you* got lined up after graduation, Pete?" Everyone knew that Pete was headed to community college next fall, probably into a plumbing program. Some of his marks this year were too low to get him into university. More to the point, if he didn't pass physics, he wouldn't have enough credits to graduate in June, not without carrying an extra course in their last semester. Why'd he taken that damn physics course in the first place?

"Thanks, man," said Pete, his voice a raspy mutter on the line. "That's real great. Maybe you should think about going into counselling. You've got a real gift for helping people see their potential."

Ethan's anger dissolved, but before he could say anything else, Pete continued, "Sorry I bothered you, man. You do whatever you want. But, hey, that's pretty much your motto anyway, isn't it? To hell with anybody else." The line went dead.

Ethan stared at the cell, wondering if more than just the call had ended. He and Pete had never really argued about anything before. Sure, they'd disagreed about things, taunted each other on the basketball court or in the pool, poked fun at each other's blunders—but nothing like this. Allie was right when she'd joked about them being joined at the hip. Pete was more than his best friend. He was like the brother Ethan never had.

Which pissed Ethan off even more. Hell, of all people, Pete understood what the Mustang meant to him. Hadn't he said so himself? The Cobra was more than just a car to Ethan. It was a connection. So why couldn't Pete just accept whatever Ethan might have to do to get it?

He looked at his cell again, debated for a moment whether he should call Pete back and apologize, then remembered what his mother had told him all those years ago: *Nothing stays the same, Ethan. The one thing you can count on is that everything changes.*

Ethan reached for his laptop, hoping the page hadn't timed out.

It turned out that Hornsby was right. Gambling online was, in fact, a lot like surfing porn, but not only in the way anybody could access restricted sites. It was also how the urge to click took over, pulling you deeper into that digital vortex, five minutes collapsing into fifty until you suddenly found yourself wondering where in hell the hours could have gone.

Clicking.

Continually clicking.

To hell with the consequences.

Chapter 23

"I thought you said it was *foolproof.*"

Hornsby's face was expressionless, but Ethan thought he saw something behind his dark eyes. Laughter? "What'd you do," Hornsby asked. "Lose it all?"

The early December breeze sweeping up from the harbour drove a shiver through Ethan, but he was barely aware of it. As he stood in his shirtsleeves in the alley behind the diner, all he felt was anger. And betrayal. "A thousand. The other five hundred I already spent."

"Tough break," said Hornsby.

Ethan wanted to smash something. Or at least throw something. Looking around the alley, though, the only thing he saw was an empty Tim Hortons coffee cup, probably dropped there by one of the workers doing the construction next door. Ethan kicked it savagely, but it skidded only a few feet before coming to rest, rocking back and forth in the breeze. "Tough break," he echoed, his sarcasm like audible acid. "Maybe for you. Me, I don't have a cent left. And I need that money."

"We all need money, kid," said Hornsby, the toothpick in the corner of his mouth bobbing as he spoke.

"You said the Martingale system was a sure thing."

"I said it was a sure thing as long as you follow it to the letter."

"I did everything you said."

"Everything?"

Ethan cast his mind back over the past three days.

He takes it slowly at first. Decides he's going to play with only a hundred his first time online. See how it goes.

Wonders how much he should bet. Go big or go home. Wants to start with ten, decides on five. Better to start small.

Gets his first card—an 8. Dealer's up card is a jack. Clicks the Hit Me button. A king. Decides to hold at 18. Dealer gets a 3 for 13. Then an ace for 14. Then an 8 for 22. Bust.

Just five bucks, but it took him only five seconds to make it. And he didn't have to carry a tray of All Day Breakfasts or Philly Steaks With Fries, either.

Your Total Winnings: $5. Bets five. First card is an ace. Hit Me. A 10.

Blackjack!

Your Total Winnings: $10. Bets five. Loses.

Your Total Winnings: $5. Thinks about the Martingale system. Bets ten. Wins.

Your Total Winnings: $15. Bets five. Wins.

Your Total Winnings: $20. Bets five. Loses.

Your Total Winnings: $15. No sweat. Martingale again. Bets ten. Loses.

Your Total Winnings: $5. Law of averages, right? Bets twenty. Loses.

Okay. Down fifteen bucks. Thinks. Thinks again. Martingale calls for a forty-buck bet. Down fifteen, but he still has eighty-five bucks. Balls and bankrolls.

Your Total Winnings: $0. Bets forty. Wins. Yes! Leaps around the room, pumping the air with his fist. Hornsby, you are the man!

Your Total Winnings: $40. Which means he's up twenty-five. Maybe he should bet ten this time. No. Martingale says stay the course. Bets five. Wins.

Your Total Winnings: $45. *Which means he's up twenty-five.*
Bets five. Wins.
Your Total Winnings: $50. *Up thirty. Bets five. Loses.*
Your Total Winnings: $45. *Up twenty-five. Bets ten. Loses.*
Your Total Winnings: $35. *Up fifteen. Bets twenty. Loses.*
Your Total Winnings: $15.
After fourteen bets, he has eighty-five of his original hundred-dollar stake and fifteen in winnings. He's broken even.

He's kept track of his bets. Won seven, lost seven. Law of averages. Classic Martingale.

Balls and bankrolls. Still has the second, but he wonders about the first.

After school the next day, he goes to the public library, dodging Allie and Pete, who are heading to the media room. As they pass the bookcase he's standing behind, he hears them laughing together about something and his fingers curl into his palms. Allie loves you, man. *He knows this. But still his nails dig into the heels of his hands.*

*When they're gone, he signs out the book he found on the library's website—*Beating Blackjack: A Winner's Primer.

That evening, he studies blackjack, is surprised at the terminology of the game. Not ridiculous words, though, like coefficient, *like* GS450 *and* SLK350. *Words that have meaning. Like* soft hands—*with aces that count as 11—and all other hands,* hard hands. *Terms like* push, *when the dealer's hand is equal to the player's, and* doubling down, *when the player still has two cards and doubles his stake, getting only one more card.*

He learns when it makes sense to double down, when your two cards total 9 or 10 or 11. You always double down with 11, unless the dealer's up card is an ace. Likewise with 10, unless the dealer's up card is an ace or a face card or a 10. Doubling down with 9 is trickier—the dealer's up card must be 3 or 4 or 5 or 6. Otherwise, you hit.

He learns when to split, *learns about* card counting, *learns there is so much more to the game than he'd imagined. In some ways blackjack is like physics, unseen forces working in the background, the dealer a kind of gravity bringing everything back to centre. But blackjack is also* not *like physics. Because these forces he understands. There is a cool logic here that seems sensible, safe.*

By ten-thirty that evening, he is ready to play again.

An hour later, his Total Winnings window reads $740.

At midnight, he has broken even.

He picks up Beating Blackjack: A Winner's Primer *again, turns the pages slowly.*

———————

He is tired the next night, yawns repeatedly into the screen. He fell asleep in English class, waking only when Allie prodded him, her face a question mark. "Up late studying," he'd murmured, which wasn't a lie.

But despite the yawning, he is ready. Large coffee, a Mars bar, and he's good to go.

By three o'clock that morning, he has nothing left. Everything is gone.

———————

"You did *everything* I said?" repeated Hornsby.

Ethan shrugged. "Almost everything."

"Almost ain't good enough, kid."

Ethan looked at the condominiums next door. Although they were still under construction, a huge sign on the street announced three-quarters of them already sold. Apparently, *almost* was fine with some people. "I didn't have enough money left after my last loss to double the next bet," he said.

"Too bad."

"That's all you got? 'Too bad'?"

Hornsby looked at him. "Whaddya expect *me* to do about it?"

"What about going back to the casino?"

"With what? You just told me you're broke."

Reddening, Ethan looked down at the cracked asphalt in the alley, where they'd met because Ethan didn't want Lil seeing him with Hornsby in The Chow Down's parking lot. Lil had told him the other day that the developer who was building the condos next door had contacted Mr. Anwar, the owner of the diner, and she and Ike had assumed it was about sharing the cost of resurfacing the alleyway. They were wrong. The developer had offered to buy the restaurant, which he wanted to turn into more condos, adding four more floors to the building. And much to Lil's dismay, Anwar seemed to be considering it. No loyalty there.

Nor, apparently, was there any here. But Ethan asked anyway. "You think maybe you could carry me this one time? I could pay you back from your winnings."

Hornsby snorted, the harsh sound bouncing off the brick walls. "Whaddya think I am, Goodwill? I don't do charity, kid." He turned to leave.

"You got me into this," said Ethan, the tone in his voice both pleading and demanding, like some of the brats he served.

Hornsby stopped and slowly faced him. "I didn't get you into *nothin'. You* came to *me.*" He spat the toothpick onto the asphalt. "What we got here is a problem with perspective. You think I'm your friend. I'm not." He turned, throwing his final words over his shoulder. "You come up with some more cash, we'll talk. Otherwise, get lost."

His break over, Ethan could do nothing more than head back into the diner.

Standing at the sink, Ike looked up as Ethan came in the door. "I saw you out back talkin' to Hornsby," he said.

"I have to clear with you who I *talk* to now?" snapped Ethan. He'd never responded to Ike that way before, frustration undermining common sense, and he half expected Ike to roar at him.

Instead, the cook merely shrugged. "That guy's trouble. If I was you—"

"Well, you're *not* me, are you?" The anger surprised Ethan, but it felt good to give in to it, to let it go, to finally respond to the weeks of criticism and ridicule the cook had directed at him. "You've been riding me since the day I got here. What's your *problem*, anyway?"

The cook's face darkened. "I'll *tell* you what my problem is, kid. You waltz in here like you're God's gift but you ain't done a lick 'a real work your whole life. I *seen* that piece 'a paper you call a resumé. Lifeguard! Most 'a the people who eat here? They might not be able to afford a place in fancy Cathedral Estates"— and here his voice thickened in a sneer—"but they damn well know what it's like to do an honest day's work. You come in here like you're slummin', doin' us all a big favour just by showin' up, then expectin' the world to pat you on the back and say 'Good job!' You get outta this life what you put into it, and it seems to me you ain't put in a thing. I know your old man's supposed to be some big hotshot, but from where I'm standin', looks like the best part 'a your daddy ran down your mama's leg."

Ethan opened his mouth, but before he could say anything, Ike thundered on. "I actually thought I seen you improvin' the

past couple weeks, thought maybe there might be somethin'
there, maybe you might be worth a damn after all. But no. You
wanna screw up your life hangin' with the likes 'a Hornsby, you
go right ahead. No good'll come of it, you can be damned sure
'a that, but don't say *I* didn't warn you." The cook turned away,
thrusting his hands under the tap as if washing them of Ethan
and whatever situation he'd gotten himself into. "Them that lie
down with dogs," he muttered, "get up with fleas."

Ethan responded with the only words that came to mind—
"Screw you! Screw the whole damn lot of you!"—and grabbed
his jacket from the hook by the door. Instead of heading back out
into the alley—he didn't want to cross paths with that asshole
Hornsby again—he shoved through the batwing doors into
the dining area, storming past an open-mouthed Lil and five
afternoon diners with forks paused in mid-air, and slammed out
the exit. Not even grease could have saved that hinge as the impact
drove the door back against the side of the building.

Chapter 24

"You're home early." Raye stood in the doorway of the family room, which Jillian hadn't had a hand in decorating, so its oak floors and sand-coloured walls made it a warm, inviting space for the comfortable leather furniture Ethan sprawled on now.

"Mm."

"I thought you were working this afternoon."

"I was." Ethan didn't feel like talking. He'd called Allie's cell several times, but it kept going straight to voice mail. Maybe her battery was dead. He'd stopped by her house, but no one was home. From there he'd gone to the library and then her dance studio, but another group—which looked to be for beginners and chronic klutzes—was being taught, so he'd left there, too. After that, he'd had no idea where Allie might be. Shopping with Bethany or her mom? She hadn't shown up at school and he'd meant to phone her earlier to find out why, but his head had been preoccupied with getting to The Chow Down and, hopefully, seeing Link Hornsby. Now that he needed to tell her what had happened, he couldn't find her.

Frustrated, he'd come home and turned on the seventy-inch LED in the family room just to have noise in the house. Two women on the Home Shopping Channel now *oohed* and *ahhed* over a skin cream that, from the sounds of things, did everything but cure cancer. Maybe even that, too.

"Thinking of ordering some?" teased Raye, nodding at the screen.

He didn't reply. Instead, he began clicking the remote, ratcheting his way up through the hundreds of channels their satellite dish brought into the house.

Raye frowned, then plopped herself down on the loveseat that formed the short side of a leather L in front of the flat screen. "What's up, Ethan?"

"Price of gas, according to C-SPAN."

"Funny."

"I'm here all week, two shows a night."

Both of them silently watched the images change rapidly in front of them, logos of various networks flashing past.

Finally, "Ethan, is something wrong?"

"Life," he muttered, his eyes still on the flickering screen.

"Anything I can do?"

He was about to say no when he suddenly turned to her. "That offer to loan me some cash still good?"

She nodded. "How much do you want?"

"How much do you have?"

"Four eighty, four eighty-five, something like that."

Ethan tried to look nonchalant. "Say, three hundred? Just for a few days?"

Raye's left eyebrow lifted, but her voice was even as she replied, "No problem. When do you need it?"

"When can you give it to me?"

"It's upstairs."

He grinned at her. "You didn't get the memo about interest?" Their father was forever lecturing them about the importance of making deposits into their accounts rather than leaving their money lying around earning nothing.

Raye grinned in return. "He shouldn't have given me Juanita," she said, referring to the huge blue piggy bank that sat on her dresser. "I'll be right back."

And in a minute she was. "Here," she said, passing him a roll of bills. She hadn't asked him what the money was for, but the unspoken question hovered over them like a glowing neon sign.

Ignoring it, Ethan took the money and stuffed it into the pocket of his jeans. "Thanks, Raye," he said. "I'll get it back to you in a couple days. Three at the most."

"No worries," she said. "I know where you live."

Standing up, Ethan grabbed the jacket he'd left lying on the ottoman and headed toward the patio door.

"Ethan?"

Both arms in the jacket's sleeves, he turned. "Yeah?"

"Is everything okay?"

He flashed her a grin. "Never better."

She looked down, and he could see a new splash of ink on the back of her hand where Jazz had been at work again. From across the room, he couldn't tell what it was. Not a dragon this time. A unicorn, maybe?

"You don't seem . . ." Her voice trailed off.

"What?" he asked, failing to keep the impatience out of his own voice. He had less than half an hour to make it to the bank before it closed. "I don't seem what?"

She shrugged. "Nothing."

He nodded. "Thanks again, okay?" And he left.

———

Afterwards, he realized he should have gone to find Hornsby and offered him Raye's cash as a stake at the waterfront casino.

But he'd remembered Hornsby's comment in the Echo, how their fifty-fifty split that night had been "a one-time low introductory offer," and he knew the guy would want an even bigger chunk this time. And besides, Hornsby had been such an asshole in the alley—*You think I'm your friend. I'm not*—that he was the last person Ethan wanted to see that afternoon.

Instead, Ethan had made it to the bank just in time to deposit Raye's three hundred bucks into his account, after which he'd gone home, logged onto MyDigitalVegas.com, and tried to transfer the money to the site. It took him a dozen attempts that afternoon for the money to go through—apparently, the bank's site wasn't as efficient as the online casino's—but after almost an hour he was good to go.

And in less than fifteen minutes, he'd lost it all.

———

"—so if you two could keep the noise down this evening, I'd appreciate it." Jack Palmer looked from Raye to Ethan, who absently moved something resembling angel-hair pasta—minus most of the calories and all of the taste, since Jillian had cooked it—around on his plate with his fork. "Is that doable?" he asked.

Ethan continued to play with his food until he felt a foot kick his shin under the table. "What?" he demanded, looking across at Raye, who was nodding toward their father. "Yeah, yeah," he muttered.

"Thanks," said Jack. "The crew should be in and out in a couple hours, and a lot of that is set-up time. The interview itself shouldn't take more than half an hour."

If he'd cared at all, Ethan might have wondered how the tech person in charge of lighting would handle the glare off those Brilliant Cream walls, since the media consultant for his father's party had decided the interview should be conducted in their living room. He'd granted CBC's Connie Althorpe an exclusive "At Home with Jack Palmer," and she was scheduled to arrive within the hour.

Ethan, however, didn't give a damn. The only thing occupying his mind at the moment was the money he'd let slip through his fingers in the last two days. First the thousand remaining after he'd paid Filthy his five hundred, and now the three hundred he'd borrowed from Raye. And that wasn't even counting the three hundred he'd paid for that damn driver's licence. On top of that, he'd thrown away his job at The Chow Down this afternoon, and he'd be lucky if his next—and last—paycheque from there came to more than a hundred bucks. That wouldn't even cover the Christmas gift he'd wanted to get Allie let alone the money he now owed Raye.

He had tried the Martingale system again, but he knew now where he'd gone wrong. The Martingale required more than balls and a bankroll to work. It also required brains. Ethan had been in a hurry, and instead of starting out with his regular five-dollar wagers, he'd begun placing ten-dollar bets, which meant he'd gone in the hole much faster. He'd been up sixty bucks when the law of averages kicked in and his initial winning streak ended. Five losing hands later, he had only fifty left, far less than the three hundred twenty his next bet should have been. What else could he do? He bet the fifty.

And lost it.

Idiot! If only he hadn't gotten greedy. Next time, he'd know what to do. Next time, he'd stick to five-buck bets, wouldn't get carried away by a few early wins.

Next time.

Chapter 25

Ethan unlocked the back door and slipped inside, feeling like a thief in his own home as he keyed the entry code into the alarm system. He'd left school after first period—Beaker had given his forged note only a passing glance before waving him off—and didn't think he'd be missed since so many others in his class were absent, one of them Allie. Pete and Seth were among the missing, too, and he wondered what the two of them might be up to. Whatever it was, it couldn't be worse than what Ethan was planning to do.

He passed through the kitchen and down the main hall, glancing into the living room where his old man's interview had taken place. He wondered if it had gone as well as his father had hoped. As he'd promised, Ethan had stayed in his room the whole evening—he hadn't felt like doing much else anyway—then he'd lain awake most of the night weighing his options. As a result, he'd overslept and missed breakfast, so there'd been no one to ask how the "At Home with Jack Palmer" thing had gone. Not that he was really interested, but at one point he could hear his father's raised voice floating up from the living room. He was probably making some point like he did in court—dramatically. Ethan had heard nothing else after that, except for the camera crew's van pulling out of the driveway a few minutes later.

Fighting the urge to tiptoe, Ethan now climbed the staircase and went through the first door on the left. As usual, he shook his head at the sign above his sister's bed: *Raye's World*. Even on this sunny day, it was like a tomb in there. The walls and ceiling were a deep purple, a tribute to her favourite band painted by Raye herself, the week before they moved into the house, and the window and bed were draped completely in black, a holdover from Raye's brief goth flirtation. But Raye's World was anything but grim. Pinned up on every available wall surface were hundreds of cartoons, some clipped from newspapers and magazines, some downloaded from the Internet, and others drawn by Raye herself. They were nothing like the cartoons in those dumb decorating magazines that Jillian sometimes brought over and left lying in the family room. Raye's taste ran to *The Far Side* and *Doonesbury* and even weirder offerings she'd clipped from magazines like *The New Yorker* and *Harper's*. She'd shown Ethan her latest find a couple of days ago, a drawing of dozens of cattle entering a tiny corral with dialogue balloons saying things like "Excuse me" and "Pardon me." Raye had laughed like crazy when she'd shown it to him, and he'd laughed as much at her reaction to it as anything else. Although he'd never said so, his sister's weird sense of humour was just one more thing that he loved about her.

Which made what he was about to do now even harder.

Moving to her dresser, he picked up the blue ceramic pig she'd named Juanita P. Orker and heard inside it the clink of coins and the rustle of something more substantial. He turned it over and unscrewed the plastic plug in the pig's belly, then shook the contents onto the black bedspread. Just as he expected, he counted nearly two hundred bucks, more than half of it in toonies, loonies, and quarters. It was so like Raye to have given him only bills the night before while she kept the more unwieldy coins for herself.

Replacing Juanita's plug, Ethan scooped up the money and shoved it into his pockets, then repositioned the pig on Raye's dresser. With the law of averages on his side—and what he knew about balls, bankrolls, and brains—he'd be able to repay all the money he'd borrowed from her by the end of the day. He was sure of it.

———————

"You don't have school today?" asked the teller at the bank, a young man who was carrying about fifty pounds more than he should.

Looking over the counter, Ethan saw that the guy's ass hung over both sides of the stool he was sitting on. "In-service," he lied.

"Gotta love those, huh?" the man grinned. "Now what can I do for you today?"

Ethan began pulling the coins out of his pockets, placing them on the counter between him and the teller. "I have a hundred ninety-six bucks that I—"

"Sorry," interrupted the teller, "I can't take all those loose coins."

"Why not?"

"Bank policy. That many coins have to be rolled." The teller reached into a drawer and pulled out several paper tubes. "These here are for your two-dollar coins, these are for loonies, and these ones are for quarters. Doesn't look like you've got enough of anything else there to roll."

Ethan tried to hide his impatience. "Can I do that here or do I need to come back?"

"There's a table in the reception area you can use if you don't mind doing it out in the open but, if I were you, I'd use the one over there." He pointed to a table behind a large pillar that held a display of banking pamphlets and brochures.

And if I were you, thought Ethan, *I'd cut back on the Cinnabons.* "Thanks. I'll just be a minute."

The teller had grinned at this and, fifteen minutes later, Ethan understood why. Getting coins into those paper tubes wasn't as easy as it looked. More than once he'd dropped a handful of toonies on the floor, and they'd rolled in all directions. He had just dived again after a bunch of quarters when he heard a voice he recognized.

"I need to see the bank manager, please."

"Certainly, Ms. Fontaine. He's with another client at the moment, but he shouldn't be too long. Would you care to take a seat?"

Ethan looked up from beneath his table and saw Allie's mother standing at the end of a counter separating this part of the bank from two offices with signs on their doors: *Manager* and *Assistant Manager* and names below them. An attractive woman in a grey suit stood on the other side of the counter.

Christ, thought Ethan. *Of all the times—*

"Do you know how long he'll be?" asked Allie's mother.

"I can check for you," the woman said.

Ethan glanced around the space and saw that the only empty chair was directly across from where he was working. Shit!

Allie's mother put her hand to her throat, her fingers toying with the necklace Ethan recognized as the one Allie and Bethany had given her for her birthday. He knew that gesture well. He'd seen it when he'd been at the Fontaines' house the day Bethany had strep throat and she and Allie's dad had debated taking her to the doctor again. He'd seen it when she was attending one of Allie's dance recitals just before Allie and her partner executed a particularly challenging move. He'd seen it the night he'd dropped Allie off after a movie, the streets slick with freezing rain that hadn't been forecasted. The woman was nervous or upset. Or both.

"No, that's okay," she said. "It's probably better if I make an appointment."

"I know he's free at one o'clock," said the woman behind the counter. "Would you like to come back then?"

Ethan watched Allie's mom tug at her necklace again. "I think it'd be better if I called him."

The woman nodded. "By all means. Would you like his card?"

But Mrs. Fontaine was already moving past Ethan's table on her way toward the exit.

Relieved, Ethan crawled out from under the table and slid the last errant coins into the sleeve for quarters. Standing up, he collected the filled tubes and remaining loose change and headed back to the lineup.

The Martingale system served him well after he returned from the bank . . . for the first hour.

At one point, Ethan had won back all the money he'd borrowed from Raye the previous night and was up a hundred eighty-five bucks—and that didn't include the cash he'd taken from Juanita that morning, which he still had. He'd lost some along the way, of course—five bucks here, ten there, and a string of bad hands had cost him forty bucks on one bet and eighty on another—but he'd kept his head and stayed the course, waiting for the law of averages to kick in when he needed it. And it had.

Until the second hour.

At one point, he considered stopping, almost clicked the End Game button, but then he slid the cursor over to Hit Me. Again and again, like his brain had separated itself from everything but the job of creating the electrical impulse that travelled down his arm into his index finger.

Ten minutes into the second hour, it was all over.

Sitting on his bed now, Ethan looked at the screen in disbelief, staring at the zero in his Your Total Winnings window.

He flung his laptop across the room.

"Hey, buddy," said Ethan.

Standing in the open doorway of his parents' kitchen, Pete looked first at his feet and then at Ethan on his back step. "Hey," he said.

"Can I come in?"

Pete glanced behind him and Ethan could see Pete's mother making a pie at the counter. Ethan nodded to her—"Hi, Mrs. Hennessey"—and she waved back, her hand covered with flour.

"Maybe I'd better come out," Pete said. He stepped inside for a moment and then reappeared, slipping on his jacket as he closed the door behind him.

Ethan moved down the steps into the driveway. Behind him, Pete grabbed the railing with one hand and nimbly swung his legs over the wrought iron and landed on the concrete beside his friend.

"You weren't in school today," said Ethan. He wanted to ask, *So, you and Seth hanging out now?* but that would've just complicated things.

"I drove Ma to Bridgewater. Doctor's appointment."

Ethan blinked, embarrassed. "She okay?"

Pete nodded. "Eye checkup. They put drops in and she couldn't drive herself home. No big deal."

"Good to hear."

The two stood looking at each other, an awkwardness settling around them like wet sand.

"I bet you're surprised to see me," offered Ethan finally.

Pete looked at his feet. "Not really. No."

Another moment passed. Then both began speaking at the same time: "Look, I'm sorry—"

They stopped, then chorused, "Jinx!" Like they were nine years old again. Ethan laughed self-consciously, and Pete joined him. Their laughter lasted longer than it needed to, as if they were delaying an uncomfortable inevitability.

"You first," said Pete, finally.

Ethan nodded, ran a hand through his hair, cleared his throat. "I'm sorry for what I said on the phone about options. I didn't mean it. You've got plenty."

Pete shrugged. "I don't know about plenty," he said, "but thanks, man."

"I was a jerk," continued Ethan. "I was pissed over what you said about Allie, but that was no excuse to take it out on you."

Pete looked away. "Yeah. About that."

Ethan glanced at his watch. The day was disappearing. "Look, Pete, I gotta ask a favour."

"Favour?" Pete's voice seemed to come from farther away than where he stood in the driveway.

Ethan didn't know how to ask what he'd come for so it wouldn't sound like the only reason he was there. But he asked anyway. "Can I borrow some cash? Fifty, a hundred, whatever." He paused, then added, "Two hundred, if you got it."

Pete turned to him. "You came here for money?"

Ethan flushed. "Yeah, look, I wouldn't ask if it wasn't important."

Pete stared at him for a moment, a series of expressions flickering across his face. Finally, "I got maybe twenty bucks."

"Twenty's good." Ethan hated the eagerness in his voice, but he plunged on. "I'll pay you back soon as I can. It's just—"

"Don't worry about it," said Pete. He reached into his back pocket, took out his wallet, then hesitated. "Ethan?"

"Yeah?"

"That's really why you came here? To borrow money?"

"Not *just* that," Ethan replied. "To apologize, too, right? But I'm in kind of a rush. Do you think you can—"

Pete held up his hand. "There's something I gotta say." He took a deep breath, released it. "I'm sorry."

Ethan felt a wave of impatience surge through him. "Look, it's not for long. I'll get the twenty back to you tomorrow. Or the next day for sure."

Pete shook his head. "It's not about the money." A car came down the street, and he followed it with his eyes until it passed. "I didn't mean for it to happen."

"What?"

"You're my buddy. My best friend. Friends don't do something like that. They don't *plan* to, anyway."

Ethan frowned. "What are you talking about?"

Pete looked toward the street again. "It wasn't Allie's fault."

Ethan could feel his impatience become annoyance. "What's Allie got to do with it?"

Pete turned to him. "She really didn't tell you?"

"Tell me what? She wasn't in school this morning."

Pete shrugged. "Yeah. I was up half the night myself." Now it was his turn to run his hands through his hair, and he kicked at a piece of concrete crumbling from the driveway's edge. "I like Allie, Ethan."

"I know you do. Who doesn't?"

"No." He took another deep breath. "I mean I *really* like her."

Ethan's eyes narrowed. "What are you saying?"

Pete looked at his feet. "You know what I'm saying."

Ethan tried to make sense of what he was hearing. "But how *could* you?"

Pete looked up, his face lined with misery. "I didn't want to. Honest. It just—"

"But you're gay!"

Pete gaped at him. "What? I'm not gay. Where'd you get *that* idea?"

Ethan ran over everything in his head, trying to sort it all out. "You've never been serious with a girl. And you haven't dated anyone for *months*. You don't even *look* at girls. I saw you at—" He thought back to their lunch at Perk Up Your Day, how Pete had ignored the server's big breasts, looked through her as she'd leaned over him, collecting their dishes while he—

While he chatted with Allie.

And when had Pete stopped dating?

After Allie arrived at John C. Miles.

And the questions: *What's Allie doing tonight? Does Allie know? How do you think Allie'll feel?*

He even knew about Ragged Ending, Allie's favourite band.

"I'm not gay," Pete said simply.

Ethan looked at the crumbling concrete that Pete was poking with his toe, began to feel the driveway vibrate under his feet. A tractor-trailer churned up the street, the sound growing as it approached then washing away as it passed. It left a smell of something heavy in the air. Oil? Rubber? Transmission fluid just before the gears seize? Everything connected in some way. Allie and Ethan, Ethan and Pete.

And now Allie and Pete.

"What didn't Allie tell me?" asked Ethan. He was surprised to hear his voice sound so normal. Not at all like the tractor-trailer that churned in his chest right now.

Pete didn't look up, just kept staring at the concrete. "It wasn't her fault, man. It was all me."

"What—didn't—Allie—tell—me?" Ethan repeated. Hearing the question a second time didn't make it more real. Nothing about this moment was real. A "zero winnings" message flashed in his brain.

"I kissed her, Ethan."

Ethan saw his knuckles connect with Pete's face before he knew he'd made a fist. Pete staggered backward, blood already beginning to flow from his nose. But he said nothing, made no move to raise his own fists.

"You kissed Allie," said Ethan. He might just as well have said *You dissed Allie* or *You pissed Allie*. Neither of those would have made less sense.

Pete nodded, the blood now dripping onto his jacket. He spat, drops of blood flecking the concrete, then wiped at his nose with the back of his hand, smearing red to his wrist. "It just happened, Ethan. I didn't plan it. I would *never* have planned—"

"*What happened?*" Ethan's words were a guttural growl.

Pete wiped at his nose again, took another breath. "We were working on that profile assignment, leaning over one of the monitors in the library. She'd just thought of this great idea about how we could frame the whole thing, and she looked up to tell me. And I couldn't stop myself. I kissed her."

"You kissed Allie." Repeating it was perhaps the only thing that kept Ethan from swinging again. Forming words with his lips gave his brain and his body something else to do. Some small thing that kept him from forming fists with his hands and lashing out, drawing more blood. There was too much of that already. Pete wiped at his nose with the back of his other hand now and then the sleeve of his jacket.

"I've had a thing for Allie from the moment I first saw her," continued Pete, "but I never did anything about it. I wouldn't. I knew how you felt about her, man."

"But you *kissed* her."

"I never meant for it to happen, Ethan. It just did."

"And Allie—?" Ethan couldn't finish the question, couldn't bring himself to say the words.

He didn't have to. "She was real upset. She started apologizing for maybe giving me the wrong impression. But she hadn't. I told her so, told her it was just me. All me."

Ethan looked down at his hand, saw two of his knuckles were bleeding where they must have grazed Pete's teeth. "She didn't tell me."

"You said you haven't seen her."

"She didn't call."

"She's got some things on her mind—"

"No shit."

Pete shook his head. "Not that. Other things."

Ethan raised his eyebrows. "What do you mean, 'other things'? She's been telling you stuff? Personal stuff?" The anger he'd felt earlier threatened to erupt again.

"You were busy at the diner and with that project you're working on. She hadn't seen much of you lately."

"And you just happened to be around to listen," said Ethan, his voice a razor. "Convenient."

"That's not how it was at all, Eth—"

"You must've just been *waiting* for something like this, huh?" Ethan snarled. "Your timing was perfect. And here I said you didn't have options. You *make* your options, don't you, buddy?"

Pete reached out and gripped Ethan's shoulder. "It wasn't like that—"

Ethan flung Pete's hand aside. "Stay away from me," he breathed. "And stay away from Allie, too."

"Ethan!"

But Ethan ignored him. He was running before he reached the street.

Chapter 26

"How much can you give me for it?"

The woman behind the counter at Delta's Estate Jewellers and Pawnshop looked again at the object in her hand. "Seventy-five."

"She paid over *two hundred* for it!"

"Look, kid, it's a specialty item. Not a lot 'a people around here are gonna wear a buckle like this. Maybe in Alberta, all those cowboys." She shrugged. "Hundred. Take it or leave it."

Ethan took it.

His smashed laptop still on the floor of his room, Ethan sat at the computer in his old man's study staring at the "zero winnings" message blinking on the screen. It had taken him less than five minutes to lose the money he'd gotten at the pawnshop. In fact, the timer at the bottom of the screen read four minutes and thirteen seconds. He'd lost every hand, doubling each successive bet so he was down seventy-five dollars after the first four. The Martingale system called for a fifth bet of eighty bucks, but he only had twenty-five left in his account. Brains, balls, and bankrolls. Why did it always come down to the third?

He bet the twenty-five, then drew a jack of diamonds after his three of hearts and nine of spades.

Sitting there at his old man's double-pedestal desk, he heard himself make a sound, something between a sigh and a sob.

He leaned forward, resting his head on its cool, glass-topped surface, his mind moving through moments of the last few weeks. He'd gambled away all of his cash and lost his job. He'd stolen money from his sister. His girlfriend had made out with his best friend, for Christ's sake. Everything was ruined. He felt broken inside, like the tree a windstorm had brought down in the yard behind their house in Herring Cove. He slammed his fist on the desk, scattering papers and envelopes onto the gleaming oak floor. He cursed as he bent down to collect them, the words piling up in the silence, then sat up, rolled the plush leather office chair backward, and got to his feet. That's when he saw them: pieces of torn newsprint in the wastebasket by the desk, a cardinal sin in their *Waste not, want not* household. Even as a child, his father had been anal about recycling—"When you have next to nothing, you find uses for what others throw away," he was fond of saying—yet Mr. Perfect had broken his own rule. Ethan forced himself to grin, trying to fill up that hollowness for a moment, trying hard to feel something besides empty. It didn't work.

Most of the papers in his hands were unopened mail. On top of the pile was an envelope addressed to his father, bearing the emblem of a financial institution that Ethan had overheard the investment adviser talking about. The envelope was thick, and through the paper beneath his fingers Ethan thought he could feel the raised numbers of a bank card. Or a credit card.

Sudden hope kindled itself inside that emptiness as an idea sparked in his head, thoughts flashing like wildfire through his brain, but then common sense gripped him. He laid the papers and the mail on the desk, boxed their edges to neaten the pile, then turned to the computer and cleared the Web browser's history, deleting the sites he had visited. One site, really: MyDigitalVegas.com.

He left the study. Glancing at his watch, he saw Raye wouldn't be home for at least another hour. No, he realized, longer than that. Today was Thursday, the day she took guitar lessons from Winnipeg Joe. Ethan was relieved. More time to consider what to do about Juanita. Funny, he thought, how easy it was to focus on a ceramic pig. Better than letting his mind wander to Allie. And Pete.

Although he hadn't eaten since the night before, he wasn't hungry. But he found himself thirsty and went to the kitchen to draw himself a glass of water from the fridge dispenser. Manufacturers didn't sell refrigerators bigger than the model his old man had purchased unless they were custom built, and Ethan often wondered why his father hadn't chosen to have one made to order—something else Jack could have complained about when it didn't turn out the way he expected. Like his son.

Standing in front of the stainless-steel door, Ethan thought again of the tree that had blown down behind their house in Herring Cove, thought about the storm that had snapped it off and brought it crashing within a few metres of the power lines.

He thought about how in the space of a few weeks his life had been turned upside down by another kind of storm, and he let his mind travel back to its beginnings—the night he'd clipped the corner of the garage with the Volvo.

No, that wasn't right. It was the morning *after* that when everything really went to shit, the moment when his old man decided Ethan should pay for the damages out of his own money, the fifty-three hundred bucks that would have bought him the car he'd wanted for more than half his life. He thought about the physics of that moment—he'd been the tree, his father the unstoppable force that brought him crashing to earth. But it was all for the greater good, right? In the service of those goddamn life lessons handed down by a grandmother he'd never even known.

Every action has a consequence.

Ethan thought of the number of times he'd clicked the Hit Me button on MyDigitalVegas.com. Yeah, every action had a consequence, all right.

A person is invariably defined by his ability to meet his obligations.

Ethan thought again about all the money he'd lost, especially the money he'd taken from Raye. His kid sister, the only member of his family who gave a damn about him, and look what he'd done to her.

Make every obstacle an opportunity.

Ethan thought about the money that had repaired the Volvo and the corner of the garage. *His* money. He'd worked hard to save it, and his old man had taken all of it and more. He thought again about the three obstacles to success with the Martingale system—brains, balls, and bankrolls—and then again about that fifty-three hundred bucks. His father *owed* him that money. That was *his* bankroll.

Ethan swallowed the last of the water, left the glass on the counter, then returned to his old man's study. Looking down at the desk, he picked up the thick envelope and again felt beneath his fingers the raised numbers of the plastic card inside. *Make every obstacle an opportunity.* Without hesitating, he tore it open and pulled out several pages, and glued to one of them was a credit card with a sticker bearing another valuable life lesson: *Just call to activate.*

Chapter 27

"This is gettin' to be a tradition," said Hornsby. "You, me, and crappy diners."

Sitting across from him at The Lobster Pot, a hole-in-the-wall in the city's north end that wasn't much bigger than its namesake, Ethan didn't even try to fake a smile. He'd spent an hour outside the waterfront casino and then walked a four-block radius around The Chow Down for nearly two more, hoping he'd spy Hornsby somewhere, but he hadn't. It was Hornsby who'd spotted *him*, pulling his rusted Echo over to the curb and asking if he wanted a lift. Ethan had nearly sobbed with relief.

He passed on Hornsby's offer of a burger or fries—"My treat," Hornsby had said, but food was the last thing Ethan wanted. Instead, he launched into an explanation of everything that had happened online. Hearing himself say it out loud, he felt even more like a loser than when he'd finally turned off his old man's computer that second time. At least he hadn't thrown it across the room.

"So, can you help me?" he asked, leaning forward in the booth. He hated that he sounded so desperate. But the truth was he'd never felt more desperate in his life.

Hornsby took a long swallow of his iced tea—*Who drinks iced tea in December?* wondered Ethan—and sat back against the red vinyl upholstery, scarred from years of zippers, sharp corners on purses and packages, and the odd knife or fork used for things other than eating. "Lemme get this straight. You maxed out the card in less than an hour?"

Ethan nodded. "Fifteen hundred. And five hundred more before that, money I took from my sister." He didn't bother mentioning the hundred he'd gotten for the buckle. What was the point? "I've gotta come up with two thousand quick."

Hornsby shrugged. "Why not just come clean to your old man? Guy livin' in Cathedral Estates could probably cover a couple thou' easy."

Ethan shook his head. He had actually considered it. Adding up the damage that day, he knew he was in over his head. He couldn't continue on the course he'd taken, couldn't keep thinking he could pull a miracle out of his ass.

But the idea of telling his old man what he'd done made him want to puke. The morning in the kitchen after Ethan had hit the garage would pale in comparison with the production his old man would make when he heard about the money Ethan had gambled away. It would be a two-act play—first, the *Shocked And Appalled* portion of the program, which included lots of yelling, then the *What Did I Ever Do To Deserve This* suffering-martyr routine Jack loved so much. Ethan could see his father now, arms folded, head shaking sadly, as if he couldn't believe that the person in front of him had actually sprung from his loins. And Ethan could only imagine the aftermath—not just the punishment he'd hand down but also what he'd make Ethan do to repay the cash. Car washes on Seminary Lane? A paper route? Something that would teach him the value of an honest day's work. Christ!

Ethan shook his head. "Going to my father isn't an option." He looked down at the table, saw that someone had scratched "LR luvs DP" in the faded laminate. For a moment he wondered who LR and DP were, wondered if they'd been able to make it work, keep it together. Nothing lasts forever, though. Just look at him and Allie.

He raised his eyes. "There's nobody else I can go to," he said. "Can you help me?"

Hornsby stared at him for a long moment. "Depends."

"On what?"

"On whether you're willin' to take some risks."

The last time Hornsby had asked him that question, Ethan couldn't have imagined how badly things would turn out. But they couldn't get much worse than this, right? "What have I got to lose?" he said.

It turned out that Ethan had a lot more to lose than he thought. They'd left The Lobster Pot to sit in Hornsby's shitbox of a car and, hearing him outline his plan for getting the cash, Ethan felt his lower jaw loosen and had to put conscious effort into keeping his mouth closed. He couldn't get out of his head what Lil had said about Hornsby that first day he saw him: *I'd steer clear 'a the guy if I was you.* And hadn't Ike told him much the same thing? Along with *That guy's bad news.* If Ethan had ever needed proof of that, he certainly had it now.

"I can't do it," said Ethan.

Hornsby leaned back in the seat, his left arm propped on the door frame. "There's lots 'a things we *think* we can't do," he said. "You'd be surprised how easy it is."

Ethan shook his head. "Not this."

"Thought you said you had no other options."

"There has to be another way."

"There's always another way."

Ethan's heart lifted. "Tell me."

The smirk around Hornsby's mouth was evident even before he began to speak. "You get yourself a big bag and start walkin' the 101 pickin' up bottles 'n' cans. Shouldn't take more'n a few hundred trips to an Enviro Depot to score what you need. Good luck with that, okay?"

Ethan turned to look out the passenger-side window, anger boiling away his disappointment. "Funny," he muttered, gripping the worn armrest.

"Look, kid," said the man, and there was no mistaking the boredom in his voice now, "you got yourself into this. You wanna get out of it quick or slow, that's up to you." He reached into his jacket and pulled out a card, handing it to Ethan. "You change your mind, call me. Now get the hell outta my car." He turned the key and the Echo sputtered to life.

A moment later, Ethan stood on the sidewalk watching helplessly as Hornsby drove off. He glanced down at the card in his hand. There was only a number printed on it, obviously a cellphone. No name, no address, nothing but the number.

In the second it took him to read it, Ethan realized what he had to do. What other choice did he have?

He would tell his old man everything.

Chapter 28

Ethan was almost sick with relief to find no one at the house when he got there at six. Raye was usually home by now, and he took her absence as a blessing. She would know something was wrong the moment she saw him and she'd be all over him. He needed the time alone to plan what he was going to say to his old man. Already he could feel his guts churn as he thought about it.

Of course, it didn't help that he'd had almost nothing to eat all day. He still didn't feel hungry, but he needed something on his stomach before he faced his father. He went to the kitchen and began opening cupboard doors, knowing what he'd find. Other guys' parents bought snacks that weren't soy-based and drinks that didn't make your lips curl back when you got a mouthful of sour. What would it be like when Jillian finally moved in for good? Ethan abandoned the cupboards and tried the fridge, settling on a container of cottage cheese. It reminded him of albino brain matter, but he thought he could force some down if he didn't look at it.

He took the container and a spoon into the family room and slumped onto the sofa. He wished he could call Allie, longed to hear her voice, longed to talk to her about the mess he'd gotten himself into, but he couldn't yet deal with what Pete had told him that morning: *I kissed her, Ethan.* Pete had said again and again that Allie had done nothing wrong—*She started apologizing for maybe giving me the wrong impression. But she hadn't. I told her so, told her it was just me. All me*—but he couldn't think of Allie without picturing her face next to Pete's, her lips touching his.

Besides, she hadn't called him in almost two days. What was up with that? Guilt?

Ethan reached for the remote and clicked the flat screen on, eager for other images to replace the ones in his head. Spooning cottage cheese into his mouth, he surfed absently, and he was three channels past it when his brain finally registered their Brilliant Cream living room. He channelled back down and found himself looking at Connie Althorpe, a monitor behind her showing his old man sitting on their white sofa: "—had an opportunity to interview prominent Halifax lawyer Jack Palmer last night in his Cathedral Estates home. Mr. Palmer, who recently threw his hat into the political arena, responded at length to questions about his work and his plans for the future. That interview will air in its entirety this evening on *Maritime Movers and Shakers.*"

The camera drew back to show Althorpe sitting beside another news commentator, this one male. "Can you give us a preview of what we're going to see, Connie?" he said.

Althorpe nodded. "As you'd expect from the city's most successful defence attorney, Mr. Palmer was extremely articulate. He was also refreshingly forthcoming. Up to a point."

"Didn't he hold up under cross-examination?" the commentator joked.

Althorpe smiled primly. "One of my questions, as you'll see, evoked a rather heated refusal to elaborate." Althorpe turned, and the camera zoomed in on the monitor. The producer had obviously intended to save the bulk of the exchange for a later viewing since the clip was brief, but it was clear that Ethan's father was upset, his face red as he said crisply, "I have absolutely no comment other than to say I'm appalled that you would ask such a question in my own home."

The image froze and the camera returned to Althorpe and

the male commentator beside her. "Connie," he said, "can you tell us what question upset Palmer?"

Ethan sat up straight, pressing the volume-up control on the remote.

"I asked him how it felt to defend a man charged with driving while intoxicated when the mother of his own children was killed by a drunk driver."

His hands trembling, Ethan reached inside the wastebasket in his old man's study and pulled out the newspaper. It was today's, delivered long before anyone in Cathedral Estates was awake. His father would have seen it before he went to work, probably intended to clip yet another article about himself to add to his glory wall.

But he hadn't. Ethan reached for the torn newsprint he'd seen earlier and dropped the scraps of paper onto the desk. Sifting through them, he could see that all the scraps were remnants of a single page, and it took him little time to piece them together. The article, headlined "Would-Be Politician Faces Personal Dilemma," summed up what Ethan had already heard, except that it included two photos. One showed the now-familiar YouTube image of the MLA's damaged car, the other a crumpled 1996 Mustang Cobra SVT, its Mystic finish imperceptible in the grainy black and white photo.

"You son of a bitch," breathed Ethan.

"I'm sorry you had to see that."

Ethan turned toward the voice. His father stood in the study doorway, his Fisher, McBurney, and Hicks briefcase in his hand. "That's sensationalism, not journalism," said Jack. "It was unfair of that Althorpe woman to bring it up."

Ethan glared at him. "Unfair or inconvenient? But it doesn't really matter, does it? You've got a media consultant to fix problems like that, right?"

"Don't use that tone with me, Ethan."

"'Don't use that tone'? You're really going to play *that* card?"

"Ethan—"

"How *could* you?"

"How could I what?" The question was natural enough, but Ethan could tell from the hesitation in his father's voice that he already knew the answer.

"Agree to defend a man like that when it was a drunk driver who killed her."

"It's not that simple, Ethan."

"Isn't it? I thought a person is invariably defined by his ability to meet his obligations," said Ethan, his face warped in a sneer. "Seems to me a person might feel at least a *little* obligated not to shit on his dead wife."

Jack set his briefcase on the floor beside him, stood looking at it for a moment before raising his eyes again. "Everything is always black or white with you, Ethan. So cut and dried. When you're older you'll understand that a person has to make compromises to ensure the best for his family."

"The best for his family," repeated Ethan. "Don't you mean the best for *you?* I expect your party will be pretty grateful if you can make that DUI charge disappear. And it wouldn't hurt your new political career to be able to call on a few favours from day one, would it." Ethan heard paper crinkling and he looked down to see he was making fists, the newsprint twisting between his fingers.

"This is important to me—" his father began, but Ethan cut him off.

"Really? Something is actually important to you?" He realized he was shouting now, but it felt good. Great, in fact. "Do you have any idea what's important to *me?*" He snorted venomously. "Or what *was* important to me?"

"If this is about that car again—"

"Do you know how long I've been thinking about it, planning for it?"

"Ethan—"

"Since the day we buried her. Did you know that?"

The surprise was evident in his father's eyes.

"Remember that big tree that blew down in our backyard in Herring Cove the week after Mom died? The one with the swing? I was sitting on it after we got home from the funeral. Someone sent me outside because Raye was napping and they didn't want me to wake her up." Ethan was surprised at how fast he was talking, how fast the memories were coming back to him. "So I was sitting there on that swing trying to remember the last thing I heard Mom say. Raye and I were with you that weekend and she called you on the phone. She was going to bring you the divorce papers, even though the weather was supposed to turn bad. She called those papers your 'early Christmas present.'" His voice cracked again, but he pressed on. "All this time, I thought it was the snow that caused the accident. I must've heard about the drunk driver at some point, but all I remembered was the Christmas present. And the snow."

He sobbed suddenly, hating himself for doing it, and he looked down at the desk and the newsprint crumpled in his hands. "After the funeral? While I was sitting on the swing? These two guys came out to the backyard for a smoke. People you worked with. They didn't see me. The swing was on the other side of the tree. I heard them talking about the car. How it was a shame, right? Car like that? Cobra SVT? They even knew about the Mystic finish." He looked up again. "I'd just lost my mom and it was a goddamn shame about the car."

"Look, Ethan—"

"At that moment, I knew I'd have a car like that one day." He paused, wiping savagely at tears, then continued, "I begged her to get it. Did you know that?"

His father shook his head.

"On the way home the day we found it, she talked about how nothing ever stays the same. But that afternoon sitting on the swing listening to those guys talking about the Cobra, I thought—" He coughed, cleared his throat noisily. "I thought maybe if I could make just one thing the same—" He stopped. He had no more words, none that would make a difference, anyway. He stood up, unfolded his fists, pulled one of the scraps free and held it up. It was a fragment of the photo with the Mustang. "*That's* what was important to *me*."

A horrible silence echoed in the study until Jack broke it. "You never told me anything about this, Ethan," he said softly.

"Like you ever asked."

"That's not fair—"

Ethan laughed harshly. "You're real big on the whole fairness thing, aren't you? People probably think that's why you became a lawyer, right?"

"It *is* why I became a lawyer."

"Yeah, right. Champion of law and order, defender of the poor and underprivileged. Bullshit! How underprivileged would you say your current client is?"

"His wealth doesn't deny him the right to a fair trial, Ethan. And he's not my only client. I've defended lots of people who were in dire straits. People in situations like my own mother—"

"For Christ's sake!" shouted Ethan. "If I hear one more story about that goddamn woman, I'm gonna—"

"Don't you *dare* talk about her that way!" his father roared.

"Right!" Ethan roared in return. "I shouldn't disrespect a woman I never even *knew*, but it's okay for you to defend a man like the one who *killed* the woman who carried me inside her, gave birth to me, and raised me while you were keeping white-collar criminals out of jail!" As angry as he was, he liked the way his voice sounded now. Stronger, more in control than he'd felt in weeks. Months.

"Your mother was no saint."

"I hope not," Ethan retorted. "There's one too many in this family already."

His father shook his head. "If you could see yourself, hear what you sound like—"

"That's what it always comes down to, isn't it," Ethan barked. "What *other* people see and hear and think."

A third voice spoke from the hallway. "Well, the neighbours are certainly getting an earful right now."

Ethan and his father turned to see Raye with Winnipeg Joe's bass guitar in her arms. "I could hear you two before I even got in the house."

"Yeah, well, too bad," snarled Ethan. "I certainly wouldn't want to shatter anyone's impression of Jack Perfect here." He strode to the door, pushing past both of them. In the process, his foot connected with his father's briefcase and sent it crashing into the wall.

Raye turned astonished eyes toward her brother, who was now heading down the hallway to the front door. He could hear her asking their father what was going on, but the reply was lost as Ethan banged open the hall closet door, yanked his jacket off its hanger, then slammed the door shut.

"What's wrong?" Raye asked, coming down the hall toward him.

"Wrong?" He gripped the handle of the front door, swung it open roughly. "How could anything possibly be wrong in *this* house?" He stepped outside, poking his hands into each of the jacket's pockets, finally pulling out a card. He looked at it, smiled grimly, and strode down the driveway.

"What're you going to do?" called Raye from the doorway.

"Do?" he shouted back over his shoulder, then realized he'd been repeating her last words. Interesting, he thought, since their old man was the one who always got the last word. Well, by God, not tonight. If anyone was going to have the last word this evening, it was Ethan Palmer. "I'll tell you one thing I'm *not* gonna do," he shouted. "I'm not gonna worry about *appearances!*" Reaching the sidewalk, he took out his cell and began pressing buttons as he stormed down Seminary Lane.

Chapter 29

"Surprised to hear from you again so soon," Hornsby said on the phone. Except Ethan didn't believe him, sensed somehow that the guy wasn't the least bit surprised. "I thought you didn't like my plan."

"I'm in, okay?" Ethan muttered, walking past Big Ben Cleveland's plantation-style monstrosity in the fading December light. The self-appointed leader of their non-existent Neighbourhood Watch, the asshole who couldn't wait to report Ethan's wrongdoings to his father, was standing on his front lawn holding a long-handled weed-digging tool. He jabbed it into the ground and twisted, his huge gut bouncing with the thrust, looking like the picture of compliance with the city's ban on lawn poisons. But Ethan knew it was all show. Earlier that day, he'd seen their neighbour's GMC Denali pulling into his garage, the back loaded down with something heavy. Even through the vehicle's heavily tinted windows, Ethan recognized huge bags of Weed & Feed, which he guessed Big Ben would spread late at night when no one could see. Watching him now while listening to Hornsby spell out specifics made what Ethan was about to do seem a lot easier. Everybody took shortcuts to get what they wanted.

Hornsby finished outlining the details, asked if Ethan had any questions, and then hung up. When he reached Monastery, Ethan looked at his watch and saw he had a few hours before he'd be joining him downtown, and he mulled over his options as he walked. He was still mulling them over when his feet decided for him.

Ethan paused beneath the wrought-iron structure that arched over the entrance to St. Anthony's Cemetery, trying to remember the last time he'd been there. The only good thing about living in Cathedral Estates was its proximity to St. Anthony's, where his mother was buried, much closer than their last home had been. Although he didn't come often, he liked knowing he could visit any time. When he'd last been here, in July, songbirds had trilled from several of the trees that dotted the cemetery, flowers were bursting around the graves, and he'd seen a gardener on a lawn tractor pulling a cart filled with soil and what looked to be a birch sapling ready for planting. For a place filled with dead people, St. Anthony's had seemed to be teeming with life.

Now, though, the trees were bare of leaves, and the few flowers Ethan could see dotting nearby gravesites were made of plastic. In the glow of the lights that lined the perimeter, he was the only person in sight. He tugged his jacket around him as a sharp breeze whistled through the wrought iron, and he stepped through the entrance.

Ethan followed the gravel path that wound along the western side of the cemetery until he came to his mother's headstone. A street light on the other side of the wrought-iron fence lit the inscription on the polished granite: *Olivia Leanne Cameron-Palmer.* And, below, the words that tore at him as much now as when he'd seen them the first time: *Beloved Mother.* Each time he came here, he expected—hoped—that his memories of her would strengthen, as if nearness to her physical remains would somehow bring into focus what he'd lost, but it never happened.

He stepped forward, tracing his fingers along the intricate

lettering, then noticed a large white spatter on the stone's curved top—birdshit. Seagull, most likely, judging from the size of it. He swore and dug in his pockets for something he could use to clean it. Nothing. He swore again.

To the right was the headstone that had made him and Raye laugh the last time they'd come here together. Twice as wide as their mother's, it marked a double plot that still had only one occupant: *Grace Althea Elliott, God's Newest Angel*. Married to Norm Elliott, their Cathedral Estates neighbour across the street, she had died last year from ovarian cancer while the Palmers' house was being built. Nothing funny there, of course. What had made Ethan and his sister roar—for ten minutes straight— was the inscription beside Grace's: *Norman Robert Elliott, Loved By One And All*. Norm had obviously saved money by getting both his and Grace's epitaphs carved at the same time. Seeing the headstone now, Ethan smiled again, but not because of those ridiculous words. In a stone vase beneath Grace's name were what appeared to be roses, remarkably red in that December setting, the flowers made of bright cloth. He grabbed a handful and rubbed and rubbed the moulded fabric across the mess on his mother's headstone, but it only smeared the white stain.

He let the ruined flowers fall from his hand, ground them beneath his heel, then jumped on them again and again, his curses puncturing the cold December air. He didn't realize he was crying until, exhausted, he finally stopped, the roses obliterated beneath his feet.

His cell rang. Sitting on the cold ground, his legs drawn up against his chest, Ethan lifted his head from his knees, pulled the phone from his pocket, and saw it was Jillian Ro-bitch-cheau this time.

The phone had rung all evening, some of the calls from Pete, but Ethan had just hit Ignore. Pete was the last person he wanted to talk to right now.

No, that wasn't completely true. The last person would be his old man, who'd begun calling from their house phone and then switched to his cell an hour ago. Ethan had let those calls ring. It wasn't like the sound was going to bother anybody in St. Anthony's, and he liked picturing his father's growing frustration each time he got Ethan's voice mail.

But now the Barbie doll was calling. Christ! Looking once more at the granite headstone—*Beloved Mother*—he tapped Ignore and got to his feet. It was already close to ten o'clock. Time to get moving.

Afterwards, Ethan thought he should have taken the bus, but with a couple of hours to kill he walked all the way from St. Anthony's to the downtown address Hornsby had given him. Even wearing his cross-trainers, his feet were sore by the time he got there, but he'd appreciated having the time by himself so he could think, get everything straight in his head. Or, as his mother used to say, "Connect the dots," something he'd suddenly remembered as he sat on the ground beside what remained of her, trying to explain to her what he was going to do. And why.

There'd been a lot of dots, but he'd connected all of them. He knew now why Link Hornsby had been outside that convenience store the night Ethan discovered Boots's ticket was a winner. What was that line they still used sometimes on cop shows? *The perp was casing the joint.* Like Hornsby had cased lots of other joints in the city during the past few months. Convenience stores and gas stations, mostly, which might have seemed like small potatoes when there were banks and credit unions waiting to be robbed. But as Hornsby had explained, banks and credit unions had far tighter security than convenience stores and gas stations, and the risks were far greater. Of course, convenience stores and gas stations *were* small potatoes much of the time. No self-respecting career thief would consider a few hundred— or even a couple thousand—dollars worth the risk—but they could offer bonanzas, too. During those weeks when the 6/49 or Lotto Max million-dollar prizes soared into the double digits, businesses with lottery terminals had sudden boosts in sales. Countless customers who came in to play their own numbers almost always got an Insta Pik—or five—and then bought their cigarettes and shit while they were at it. And the smaller the operation, the less likely that there was manpower available for making multiple bank deposits throughout the day, which meant lots of cash lingering on site. So during weeks when jackpots were huge, those convenience stores and gas stations could offer some pretty substantial returns with—how did his father's investment adviser put it?—"a modicum of risk."

Hornsby had told him some of this, of course, though not all of it. Ethan had to connect the rest of the dots, but he was pretty confident in his conclusions. He'd remembered seeing in the news how police had identified the perp's M.O., and it was the same as the set-up Hornsby had told him about tonight's job: lots of cash in the safe awaiting deposit, only one person working, surveillance system installed by Atlantic Alarms, and on and on. A robbery just waiting to happen.

When Hornsby had suggested it that afternoon in his Echo, Ethan thought he was joking at first, then wondered why he'd risk telling someone else his plan. But it wasn't hard to connect those dots when you thought about it. Wasn't Ethan already a criminal? Hadn't he been breaking the law for weeks, gambling online, buying an illegal driver's licence he'd paid for with some of his lottery winnings? And hadn't he told Hornsby he'd stolen money from his own sister and fraudulently activated and used his father's credit card? Ethan wasn't exactly in a position to rat out Link Hornsby. Besides, the legal system would go easier on Ethan—a minor and first-time offender from a good family—than on Hornsby if he got caught. And Ethan was motivated, desperate for cash. Even with a sixty-forty split, he would have enough money from tonight's anticipated take to pay off what he owed everyone *and* buy Filthy's car.

Sitting in Hornsby's rusted Toyota Echo earlier that day, Ethan had wanted nothing more than to take him up on his offer to get back the money he'd lost and clear the slate once and for all. But nothing he heard could sway him to take part in a robbery.

That was this afternoon. Before he'd learned what kind of man his father really was, someone who would sell his soul for a sound bite, all in the name of appearances. After that revelation, Ethan didn't give a damn *how* he solved his problem as long as it went away. And weren't store owners insured for things like this? Ethan looked ahead at the sign hanging over the deserted sidewalk and grinned at the words glowing in neon green— *Anwar's Convenience, 24 hours, We have everything you need*— and felt a zither of excitement run through him.

Chapter 30

As it turned out, what he'd felt wasn't excitement—it was his cellphone vibrating, alerting him to an incoming text. From Jillian. He nearly laughed when he saw each word typed fully instead of in the shorthand he was used to seeing, complete with capital letters and punctuation: *Ethan, please come home. You don't know everything.*

Well, if her message was supposed to soften him up, give him the warm fuzzies, that walking clothes rack was even dumber than he thought. He jabbed the Delete key with his finger and watched the words vanish.

It was true, though. He *didn't* know everything. Like what would happen in the next few minutes. He could feel gooseflesh form on his neck, and it wasn't all due to the frigid wind gusting off the harbour three blocks away. But what had Hornsby told him? *Win-win, kid.* Even if he got caught, nothing was going to happen to him. And there'd be the added bonus of seeing the look on his old man's face. *Wouldn't play well for the voters, would it?* he thought. Well, maybe his father should have *asked* Ethan before accepting that nomination. Would it have killed him?

Despite Ethan's sudden nervousness, he knew Hornsby had taken care of everything. He'd planned it all out to the letter and had no doubt taken care of the alarm by now. And hadn't he done this kind of thing many times before? Ethan focused on the infusion of cash his bank account was going to get from

Mr. Anwar, the asshole who was probably in the middle of selling The Chow Down and putting Lil, Ike, and Rake out of work, along with Jeannie, the other part-timer he'd never met. Not that Ethan gave a shit about Ike, but he'd come to think a lot of Lil, who'd been so good to him. Good to everybody, really. And not just good *to* them but good *for* them. She made everyone who came through the diner's doors—even that goddamn two-chinned Clarence—feel that they were welcome, that she was truly glad to see them, that their being alive and well and present actually mattered to her. *People got a whole lot to tell you if you take the time to listen,* she'd told him. *And you don't just hear it in what they say.* When The Chow Down closed, where would her regulars go? Where would Boots McLaughlin go?

Ethan felt a wave of regret at the thought of the little man now. He suddenly wished the lies he'd told Allie had been true, wished he'd actually handed him that money and watched the guy's face light up. And Lil's, too, because she would've been so happy for Boots. Not fake-happy, but honest-to-God, in-your-face, over-the-moon happy. *For* him.

Moving along the empty sidewalk through pools of darkness, Ethan stepped over a branch a gust had likely brought down and found himself thinking about what Pete had said to him on the phone. *All you think about is yourself. You're so wrapped up in what you want, what you think you need, that you don't give a damn about anyone else.*

And that wasn't all. *You do whatever you want. But, hey, that's pretty much your motto anyway, isn't it? To hell with anybody else.*

Ethan had been pissed at Pete's comment, but as he walked past Anwar's Convenience now, he slowed his pace, wondering about the last time he'd done anything for somebody else without feeling obligated to or without getting something out of it himself. Even when he'd sprung for that dinner at Carruthers, he'd done it because he'd felt like such an ass for forgetting his and Allie's anniversary. Not because he loved her, which he did, but because he'd been too busy thinking of himself to remember their anniversary in the first place.

He thought of all those times he'd criticized his old man for putting himself and his work above everything else. And all those times Ethan had prided himself on being nothing like him. He was wrong. Even the photo on his fake driver's licence said otherwise.

Approaching Hornsby's car, parked several doors beyond Anwar's Convenience, Ethan thought about the actions that had brought him to this point right now. And not just the lying and the stealing he'd done but what he *hadn't* done, too. Like spend time with Allie. He hadn't even called her to find out why she'd been absent from school the past two days. What was worse, though, was that he hadn't even told her yet how he really felt about her, that he loved her more than anything. Three simple words, but he'd been too busy with other stuff. Screwing up his life. *I'll change*, he thought. *I'll just do this one thing and it'll be over. After tonight, everything will be fine. I'll make sure of it.*

Coming abreast of Hornsby's car, he saw through the windshield the tattooed man he'd originally thought was in his thirties but now knew was much older. Hornsby leaned over and shoved the passenger door open. "You took your goddamn sweet time!" he snarled. "We only got a small window to do this, now get in!"

Ethan slid inside and shut the door. On the Echo's scratched console, draped around the gearshift, was a pair of wire cutters. Hornsby reached under his seat and brought out a cloth bag. Opening it, he pulled out a black toque with holes for eyes and a mouth, and he tossed it into Ethan's lap. Then he pulled out something else.

"Christ!" breathed Ethan. His heart began to hammer.

"She's a beauty, ain't she?" said Hornsby, stroking the gun. "I call her Perse."

Ethan blinked. "Purse?"

"For Persuader."

For a brief, ridiculous moment, Ethan thought about a line from a comedy he and Pete had watched once, something about people who gave names to objects and body parts. Wished he could laugh now like he'd laughed then. "Is it loaded?" he asked, his voice quavering.

"You'd be surprised how little it matters," Hornsby replied. "Just so you know, though," he said, patting a bulge in his jacket, "*this* one is."

As if underlining the moment, Ethan's cellphone burbled, signalling another text.

"Jesus!" snarled Hornsby. "Turn that thing off!"

Ethan looked at the cell's screen. The text was from his father: *whr r u? call! please! cant find—*

Hornsby tore the phone from his hands. "We don't got all night!" he said, tossing it into the back seat. Then he pressed the Persuader into Ethan's hand. "Here, take it," he said.

The gun was heavier than it looked. And ice cold, like Hornsby's eyes. Ethan's heart slammed against the wall of his chest as though trying to get out. Because that's what Ethan was doing now, too—looking for a way out. How the hell did he get here? He was about to commit a robbery—a goddamn *armed* robbery—masterminded by a guy he'd twice been warned to steer clear of. And why? He could blame it on a hundred things, of course, but it all boiled down to one: a twenty-buck bet that he couldn't get from Seth's place to Cathedral Estates in ten minutes. Christ! "L-look," Ethan stammered, laying the gun beside the wire cutters. "I can't do this."

Hornsby stared at him for a moment and then, impossibly, he smiled, the expression reptilian in the glow from the car's instrument panel. "Nerves, kid. Everybody gets cold feet the first time."

The first time. If Ethan could have been convinced even two heartbeats earlier to go through with this thing, it only took hearing those three words—and their implication that this wouldn't be the *only* time—to reaffirm he'd been about to make the biggest mistake of his life. "No, it isn't nerves," he told Hornsby. "I can't do this. I won't."

Hornsby glowered at him. "You *owe* me."

"How do *I* owe *you?*"

"You think I *won* all that money in the casino? The money I gave you in the Park 'n' Pay?"

"I *saw* you win it."

"You saw me *play*. I won a few hands, sure, but you were standin' too far away to see what I cashed in. Why d'you think I had to split fifty-fifty instead of sixty-forty? I topped up your winnings with my own dough."

"Why?"

Hornsby snickered. "You really that stupid, kid?"

No, Ethan *wasn't* that stupid. Not anymore. He'd just connected the last pair of dots, the ones that explained why a small-time thief like Hornsby drove a rusted Toyota Echo with a gouge down the driver's side. It wasn't because of any *Waste not, want not* lifestyle choice. It was because there was no such thing as beating the odds. When it came to gambling, the only winners were the ones who owned the house. The rest were just suckers. And Ethan had been the biggest sucker of them all, exactly what a low-life like Link Hornsby had been looking for. He'd even been warned. *Them that lie down with dogs get up with fleas.* Well, fleas or not, Ethan Palmer was getting up right now. He reached for the handle and opened the door.

"You *ain't* walkin' out on me," Hornsby seethed.

Ethan tossed the toque aside and climbed out. He heard the driver's door swing open, its rusty hinges complaining before it slammed shut. Footsteps. And then Hornsby was in his face.

"You *owe* me," the man repeated. "You're *mine*, asshole."

"I'll pay you back," said Ethan, stepping away.

Hornsby's laugh was harsh, guttural. "Yeah, like you're gonna pay back your old man? And your sister? And who knows *how* many others? I don't take IOUs, you little pissant."

"You'll have to," Ethan said, turning and heading in the direction of the bus stop a block away. He wanted to see Allie. *Needed* to see her. Nothing was going to stop him.

"Look, you miserable piece of shit," hissed Hornsby, who'd come up behind him so quickly that Ethan jumped. "You're doin' this whether you want to or not."

Ethan felt something hard press into the small of his back as a hand grabbed his shoulder, stopping him. He felt his legs turn to water, and his heart, which had slammed into his chest wall only moments earlier, seemed to stutter. He had to force out his next words: "D-don't shoot."

In the shadows between the street lights, a gun jammed into his back, Ethan heard Hornsby rasp in his ear, "That's up to you, dickhead. We had a plan and we're stickin' to it. Now suck it up and let's get this over with."

Ethan's mouth had become the Mojave. "I can't," he croaked. "I thought I could, but I can't."

He felt the barrel of the gun prod deeper into his flesh, felt the hair on the back of his neck leap to attention, felt his heart abandon its stutter and pummel his rib cage as the voice in his ear growled, "You chose the wrong time to grow a pair, asshole. *Nobody* backs out on Link Hornsby, you got that? *Nobody.*"

Ethan heard a sound in the darkness, and some part of him realized his mouth had made it. A pleading sound. The sound your brain manufactures when it realizes it's probably the last sound your mouth will ever make.

Then there was another sound and Hornsby grunted thickly, staggering backward.

"You leave my brother *alone!*"

Despite the shadows, and despite how quickly the next events unfolded, they would be forever etched into Ethan's memory. He turned to see Raye holding a tree branch that she'd just slammed into the back of Hornsby's head. Or tried to. Because of her height, the unwieldiness of the branch, and—probably most of all—her poor eyesight, she'd missed and glanced his shoulder.

Hornsby whirled to face his attacker. "What the—"

This time the branch hit him squarely in the temple and Hornsby roared, nearly dropping to his knees as Raye struck him yet again.

"Raye!" Ethan shouted. "Get out of here!"

"Not without you!" She raised the branch one more time, shouting at the stranger in front of her. "You leave my brother alone or—"

Afterwards, Ethan would think about the sound the gun made when it fired. It was nothing like he'd heard in all those movies. Not the crack you might expect. Loud, sure, but without the hard edge. Like a mirror breaking inside a mattress.

He would also think about the look on Raye's face when it happened. Astonishment? Maybe, but more than that. Something like outrage.

And then she fell.

At some point, Hornsby must have run to his car and squealed off. All Ethan could see was Raye crumpled on the sidewalk. Oddly, his mind replayed the video of that deer leaping into the coffee shop, and some part of him now understood what the creature had felt, the sheer terror of slamming into something you didn't see coming and feeling everything crash down around you. He screamed his sister's name, gathered her into his arms, and staggered to his feet. Stumbling under his burden, he almost went down, and he sobbed as he struggled not to drop her. He felt like someone had scooped his guts out, but he forced the

hollow shell of his body forward, praying that Anwar's claim—
We have everything you need—was really true.

The clerk, a young man with a goatee and a safety pin through
one eyebrow, was standing wide-eyed in the entrance as Ethan
approached. He held the door open so Ethan could carry Raye
inside.

"Call 911!" Ethan yelled, laying her gently on the tile floor.
"She's been shot!" A red flower bloomed through her coat in the
centre of her abdomen.

The young man picked up the phone, then looked helplessly
at Ethan. "There's no dial tone. It's dead."

Ethan remembered the wire cutters and moaned. "Use your
cell!"

The young man winced. "I don't have one."

"Here! Take mine!" One arm still around Raye, Ethan
reached into his jacket. And then cursed as he remembered
Hornsby flinging it into the back seat. "I don't have it! You have
to get to a phone!"

The young man looked at the cash register behind him. Beside
it on the counter lay an open magazine and half a candy bar.

"For Christ's sake, *go get help!*" Each utterance an exclamation.
For an odd, brief moment, Ethan wondered if he'd ever be able to
speak again without screaming. He hugged Raye to him, put his
hand on her belly to keep her life from pouring out, and wept.

Chapter 31

His father and Jillian got to the emergency room ten minutes after the ambulance did. Ethan looked up as they burst in, seeing them without seeing them. Shock, he would later learn, had a way of doing that, protecting the brain and the body from things they weren't ready for.

"I'm Jack Palmer," he heard—but didn't hear—his father say when he reached the admitting desk. "My daughter was just brought in. She's been shot?"

The woman at the desk nodded. "She's in surgery."

Ethan saw—but didn't see—Jillian put a hand to her perfect red mouth. Had she actually stopped to apply lipstick, worried about showing up at an emergency room without makeup?

"How soon will we know something?" Jack demanded.

"They've only just started. It could be some time, Mr. Palmer. I'll let you know the moment I hear anything. In the meantime, you and your family should make yourselves comfortable." She waved toward the waiting area like a realtor selling floor space.

That's when his father saw him. "Ethan!" He rushed over. "What the hell happened?"

Behind him, Jillian echoed, "Yes, Ethan, what happened?"

Ethan looked up at them, his face slack. He'd stopped sobbing in the ambulance. Not because he didn't want people to see him cry. He was all cried out. Now all he felt was a kind of numbness.

"Ethan?" His father's voice again.

He let the numbness hold him for a moment, let it work its

way through him before he attempted to find the words he needed. "She was protecting me," he heard himself reply.

And he was wrong. He wasn't all cried out after all.

———

"We've managed to piece together most of what happened, Mr. Palmer," said the policeman wearing a name tag with *Constable Leonard Richards* printed on it.

Ethan remembered talking to him earlier. He wasn't sure when. Sometime between when his father had arrived and now. But he wasn't sure when *now* was. The clock on the wall said 3:47, but that had to be wrong. He hadn't been here that long. It wasn't possible. He remembered the clock in the Echo had read 11:23 as he'd gotten out of the car. Or 12:31. Or maybe it was 13:21. Did older cars use twenty-four-hour clocks? He remembered two 1s, anyway. And a 2 and a 3. And Raye lying on the sidewalk.

The paramedics thought he'd been shot, too, because of the blood. It had been all over him. It was still on him now. Whenever *now* was.

"What do you know?" his father asked the constable.

"You say your daughter left the house right after your son?"

Jack nodded. "Yes, yes, we've been all through this."

"Your son wasn't aware she'd followed him."

She *couldn't* have, Ethan thought. Not all that way on foot without him seeing her. To the cemetery? He'd sat there for hours. Then all the way downtown to Anwar's Convenience? Surely she hadn't followed him, hadn't watched over him all that time, shivering in the December darkness.

"Apparently, your son was mixed up with an offender we've had our eye on for some time," Richards said.

"You know who shot my daughter?"

"Yes, sir. Your son said his cellphone was in the guy's car. We traced it and picked him up a few minutes ago. They're taking his statement now. No sign of a gun yet, but they'll do a residue test on him. I'm sure it'll be positive."

Jack nodded. He looked across at Ethan as he asked the policeman his next question. "You said my son was involved with this person. This wasn't a random act then? A mugging gone wrong?"

"No, sir, we don't believe it was."

In the seat to Ethan's left, Jillian put a hand to her mouth. Not perfect now, though. She must have fallen asleep in her chair at some point because her lipstick was smudged. There was red on the back of one hand.

Ethan looked down and saw that both of his own hands were red. Like he'd dipped them in paint. Someone had given him something to wipe them off, but all he'd managed to do was smear it. Even the skin under his fingernails was red.

"You say you've had your eye on this person?" his father asked.

"Yes, sir. He preys on teenagers. Grooms them, you could say."

"How?"

"Introduces them to gambling, makes it look like a sure thing. Then when they're in over their heads, when they're really desperate, he offers them a way out. Uses them to do his dirty work."

Jack glared at the constable. "You *know* all this? Why is he allowed to continue? How does he get away with it?"

"Intimidation. We haven't found a kid yet who's willing to testify against him. And then there's—" Richards stopped, clearly uncomfortable.

"Then there's what?"

The constable squared his shoulders. "The families, sir. Lately, he's been targeting kids whose parents are well connected, people who'd rather have the whole thing go away if their kids got caught. People who can afford lawyers who make that sort of thing happen." His last words hung in the air for a moment, almost visible in the waiting area.

"I see," Jack said finally. "Thank you, constable."

"You're welcome, sir." Richards paused. "If you don't mind me saying, sir . . ."

"Yes?"

"I see a lot go wrong in my line of work."

"So do I."

Richards nodded. "Of course. I'm sure you do. It's just that with young people there's often so many other things involved, so much below the surface. There's seldom just black and white, if you know what I mean."

Ethan saw that his hands weren't really red after all. They had been at one time, but they were brown now. The blood had long since dried. *Paint's got the same colour-changing pigments in it that they use in American money.* So much blood. He wondered if it would ever come off.

"Thank you, constable," Jack said again. He watched Richards leave, then got up and crossed the space that separated him and his son. Kneeling down, he put a hand on Ethan's shoulder. "There'll be time later to sort all this out," he said.

Ethan looked at his father's hand. It was warm, even through the thick jacket he still wore. A nurse had asked him earlier if he'd wanted to take his jacket off, but Ethan had shaken his head, hugged his arms about him. It had soaked up so much blood he was afraid to remove it. They'd probably put it in one of those medical waste bags and throw it away. This was Raye's blood. He was taking care of it for her. Just like she'd been taking care of him.

He began to sob again.

"You must have more information now," said Jack standing at the nurse's desk. His voice had changed. Ethan had never heard him plead before.

The woman at the desk had just returned. She kept her voice low, and Ethan wondered why. It was 4:51 and they were the only people in the waiting area. Earlier, a reporter had arrived, but a man in a security uniform asked him to leave. The reporter had been angry, had complained loudly about his rights, but the security guard hadn't budged. Shortly after that, paramedics had wheeled in an elderly woman suffering from chest pains and took her straight to a room, leaving Ethan, his father, and Jillian alone again.

Ethan had wondered what that woman's room might look like. Those thoughts had helped keep him from thinking of the room that Raye was in now, a sterile operating theatre gleaming with stainless steel, the only colour the white of the sheets and the walls. Like their Brilliant Cream living room. He couldn't stand to think of her there, small and frail on that table in the middle of something like January.

He was kidding himself, of course. There was another colour besides white in that room. Lots of it.

The woman at the desk had earlier reported that the doctors were having trouble stabilizing Raye. She'd lost far too much blood. And the bullet had ricocheted inside her belly, scrambling her guts. That's not how she'd put it, of course, but the outcome was the same. Hearing that, Ethan had wondered if he'd helped tear Raye's insides even more when he'd run with her in his arms instead of trying to stop the bleeding on the sidewalk like his Red Cross course had taught him to. That was something else he didn't want to think about. *Couldn't* think about.

His father returned to the waiting area now, sat heavily in

his chair. "It's not good," he said. "They've been working on her this whole time." He put his hands on his knees, stared at them hard. "They fix one thing and then find there's something else."

Ethan saw his father was gripping his knees with his hands, his knuckles white against his slacks like he was holding on. Or trying to. "I guess there's always something else," Jack added, and then his voice broke and he was crying.

It was as though someone had thrown cold water on Ethan, every fibre of his body and his brain clamouring for his father to stop. Jillian put one hand on the back of Jack's neck, the other on his shoulder, rubbing it in small circular motions.

Filthy had gently caressed Shawna's belly in a similar way. Such a simple act, but it had reminded Ethan of something then. Now he knew what it was. It was perhaps his earliest memory, an afternoon when he was not yet four. He'd been on the swing in the yard of their Herring Cove home, his father pushing him while he'd giggled "Higher! Higher!" His mother had come to the back door, and he'd waved to her as she stood watching them for a moment then called for them to come eat. She'd been away somewhere that afternoon and had returned with fried chicken, Ethan's favourite, and he'd hurried inside and climbed into his chair at the table. As he watched his father cut up some of the savoury white meat for him, his mother had told them about her day. Ethan wasn't listening—his mouth was watering and he had eyes only for the chicken—but after passing Ethan the plate, his father got up and stood beside her, placed his big hand on her belly, stroked it in small, slow circles. His own hands already covered in chicken grease, Ethan had turned to them, wondering why they weren't eating. But he'd seen his father's hand on his mother's belly and somehow knew that something special was going to happen. And nearly eight months later, it did.

Seeing that moment in his mind now, Ethan wondered what others he'd forgotten. And then they swam into memory. His father's strong hands gripping Ethan's as he wobbled on skates. His father running beside him as he pedalled without training wheels for the first time. His father showing him how to swing the bat, add double-digit numbers, hold the kite string, swim.

His father was right. *There's always something else.* Ethan reached across and put his hand on his father's arm, squeezed it.

Jack Palmer looked up. His voice like gravel, he said the last thing Ethan expected to hear. "Please forgive me."

"Your grandmother was a drunk, Ethan," said Jack, his voice still husky although he'd managed to stop crying. "Even before Dad died, I'd find bottles in the washing machine. It was one of those old wringer models with rollers that squeezed the water out of the clothes before you hung them on the line. Dad had found it in a dump and got it working again. You've probably never seen one. My life was like those rollers, trying to squeeze out anything that might keep us going for one more day."

He'd been talking for a while now, sharing with Ethan the woman behind the myth he'd manufactured while both of them tried not to look at the clock on the wall, its second hand sweeping around and around.

"I was the oldest. It wasn't easy making people think everything was fine. She'd be in bed passed out half the time. When people from social services would come around, I'd tell them how she'd been up all night washing clothes she'd taken in from neighbours. But she never did that. *I* was the one who went around the village asking people if they'd like their laundry done. *Begged* them. The few who gave me theirs never knew that I was the one who washed it, hung it out to dry, folded it. They just knew I picked it up dirty and returned it clean. But the laundry helped make people think my mother was functioning like a regular person."

He paused, took a long breath before continuing. "I had my hands full making sure the house was clean and my brother and sister were fed. If I wasn't home when she got the welfare cheque, she'd blow it on liquor, so I skipped school on the days the mailman delivered it. If she was out cold, I'd forge her signature and hike to Windsor and spend it all on groceries." He shook his head. "It took me a while to learn how to put some aside for the power bill, clothes, everything else."

There were moments as Ethan listened that he thought his father was making it all up, giving himself something to say and Ethan something to listen to so they'd keep from going over to that nurse's desk again. But then he'd realize that the thing his father had made up was hanging above the fireplace in their living room.

"Of course, even if she didn't spend it on booze, the welfare cheque was never enough. I did other jobs. Weeded gardens, chopped firewood, raked leaves, shovelled snow, anything that would bring in a few bucks. I'd hide the cash in a coffee can under the woodpile, dip into it when we needed it." He dragged a hand through his hair. "I dreaded holidays that other kids looked forward to, like Christmas. I'd try my best to save a few dollars so I could put something for Carol and Paul under the tree." He grunted softly. "Tree! More like a bush. If it grew in a ditch, I figured it was fair game."

His father stopped talking then, seemed to be picturing in his head bushes masquerading as Christmas trees. Or empty cupboards or a wringer washer with liquor bottles hidden inside. Ethan couldn't stand the silence, needed to fill up the emergency-room waiting area with words that weren't about Raye. "What did you do when you didn't have enough money?" he asked.

His father looked down. "It's not what *I* did," he said, his voice thick with disgust. "She'd walk into town and bring some guy home. Tell Carol and Paul and me to make ourselves scarce, which was easier if the weather was good. Harder when it was storming and you lived in a two-room shack. Those times, I'd get Carol and Paul to pretend we were camping and I'd string up a sheet like a tent. I'd get them under it, tell them ghost stories with lots of noises so they wouldn't hear what was happening on the other side of the wall."

"They never knew?"

"They were younger than I was, but they weren't stupid."

"They never talked about any of this," said Ethan.

"I wouldn't let them."

"Why did you . . ." Ethan didn't know how to finish the question.

"Why did I want you to think she was this amazing person?" Ethan nodded.

His father looked away. "I had no one to look up to when I was a kid. It was important to me that you and your sister did."

Ethan noticed he'd said *your sister* and not *Raye*. Wondered if it was a conscious decision on his part, as if he were preparing himself for something.

"I'd spent so much of my growing-up time pretending to be somebody else," his father continued, "that I never really stopped. I was always trying to be more than who I was, more than the kid from a two-room shack whose mother whored herself for booze."

"But—"

His father put up his hand. "Let me finish, Ethan. You need to hear this. And I need to say it." He cleared his throat. "I did everything I could to escape that life—earned scholarships that helped with tuition, worked construction and took janitorial jobs for the rest. I told my university classmates that both my parents were dead." He grimaced. "My roommate found a photo of the shack we lived in. One of my mother's tricks had taken it. He'd brought a Polaroid camera with him and paid her extra, probably to take pictures of her naked. He took a couple shots outdoors, too, one of our house and one of my mother standing beside the sheets I'd just washed. I'd stuck both those pictures inside a dictionary. I don't know why. It doesn't matter. The photo of our house fell out and my roommate picked it up, asked me about it. I froze, told him it was a picture of our henhouse. He said it was the first henhouse he'd ever seen that had curtains in the windows. I tore it up the minute he wasn't looking." Turning away, he continued, "I should've torn them both up."

He took another deep breath. "I didn't tell my mother when I graduated. I was afraid she might come to the ceremony." He shrugged. "Not that she would have. She was never sober. The only thing she cared about was the cheque I'd started sending her every month. God help me, I was actually relieved when she died. I wasn't her son any longer."

He stopped, buried his face in his hands so his next words were muffled. "But I was, as much as I tried to change that."

Looking at him, Ethan suddenly understood why his father didn't drink: he was afraid he'd turn into the kind of person a son would rather pretend was dead. Would *wish* was dead.

A moment passed, and Jack finally pulled his hands from his face, wiped his nose with a tissue Jillian handed him, cleared his throat again. "I think I went into law because it seemed like the farthest thing possible from that Hants County life I'd been hiding all those years. I thought maybe if I was somebody important, like a lawyer, it would finally be behind me." He sighed. "Then, maybe if I was the best lawyer in the best firm, I could be happy. Or if I lived in the best part of the city, I'd be content somehow. But I wasn't. So I thought maybe—" He stopped, his jaws clenching, and Ethan knew he was biting back another sob.

"Maybe if he got elected."

Ethan glanced at Jillian, surprised by her sudden input, then turned again to his father.

He nodded. "If people voted for me, then . . ." He paused. "It's all about seeking approval. I've finally begun to understand that." He looked at his fiancée, smiled wanly. "I started seeing a therapist in October, Ethan."

"A therapist?"

"Jillian convinced me. *Forced* me, really. The day I took your savings to pay for the Volvo, she gave me a phone number. And an ultimatum."

Ethan looked again at his father's fiancée, knew now that she hadn't put her makeup on before she came to the hospital. She hadn't taken it off, probably had driven the streets in search of him and his sister for hours. He could see lines around her eyes. It was almost morning.

"She threatened to leave me if I didn't," his father said. He took another long breath. "I drove your mother away all those years ago, Ethan. I wasn't going to do the same thing again." He shook his head sadly. "And there was something I *should* have done. The therapist gave me an assignment."

"Assignment?"

"Homework, I guess you'd call it. He said I had to tell you and your sister the truth about your grandmother. But I couldn't. I didn't want you to know what a fraud I was." He lowered his head, and his next words were addressed to his feet. "So instead I agreed to defend the kind of man who'd get behind the wheel of a car drunk. The kind of man who killed your mother." His next words were barely audible. "I'm sorry, Ethan. I know I drove you to do whatever brought us all here. How you must hate me."

"There's something else you don't know, Ethan." This from Jillian, whose voice was stronger than Ethan had ever heard it.

"Don't," said Jack.

She shook her head. "He needs to know," and Ethan remembered the text she'd sent him. *You don't know everything.*

"What?" he asked her.

She looked at Jack. "Don't make me be the one to tell him."

He sighed, the sound ragged as if some interior part of him were separating, tearing away. "Your mother—" he began, then turned stricken eyes toward Jillian, who nodded encouragement. "Your mother was an addict, Ethan."

"*What?*"

"Prescription drugs. It's why I left her. I couldn't put up with it. I wouldn't. I loved her, but I wouldn't go through all that again."

"No," said Ethan, shaking his head. He had no memory of his mother like that.

"She was good at hiding it. Better than most. It was when my career began to take off. You and your sister were both small and I was working eighteen-hour days. She was lonely, I know that. And overwhelmed. Who wouldn't want something to make the days easier? It started with antidepressants."

"I don't—" Ethan began, intending to say that he didn't believe it, but what he could feel coming out was *I don't want to hear any more.* Jillian placed her hand over his and squeezed. He didn't pull away.

"It was my fault," said his father. "I was so focused on my work. When I finally realized what was happening, I tried to help her. Do you remember those extended visits she used to take to your grandparents' and your Aunt Carol would come stay with you?"

Ethan nodded.

"Stints in rehab. She'd come home clean and promising this time would be different. But it never was."

"Why are you telling me this now?" whispered Ethan, his free hand tracing *Beloved Mother* on the cold, hard granite of his memory.

His father stared at his feet.

"Tell him," Jillian said again. "He deserves to know."

"She—" He took a long, quaking breath. "Your mother was high the day she was killed."

"But the other driver—"

"—was drunk, yes," said his father, raising his head. "His autopsy proved he was DUI. But so did hers."

My mother? DUI? Ethan's brain had no way to process this information. Instead, it searched for safer territory, leaping to the physics of that moment on the highway, conjuring the coefficient of static friction in relation to the normal force. And then, as if seeking that normalcy, his brain two-stepped again, clutching at the laws of averages and probability, wondering what planets had aligned, what forces had conspired to create the head-on collision of two cars driven by similarly afflicted human beings. It was too much. He shook his head, trying to clear it, trying to understand. "Then how—?"

"I called in some favours, had that information suppressed."

"Why?"

"I didn't—" He tried again. "I didn't want—" But he couldn't finish.

Jillian said it for him. "He didn't want you ever feeling about your mother the way he felt about his own."

Ethan felt the numbness return. His head was suddenly too heavy for his body, and he leaned forward, his elbows on his knees. He felt his father's hand on his shoulder, heard him try to speak again but fail.

"That's why he got so upset at that reporter who came to the house," said Jillian. She placed her other hand on his father's arm, closing the triangle they made in that waiting room.

Jack finally managed to force out words. "I didn't want someone digging it all up again, maybe finding out the whole truth." He shook his head sadly. "I know you'll think I was worried about my image, but it wasn't that. I just—" His voice broke but he struggled through it. "I didn't want you and your sister to be hurt. I love you both too much to let that happen."

Ethan heard those words echo in his head as though coming to him from the end of a very long corridor.

I love you both too much.

I love you both.

I love you.

"Tell him the rest," said Jillian.

"That's enough."

"No, it's not," she said, her voice firmer. She looked at Ethan, squeezing his hand more tightly. "He agreed to defend that politician—"

"—because of my mother," Ethan finished for her. What were his father's words? *He made a mistake!* So had Olivia Leanne Cameron-Palmer, Beloved Mother.

And so had Ethan. More than one. Too many to count.

Something caught in his chest. There was so much he understood now, and so much he'd probably never understand. And there was so much he wanted to say. "Dad—" he began.

"Mr. Palmer?"

All three looked up at the doctor who loomed over them, his face ashen and drawn.

Chapter 32

The classroom buzzed with conversation. Ms. Moore had stepped across the hall to the AV equipment room to find a replacement bulb for the data projector, and most of the students were using the opportunity to catch up on gossip about the Senior SnowBall the evening before: who'd gone with whom, who *hadn't* gone with whom, who'd broken up with whom afterwards. Many of them, though, were talking about who'd been seen making out in the teachers' lounge, a tidbit of particular interest to the seniors since someone claimed to have caught Mr. Becker and Ms. Moore in a compromising clinch. Beaker and Moore-or-Less. Yet the world still spun on its axis.

"I got a letter from my dad yesterday," said Allie.

Ethan looked across the aisle. It was still awkward between them sometimes, but they were getting beyond it. The hardest part was seeing her and Pete together. But they were good for each other. Good *to* each other.

Ethan still loved her, still lay awake most nights cursing himself for what he'd lost. No. For what he'd thrown away. He'd come to realize how much he'd taken Allie for granted, how much of their relationship she had shouldered while he'd just been along for the ride. She'd put up with so much the whole time they'd been together. Allie was a person who remembered six-month anniversaries, bought just-right gifts, knew exactly what to say to boost his spirits when he needed it. Yet when she'd needed him most, he hadn't been there. Not that this had ended them—she was the most understanding person he knew, and she'd been overwhelmed for him when she'd learned about Raye. But what she couldn't put behind her was Ethan's gambling, not after what it had done to her family. Twice.

While Ethan had been busy shattering his own life, Allie's dad had been doing the same, graduating from lottery tickets to the waterfront casino, spending his lunch hour playing first the VLTs and later roulette. He'd racked up thousands on his credit cards and, without his wife's knowledge, had taken a second mortgage on their home. Which was why Allie's mother had been at the bank. Tugging on her necklace.

"What'd the letter say?" Ethan asked Allie now.

She shrugged. "I haven't opened it yet."

He reached across the aisle and put his hand gently on hers. "You will," he said.

Ethan could see Pete across the room watching them out of the corner of his eye, so he drew his hand back. Not that Pete had anything to worry about. Allie's heart belonged to him now. Pete, too, was a person who remembered anniversaries and bought just-right gifts. In fact, he'd given Allie a pin yesterday for no other reason than to mark the beginning of their second week together, and Ethan had seen immediately how perfect it was: a silver dancer whose arms and waist formed the letter A.

With Allie's help, Pete was passing physics. Actually, *better* than just passing. She'd somehow shown him how to tap into that mechanical ability of his, shown him how to use it to make the physics make sense. She was amazing. Ethan had known it all along, of course, but he wished now that he'd *told* her how special she was. Wished he'd told her again and again. Not that this would have saved them, but it might have given him some comfort as he lay looking at the ceiling each night waiting, hoping, for sleep to come. He knew now just how fleeting life could be.

Pete, on the other hand, was the kind of person who never missed a moment to share how he felt with the people he cared for, telling Allie daily how much he loved her. *Showing* her. It was hard for Ethan to hear them, harder still to see them together. Outside of class, they were always holding hands. They tried to be discreet at first, their fingers brushing as they passed, but Ethan had told them not to be so foolish. They shouldn't have to hide the way they felt. But he still had to look away when he saw them approach each other, couldn't bear to witness what he himself now missed so desperately.

He missed Pete, too. Pete had come right over the second he'd learned about Raye, his nose still swollen and one eye blackened from the punch he'd taken. That was the kind of friend he was. Ethan was sorry for the way he'd treated him that day in his driveway, but no amount of apologizing could lessen the shame and regret he felt over what he'd done. Of course, it was more than shame and regret that Ethan couldn't get beyond now, more than shame and regret creating this distance between them. The rest of it was knowing how Pete had felt about Allie all that time. Thinking back, Ethan realized Pete's feelings for Allie shouldn't have come as such a surprise—Pete always hanging out with the two of them, Pete listening to Allie's every word, Pete following her face with his eyes. For Christ's sake, he'd even enrolled in physics because she was taking it.

A few days after Allie broke up with Ethan, Pete had called him and asked if they could talk. They'd gone down to the Arm and stared at the water for a while, stood shivering, shot the shit until Ethan couldn't stand it anymore and finally forced Pete to say what was on his mind. Although Ethan knew what was coming, he hadn't reacted well. Had, in fact, torn into Pete, asking how he could be such an asshole after everything Ethan had just gone through, then shouted, *Sure, you're welcome to my sloppy seconds!* On and on. That was the kind of friend *he* was.

Pete had let him rant, and when Ethan had finally run out of steam, could think of nothing else cruel to say, Pete had apologized, told Ethan he had every right to be upset, that he was a jerk for asking if he could date Allie. He'd never mention it again.

It had taken Ethan two days before he could give Pete his blessing. Seeing what Allie was going through changed his mind. All that stuff with her father, her parents' separation, needing to sell the house to pay their debts. At least her dad hadn't gotten his hands on the girls' education funds, which were in their own names. Small comfort, though, when everything else had fallen apart. No. Been *ripped* apart.

All of it had taken a heavy toll on Allie. When Ethan had finally come out of his own fog, he could see it. She seldom smiled, had stopped laughing altogether, even stopped dancing when she walked, her feet earthbound like everyone else's. And although they were no longer a couple, it killed Ethan to know there was nothing he could do for her.

But of course there was. She deserved the support of someone who cared for her. Someone who didn't have the same baggage that had dragged down her dad. Someone like Pete.

"You sure, man?" Pete had asked when Ethan called him. Ethan couldn't tell him in person. Couldn't handle seeing the expression on Pete's face that he'd seen in his own mirror the night he'd taken Allie to Irene's Ice Cream Emporium for the first time. Could that really have been over seven months ago?

"Yeah, I'm sure," Ethan had said.

It was natural that he and Pete would stop hanging out after that. It would have been too weird. But he missed his buddy almost as much as he missed Allie.

When it came to her, Pete took nothing for granted. He understood that she was vulnerable, that more than anything else she needed a friend she could count on. And he was definitely that. In return, she offered to help him with his physics, and pretty soon they were spending every afternoon and evening together. She was as surprised as he was when her feelings for him changed, when she stopped thinking of him as just a friend.

Before revealing to everyone that they were now a couple, Allie had taken Ethan aside to tell him first, wanted to be sure he was okay with it. Ethan had lied, even hugged her and wished her the best, but in the week since, he had found excuses to avoid them when he could. Like the evening they came over to interview his father for their video profile. He offered to work Lil's shift for her that night just so he had a reason not to be in the house.

Returning to The Chow Down had, surprisingly, been the easiest of all the getting-back-to-normal things he'd done after that terrible night that still haunted his dreams when he slept at all, jolted him to cold-sweat consciousness shouting Raye's name. He hadn't thought he could ever go back there after how he'd behaved that last time, even to pick up his cheque for the final hours he'd worked, but the phone rang one afternoon and it was Ike calling to see if he was okay. Ike had heard about what went down at Anwar's Convenience—had heard some of it from Mr. Anwar himself when the owner stopped by to tell them he had no intention of selling The Chow Down. Ike wanted Ethan to know how sorry he was, that he knew how easy it could be for a young person to fall under the influence of someone like Link Hornsby. He didn't mention his son, Mike, but he didn't have to—those were two more dots Ethan had connected on his own. And before Ike hung up, he'd told Ethan that he still had a job if he wanted it.

Ethan *did* want it. He had a lot of money to pay back and the pool wasn't hiring. Plus he still owed Boots McLaughlin his half of that lottery win, and he intended to make good on his promise to Allie. He could do that much at least.

"Found one!" Ms. Moore said, brandishing a bulb as she returned to the classroom. Ethan thought he noticed colour in her cheeks, even more than usual, and he remembered there was a connecting door between the AV equipment room and Beaker's science lab. Ordinarily, he might have groaned at that thought, but today he grinned. It felt good to smile again. It had been a long time since his face had formed that expression without his having to force it.

Replacing the bulb in the data projector, Ms. Moore said to the class, "I want to thank those students who volunteered to share their video profiles with us. I thought we could spend this last class together before Christmas break viewing some of the excellent work that was turned in. I previewed all four of the profiles you'll be seeing today, and I have to say they're remarkable. Pete and Allie, your piece on Jack Palmer is outstanding, especially the segment where he talks about withdrawing from politics. I hope you don't mind, but I showed it to a friend who produces a television news program, and she'd like to talk to you about airing it. I have her card here if you're interested. Discuss it with your parents first, okay?"

Ethan watched Allie turn wide eyes toward Pete, and he gave them both a thumbs-up. Ethan wasn't at all surprised by the teacher's praise. His father had told him afterwards how impressed he'd been by all the research the two had done, how he'd opened up to them on camera, talked honestly about how his childhood had influenced both his work and his personal life. He hadn't intended to, and probably should have cleared everything with his media consultant first, but since he'd already decided not to run for office, that was all water under the bridge. There were far more important things in his life that required his attention now.

The teacher continued to talk, commenting on two other video assignments the class would be seeing. Neung Minh had profiled her grandmother, one of the many refugees who escaped Communist-controlled Vietnam in the 1970s using makeshift boats. Jakob Singer had chosen as his subject his great-uncle, who had survived the anti-Semitic pogroms in Poland after World War II. "Both of these are extremely compelling," said Ms. Moore, "not only because of the important historical nature of the events they depict but also because we hear those events described by people who actually experienced them."

The teacher touched a key on her laptop and the image of a video player leaped onto the projection screen. "To begin, though," she said, "you'll be seeing the profile by the first student who volunteered to share." She smiled warmly in Ethan's direction. "What impresses me about this one," she explained, "isn't its political or historical significance but rather its heart. I admire the very personal way Ethan has chosen to honour his subject. Matt," she said, nodding to the person sitting near the door. Matt Cushing reached up and flicked the light switch, throwing the curtained room into semi-darkness.

The teacher moved her cursor to the controls at the bottom and clicked Play. Opening credits crawled onto the black screen, revealing Ethan's name and the name of the course, both dissolving to a shot of Ethan standing on the Angus L. Macdonald Bridge staring intently at the grey undulating surface below as if looking for something he had lost. The Ethan on the screen turned to face the camera and spoke: "In recent years, Halifax's municipal government has spent millions of dollars trying to improve the quality of the water in our harbour. Despite the cost, most people appreciate the importance of this project. Like so many First Nations cultures tell us, we don't inherit this world from our parents—we borrow it from our children." As the camera slowly panned the harbour and the islands beyond, Ethan continued to speak: "It's ironic, and more than a little sad, that some people are quick to recognize significance on a global scale yet fail miserably to see what's important in their own lives. I'm one of those people."

The scene changed, the screen now filled with a large dot on a green background. Slowly, the camera pulled back and other dots entered the frame. "Maybe," came Ethan's off-screen voice, "it's because we're just too close to be able to see it clearly." The camera zoomed out to reveal the bench in front of John C. Miles High School; from afar, the dots on the painted wood coalesced into a remarkably realistic portrait of Lady Gaga. "It's only when we have distance, a different perspective, that we see what we've been missing all along."

The scene shifted to an interior shot of the Halifax Shopping Centre, Ethan standing amid a sea of consumers darting from one store to another, holiday music playing in the background. "Christmas shopping. Everyone racing around trying to find the perfect gift. It's pretty much impossible unless you know what's important to the people you're buying for." The camera panned the shoppers, then zoomed in for a close-up on Ethan's face. "Not long ago," he said, "someone suggested that I spend some time finding out what's important to me. At that moment, I already knew. Or I thought I did."

When the camera pulled back this time, the onscreen Ethan was no longer in the shopping centre—he was standing in a driveway beside a black 1996 Cobra SVT. The camera circled it, showing rusted rocker panels, front and rear fenders covered with nicks and dents, tires that had parted with most of their tread, a starburst crack in the windshield under the rearview mirror, before returning to Ethan's face. "Now, though," Ethan continued, "I know differently."

His face dissolved into a still photo of a laughing, blue-haired Raye, the words *Rayelene Constance Palmer* appearing beneath it. What followed was a visual montage of moments captured in photographs: Raye as a baby, her tiny hand gripping the much larger finger of an adult; Raye as a toddler, her face aglow with both fear and delight at having navigated her first steps alone; Raye as an eight-year-old in an ugly dark uniform, the sash across her shoulder covered with Brownie badges. The next image fluttered into action, a video Ethan had taken with his cell a couple months ago: thirteen-year-old Raye reverently holding a battered bass guitar in her arms as she coaxed tentative notes from it. These notes morphed into professionally recorded music, the original "Smoke on the Water" from Deep Purple's 1972 album *Machine Head,* which Ethan had recently discovered in Winnipeg Joe's music store.

When he'd decided to embed a portion of the song into the profile he was creating, Ethan had listened to the words for the first time. Of course, the song wasn't new to him—Raye had played it more times than he could remember—but because he'd never before paid attention to the lyrics, he was surprised to learn about the real-life event it recounted, a 1971 fire in Montreux, Switzerland. Deep Purple had gone there to record *Machine Head* in one of Montreux's casinos. On the fourth of December, a concert-goer foolishly shot a flare into the casino's ceiling, starting a fire that razed the building. Hearing the band sing about the burning of a gambling house on that long-ago December evening, Ethan had felt a chill shudder through him. He felt that same chill now. It was on the fourth of December that Raye had followed him into the longest night of his life.

Deep Purple's song melted incrementally into the background, becoming something else, something muted and indistinguishable, as images of Raye at various ages layered the screen. "It's amazing," Ethan's off-screen voice resumed, "how a person can share the same house with you nearly your whole life yet not once do you tell her how much she means to you. Not once do you even consider what it might be like never to have the opportunity again to make her understand how remarkable she is. To tell her how weird and absolutely wonderful a human being she's become." The background music grew louder, swelling into the refrain of "Running on Empty," Jackson Browne singing of aimlessness and loss before fading away. "And then," said Ethan, his voice catching momentarily before continuing, "something happens that makes you regret all those opportunities you let slip by."

The room suddenly echoed with the sound of a single gunshot as newspaper clippings cartwheeled onto the screen, their headlines screaming the events of that night:

Teen Gambling Leads to Tragedy.

Daughter of Prominent Lawyer Shot.

Girl Takes Bullet Meant for Brother.

"What do I think is important now?" asked the onscreen Ethan back on the Macdonald Bridge. "What do I *know* is important?" He glanced away, swallowing hard before turning back to the camera. "Only one thing: moments when you can tell the people you love how much you care for them. I've wasted too many of those, and that's a mistake I'll never make again. For anyone watching this now who may not know her, I'd like to introduce my sister, Raye. She saved my life."

The onscreen Ethan dissolved once more as a final image of Raye appeared. Her face pale and thin, she stood supported on one side by a crutch and on the other by a lanky Brad Clahane. Above them hung an arch made of silver balloons and a tinsel-covered sign bearing the words *Lakewood Junior High Christmas Dance.* Even behind brand-new eyeglasses—the colour of which matched her blue hair and dress perfectly—the twinkle in Raye's eyes was unmistakable. She'd been smiling at Ethan as he took the picture, beaming as he'd told her yet again how beautiful she was.

Author's Note

I've never been big on conspiracy theories, the elaborate connections people make to prove that individuals and organizations have been working together to commit outrageous acts. I once had a sociology professor who was convinced—and who attempted to persuade his students—that personal electronic devices were invented by governments intent on keeping citizens isolated, insulated from each other, so they'd be more compliant, less likely to rebel and join forces against political corruption. I recall laughing at his claim, but I recently had occasion to remember it. I was riding a subway when a power failure on a section of track ahead stranded our train between two stations during rush hour, which meant that many of the people jammed into our car (mostly twenty- and thirty-somethings) were forced to stand wedged together for nearly an hour. Increasingly annoyed by the likelihood that I'd be late for a meeting, I expected to grumble about the delay with the people around me. But I was surprised by the silence that descended on the occupants of that car. Although many of the passengers were wedged beside people who were clearly their companions, very few of them spoke, most choosing instead to text on iPhones, listen to iPods, or surf on iPads—isolated, insulated from each other despite extremely close quarters. It was a sobering moment.

I experienced a number of equally sobering moments while conducting research for *Running on Empty*. I was stunned by the percentage of high school students who gamble—some sources indicate that as many as one in three wager money on a regular basis—and by the early age at which many of them turned to gambling, some as young as seven. And I was dumbfounded to learn of the number of teenagers who struggle with gambling addiction—one source suggested that number in the United States alone is in the hundreds of thousands. During an interview with an addictions counsellor, I learned that for every teenager who seeks help for a gambling problem, there are many more who elude discovery. While they may be up to their ears in debts owed to friends, family members, and bookies, most continue to have a roof over their heads and food in their stomachs because they have parents who provide these essentials. Teens don't default on mortgages like adults do, so they avoid detection more easily.

Of all the things I learned while researching teen gambling, the most disturbing was the way our society encourages it. Film after film honours risk-takers, revering those who live on the edge while subliminally sneering at those who choose not to take chances. Reality TV programs not only make gambling a form of entertainment but glorify the individuals whose lives are governed by it. And people in the media aren't the only ones guilty of creating this culture of betting and bookmaking. Few adults would even consider giving a pack of cigarettes to a child, but an alarming number think nothing of including lottery tickets in children's birthday and holiday gifts. And what student hasn't brought home from school at least one handful of tickets to sell on a draw of some sort? And what adult hasn't said to a child, "I *bet* you . . ."?

What does all this have to do with conspiracy theories? During my research, I encountered an individual who claimed that some Internet sites for young children—like those in which youngsters earn points to support virtual pets—have been created by branches of organized crime. Their intent, this person claims, is to groom a whole new generation of risk-takers who will more readily accept gambling in their lives. Do I believe this? I didn't at first. Now, after everything I've read and viewed, I don't know. If nothing else, it's at least worth thinking about, keeping us all mindful of how easily—and insidiously—attitudes can be shaped. The more important question is how to cope with the tremendous toll that gambling takes on individuals, their families, and society as a whole. If you or someone close to you struggles with a gambling addiction, there are people who can help. A simple Internet search will identify those in your area. Call them. Today.

As always when I finish writing a novel, there are people whose support I would like to acknowledge. Among them is my agent, Marie Campbell, who willingly represented a novel about a serious issue despite working in a market that's increasingly driven by fantasy and dystopian literature. As well, I'd like to thank the incredible team of professionals at HarperCollins, who continually demonstrate how committed they are to their craft. I especially want to thank my editor, Hadley Dyer, whose vision of the story kept me on track when I seemed all but determined to derail. In particular, I'm grateful for her editorial exacto knife, which slivered ten thousand unnecessary words from an early draft. William Faulkner is among the people said to have advised writers, "Kill your darlings." I'm indebted to Hadley for killing mine.

Finally, I would like to thank my wife, Debbie, who urged me to write a story about teen gambling. I'm often asked by beginning writers to identify the single element most important to an author's success, and my answer is always the same: a great wife (or a great husband or a great partner). I began writing in 1988 and, throughout all the years that have followed, Debbie has been my first reader, my first editor, and my very own cheerleader. I could never have begun this journey without her. It is my wish for any would-be writer reading this now that you, too, will find a partner equally as supportive and as committed to your success.